BAD DOG

A DCI ROBERT KETT NOVEL

ALEX SMITH

RELENTLESS
MEDIA

ALSO BY ALEX SMITH FROM RELENTLESS MEDIA

The DCI Robert Kett Thrillers

Paper Girls

Bad Dog

Three Little Pigs

Whip Crack

Run Rabbit Run

Stone Cold Dead

Every Mother's Son

Sweet Briar Rose

Jaw Breaker

Cry Baby: A Novella

The Softley Softley Thrillers

The Harder They Fall

Hard Luck House (Coming Soon)

Other Books

Six Days, Six Hours, Six Minutes

For Barry, the Big Dog

PROLOGUE

Thursday

It just wasn't the same without the dog.

Maurice had been a little bastard, sure. Half pug, half god-only-knew-what-else, he had never *not* been neck-deep in cow shit on their daily walks across the fields. He'd spent most of his life trying to hump every fence post, grassy hillock, or bemused ewe he crossed paths with, even when he was pushing fourteen and his fur was more grey than black. Roger Carver had spent the best part of each walk either yelling at the dog, rescuing the dog, or carrying the dog home because his little legs were tired. Maurice had been a royal pain in the arse.

But what he wouldn't give now to have him back.

Roger sighed, a little more dramatically than he'd intended. The evening air was thick with dust, and the recently harvested corn-stubble crunched beneath his boots. To his left the fields stretched for miles, bright and open, sighing with relief now that the weight had been lifted from them. To his right was the woodland, dark and ancient, the trees already burnished with oranges and browns. Autumn was well and truly here, and it was going to be a cold one. He'd lived in this part of the world long enough to be able to judge the seasons, even in the notoriously unpredictable East Anglian climate.

"Not enjoying yourself, then," said Sally from half a dozen paces behind him. It sounded like an accusation, and when he glanced over his shoulder at her sour expression he knew that's exactly how she'd intended it. He felt a sudden rush of anger—maybe even hatred—and he swallowed it back down. He looked instinctively for the dog, that same awful hammer blow to his heart when he remembered Maurice wasn't there. That he'd never be there again.

Stupid little bastard.

"I'm fine," he said, hearing the passive aggression in his voice.

"Yes, you're *fine*," she shot back, thick with sarcasm. "You're always *fine*."

How had they got here, he and Sally? They'd only been together seven years. Surely that wasn't long enough for the foundations of their relationship to rot away. They were both young, he a couple of months north of thirty-five, she a few weeks south of it, with good jobs and no kids—no desire for kids, either. The world was theirs, and they'd been so keen to take it. Maurice had been their one commitment, the old dog the only thing keeping them on the leash. With him gone, anything was possible.

According to Sally, at least.

"Look," she said. "You admitted it yourself, he was in pain. It was his time."

They were approaching the end of the field, the ridges

of hard soil threatening to turn their ankles. Ahead, where the land met the woods, was a battered stile, and Roger knew that somewhere on it was a carving—*Rog + Sal + Maurice 4 eva*—that they'd made with Sal's apartment key when they'd first started dating.

"I know," Roger said. "It's fine. I said it's fine. What else do you want me to say? You killed my dog?"

The words were out of his mouth before he could stop them, but there was no taking them back. He heard Sally suck in a breath, braced himself for what was about to come. But she didn't reply, and when he looked back he saw that she'd stopped walking. There was enough sun left overhead for it to reflect in the tears that clustered in her eyes, that carved trails down her dusty cheeks.

"That's what you think?" she said.

Roger shrugged, cleared his throat. He reached out and took hold of the stile, the wood damp to the touch.

"No," he said. "But you insisted. You wouldn't let it go. He could've had surgery. He might have had years left."

Sally shook her head, her hands wrapped around her chest so tight that her white coat looked like a straitjacket.

"He was dying," she said. "The vet said so. I thought... I didn't march you in there. I thought this was what you wanted?"

"It's what *you* wanted," Roger said. "It's what you always wanted. You just wanted rid of him."

He waited for the pleas, for the apologies, for the excuses. But instead the sadness etched into her expression became something else.

"Go fuck yourself, Roger," she said.

She turned and walked away, stumbling in her welly boots.

"*What?*" Roger said, almost choking on the word. "No, fuck *you*. Bitch."

He left her to it, clambering over the stile and pushing through the hawthorn bushes that grew on the far side. He made it three steps into the next field—the anger pulsing inside his head with every heartbeat, making the sky dance—before forcing himself to stop.

"Fuck," he muttered.

He was angry at Sally because she was right. Maurice had been at death's door. Yes, they could have cut him open and sliced out enough of his cancer to keep him going, but he'd have been in constant pain, and he would have needed daily medication—and that's if he'd survived the operation and recovery period. The poor sod couldn't even see any more, could barely shuffle more than a few feet. He'd had the most amazing life, and she was right—it had been the right time for him to go.

In the distance, he heard Sally scream in frustration. And this time he didn't blame her. He was being an arsehole.

"Fuck," he said again, turning and fighting his way back to the stile. "Sally!" he yelled. "Sal, wait up, I'm sorry."

There was no sign of her in the field, which meant she had to have broken into a run. Roger set off after her, the ground crumbling beneath each step and making him feel like he was running in a dream, not getting anywhere. He kept his eyes down to navigate his route, staring so intently at the earth that he almost missed it—a flash of white in the trees to the left.

He stopped, his heartbeat the only sound in the world. For a second he thought he'd imagined it, but he squinted into the woods that edged the field and saw it again. Something white, moving fast.

"Sally!" he yelled. Why the hell was she going that way? It wasn't exactly a forest, just a strip of ancient woodland that stretched from their village down towards Beccles, but the trees were old, and they kept the last of the day at bay. Night had arrived early in the woods, and shadows crawled between their gnarled trunks. Roger shivered in his Barbour jacket.

Just leave her, he thought. *She'll come around.*

But he'd been in the wrong, and the longer he left it without an apology, the worse it would be.

"Sally!" he called, scrabbling up the low embankment and grabbing a branch. He hauled himself into the shade of a monstrous yew tree, the air instantly ten degrees cooler. Where had she gone?

He stepped carefully over the roots, blinking the harvest dust from his eyes and trying to make sense of the shifting darkness. There, a glimpse of something white, gone in an instant.

"I know you loved him," Roger said, his words swallowed whole by the trees. "He loved you too. I'm sorry for what I said, I'm still upset."

Her reply was a whisper, or maybe her voice too was rendered inaudible by the crushing weight of branches and leaves overhead. Roger hesitated, looking back. The field seemed further away than it should be, the day too dark. He'd never liked the woods, not since he was a kid and he'd got lost in Thetford Forest on a school trip—for less than an hour, but that was long enough when you were nine. Nothing made you feel smaller than the trees, nothing made you feel more vulnerable.

"I'll tell you what," he said, venturing forward again. "Let's get away for a bit. Let's just take some time and go somewhere."

A twig snapped beneath his foot with a sound like a gun going off. His heart just about exploded and he clamped a hand to his chest.

"Sally?"

There was another noise ahead, but this one didn't sound like Sally. It didn't sound human at all. It was a low growl, almost dog-like but louder. Maybe somebody was walking their dog through the woods. It wasn't a common route—they'd hardly met anyone in all the years they'd been crossing the fields—but new people were moving this way all the time thanks to the big estates they were building.

He pressed on, using the huge trunks to steady himself as the ground got rougher. Every now and again he'd catch a glimpse of Sally's coat, closer with every step. She was sitting down. *Lying* down, maybe. Waiting for him, he hoped. Maybe they'd hug, tell each other they were sorry, then head home. Maybe this really could be the start of something new between them, a kind of freedom. Roger stepped into a puddle of sunlight as he had the thought, feeling a powerful surge of relief—one that almost bordered on joy.

It didn't last.

He climbed down from the torso-thick root of another tree, and suddenly she was there.

At least, part of her was.

One arm, clad in white, stuck out from behind a clump of bracken. It twitched, the hand bouncing on the ground like it was beckoning him. Now that he'd stopped walking he was aware of a sound—something wet, something *crunching*.

He opened his mouth to speak Sally's name but found nothing in his lungs except dust. Keeping one hand on the tree he took a step to the side, then another, and every time he did, more of his girlfriend slid into view—her elbow, her bicep, her shoulder, her neck.

At first, he couldn't figure out what was all over her skin, because in the darkness of the forest it looked like ink. It was only when he took another step that he saw the blood on the lapel of her coat, so bright and so red that it looked fake. And that's the first thing that came into his head, that this wasn't real, that it was a trick, a *prank*. Even when he stumbled towards her and saw her face, her eyes open and pleading and desperate, he couldn't believe it.

Because what he was seeing was impossible.

There was something sitting on her. Something big, hunched, its body covered in clumps of matted hair, so dark that it looked like it was made of nothing but smoke and shadow. The deformed lump of its head lifted for a moment and it sniffed the air through the ragged holes of its nostrils. Then its muzzle plunged down into Sally's chest, making her grunt.

No.

The fear was unlike anything Roger had felt in his life, it was a living thing inside him, cold and dark. Sally stared at him, her mouth opened, and even in the gloom of the forest Roger could make out the word on her bloody lips.

Please.

She lifted her arm and the creature pinned it back down with its paw. She tried again, as if expecting Roger to grab her hand and pull her away.

He didn't. He couldn't.

The creature—a dog, surely, a *hound*—lifted its head again and looked back through the trees. Its eyes were two silver pennies, full of nothing but hunger and death.

But beneath them, its grinning lips were almost human.

It sniffed the air. It stared at Roger. And beneath it, Sally reached for him with the very last of herself.

I'm sorry, he said. He screamed it inside his head, hoping that she would hear him even though he was silent, even though his back was to her, even though all he could do was run. *I'm sorry! I'm sorry! I'm sorry!*

CHAPTER ONE

Friday

"How are you feeling, Robbie?"

DCI Robert Kett did his best not to scowl, but it was hard not to. The man sitting opposite him in the dusty little room at the back of the Norfolk Constabulary HQ had a face that made you instantly want to punch it. With his squirrel-like cheeks and his succession of chins—all doing their best to hide behind a soft, downy, woodland beard— the guy looked every inch the psychologist he was supposed to be. His wet eyes blinked so rapidly that the flapping sound of it was like a dripping tap.

It was his smile, though, that made Kett feel like he was going to scream. It was as soft as cheese and warped with a contrived sympathy. *I'm here for you,* the smile was supposed to say. *I feel your pain, you can tell me anything.* But the only message Kett got from it was, *Hit me as hard as you can!*

"Huh?" said Kett, realising he hadn't heard a word the man had been saying. He lifted his hand and gently rubbed his shoulder, feeling the thick bandages beneath his shirt. There was still pain there, from the knife wound he'd sustained on his last case, but the painkillers kept it quiet. Right now it was more the memory of pain. It didn't really exist anymore.

Like Billie, he thought. *Like your wife. Just a memory. Just a ghost.*

"I wondered how you were feeling?" the psychologist said. It was the same question Kett had been asked by everyone since he'd woken up in hospital a little over six weeks ago. And he gave the same answer now.

"I'm fine."

It was a lie, of course. He was about as far from fine as it was possible to be. The fight with Raymond Figg had left him with a puncture wound in his shoulder and a nasty slash across his chest. Both of them would heal eventually, but it was the scars inside him he'd feel for the rest of his life. He could still see those three newspaper delivery girls, snatched from their lives and dragged right to Hell. Bound, beaten and almost murdered. They were all okay now, he knew—Superintendent Colin Clare kept him updated on their progress, and Maisie and her mum had actually come to visit him in the ward on two separate occasions—but it could have turned out so differently. Kett wasn't sure if you ever got the stench of a case like that out of your soul.

"Robbie," began the psychologist, resting his pencil and notepad on his beige trousers. "This may not seem important, but passing a psych evaluation is essential to returning to duty. I'm here to help you, but I can only do that if you're honest with me, if you're forthright."

He rolled the last word around his mouth like a mint

humbug. Kett felt his face crease into another scowl and he ran a hand over it, as if he could pull the expression away. Other than the psychologist's nasal voice the room was impossibly quiet, and if it wasn't for the book-sized window in the far wall—which let in the merest trickle of morning light—he could have easily convinced himself that it was a tomb.

His tomb.

The silence was almost physical, pressing down on him, and he sucked in a breath that sent pain creeping into his shoulder.

"First of all," he said, chewing on his words. "It's not Robbie. It's DCI Kett."

"So, you still think of yourself as a policeman above all else," the therapist replied without missing a beat. He picked up his pencil and scribbled something. Kett wondered if he was writing down the instructions for how to remove a pencil that had been inserted into your backside —because if he wasn't careful he was going to need them.

"I don't understand the question, Mr, ah... Sorry, I've forgotten your name."

"Call me Richard," the man said.

Dick, Kett thought, remembering that the therapist had introduced himself as Richard Johnson. *Dick Johnson.* Some names just said it all.

"Richard. Right." Kett cleared his throat. "I'm fine, Richard. It was a bad case, with some bad people. But two of those bad people are dead, and one isn't coming out of prison for decades. We made sure of that. I'm alive, the girls are alive, and life goes on."

"Life goes on," the man said, tapping his pencil on one of his chins. "That's an interesting choice of phrase."

"Is it?" Kett asked, genuinely confused.

"Is it?" Richard echoed, making more notes. Kett looked around the small room, wondering if there was a camera here, if at any moment now Pete Porter and Kate Savage and the rest of the team would come barging in, laughing their heads off. But there was nothing, just him and Richard and that same awful silence.

"Look, I know why I'm here," said Kett. "I understand I need to pass a psych. But honestly, I'm fine."

He did his best to smile, but it couldn't have been very convincing because Richard tutted, then made another note on his pad.

"How are things at home?" the psychologist asked.

"They're fine too," said Kett.

That wasn't strictly true either. Alice, Evie and Moira seemed happy in their new house, and the two older girls had finally started to relax at school and nursery. But there had been a current of anxiety between them all since Kett had left the hospital. It was his fault, of course. He'd brought them up to Norwich so that they could live somewhere safe, and their first experience in the city had been their father getting stabbed. Alice had been clingier than ever, and Moira seemed even more unsettled than she had in the days after Billie had gone missing.

Billie.

Kett spoke her name beneath his breath, as if it might somehow conjure her. He closed his eyes and saw her there, but she was more of a phantom than ever. He'd found, to his horror, that in the last couple of weeks the image of her face had started to fade at the edges, like she was an oil painting dipped in water. He knew that sooner or later he wouldn't be able to picture her at all.

Until she came back, of course. Until she came back to him.

He sighed, feeling that same weight of darkness sitting on his stomach, on his chest. The black dog, some people called it. The feeling that no matter what he did now, he'd never be free, he'd never feel right again.

"I've been doing this job a long time," Richard said. Kett opened his eyes, seeing his pulse flash against the shadows like a disco light. The psychologist leaned forwards. "Your words say one thing, but your body says another. I know a fine man, Robbie, and you're not one."

"I'm fine," Kett growled. "Just sign your goddamned form and send me back to work."

The psychologist tapped his pencil against his knee, then against his pad, all the while studying Kett like he was some laboratory rabbit.

"Can I ask you about Billie?" he said. "Your wife."

"I know who she is, *Richard*," said Kett, swallowing hard to try to dampen the anger that was building inside him.

"Do you miss her, still?"

Kett actually had to clamp his lips between his teeth to stop the tirade of abuse that threatened to spill out of him. Did he miss her? Did he miss his wife after she was snatched from a London street in the middle of the day five months ago? Did he miss the mother of his children? The woman he wanted to spend the rest of his life with? The woman who could be dead or alive or somewhere in between but he had no idea, no fucking idea, because he didn't know where she was? *Do I miss my fucking wife? What do you think the answer to that question is, you fucking moron?*

"Yes," he said after a moment.

Richard made a note of it, then leant forward again, tapping his pencil against his teeth.

"Robbie, is there anything—"

"Can I tell you a story?" Kett interrupted, leaning forward himself so that he was close enough to headbutt the psychologist if he needed to. Richard swallowed uncomfortably, but he held his ground.

"You may," he said, the pencil still *clack clack clacking* against his incisors.

"Years ago I worked a case," Kett said, keeping his voice low. "Back in the Met, this was. I was a young DC, fresh off the carousel. I was called to a warehouse close to Docklands, a real dump. Pete was with me. Porter, that is. The place had been on the market and a surveyor was in, measuring up, for flats probably. Anyway, as he's pootling around he discovers a body, half-buried beneath a section of roof, just the legs sticking out—kind of Wicked Witch of the East style. So he calls us, of course, and I get the lead. We clear the metal and rubble to get a better look and we see a man there. And do you know how he died?"

Richard shook his head, his eyes so wide they looked like pickled eggs. The pencil was tapping faster now, like a metronome.

"Somebody had rammed two pencils into his face, one into each eye. Both had penetrated the orbital socket and punctured the frontal lobe, effectively lobotomising him."

Kett made a point of looking at Richard's pencil, which abruptly stopped drumming.

"Imagine the force needed to do that," he said. "To push a pencil into somebody's skull. But it *can* be done."

It was hard to tell in the gloomy room, but Richard seemed to have lost most of the blood from his face. He leant behind him and placed the pencil on his desk, then faced Kett. He opened his mouth to say something before turning to his desk again, opening a drawer, and putting the pencil inside.

"Um..." he said as he slid the drawer shut.

"Um indeed," said Kett. "That's an interesting turn of phrase. So how about it, Richard, are you going to sign me off?"

Before the psychologist could answer, somebody knocked on the door. They didn't wait for a reply before opening it, and Kett was surprised at the relief he felt when he saw Superintendent Clare's face glowering down at him.

"Excuse me," said Richard. "You can't come in here. This is a confidential session."

"Oh shut up, Johnson, you great prune," said Clare. "Sign him off, will you?"

"There's absolutely no way I can do that," said Richard, shaking his head. "You have to understand that DCI Kett suffered severe physical and psychological trauma at the hands of a dangerous criminal, that he is suffering from anxiety and quite probably depression, that the incident involving his missing wife has scarred him and has the potential to make him reckless and dangerous. There is a self-destructive streak inside him that could go off at any time and take everyone else out with it. He is in no fit state to undertake any kind of active duty. He needs rest, he needs time with his children, and he needs to see me on a weekly basis until I feel he is well."

"He needs to be signed off," said Clare. "And you're going to do it right now or I swear to god I'll lock you in here and stick the key so far up your backside you'll have to wait a week for it to appear again. We need him, and we need him now."

"Why?" asked Kett.

Clare turned to him, his expression dark.

"Because we've got a dead woman in the woods, and a monster on the loose."

CHAPTER TWO

THEY RODE OUT IN CLARE'S CAR—A BEAST OF A Mercedes that looked like it belonged in the 1980s. It had not one but five pine-scented air fresheners hanging from the rear-view mirror and the smell was so strong that it sat at the back of Kett's throat. He cranked the window down as the old car groaned up the slip road onto the dual carriageway, the wind roaring.

"Sorry," said Clare.

"It's fine," said Kett, trying not to gag. "I mean, five of them seems a little extreme. How do you actually breathe in here?"

Clare glanced at him, confused. Kett gave the air fresheners a flick, unleashing another blast of toxic air. He'd been to plenty of pine forests in his time and none had ever smelled remotely like this. In fact, the only place he'd been which had actually smelled like this was a Portaloo.

"Oh, right," Clare sniffed. "It smells a bit in here, yes. It's the kids. Teenagers, they're disgusting. All those bloody PE kits. I'll open a fresh one, they're in the glove box."

"No!" Kett said. He looked at Clare, wondering if there

was so much hair in the Super's nose that he had no sense of smell. "Christ no. It's fine, honestly. What were *you* apologising for?"

"Richard Johnson," Clare said, overtaking a bus. The car juddered alarmingly, everything rattling—including Kett's bones. "Old Double Dick. That man looks like a baked potato and he's about as useful as one. Loves the sound of his own voice. But he's the Chief Constable's cousin's husband's brother's hamster's son, or some bollocks, so we can't get rid of him. He'll sign your psych evaluation."

Clare looked over again.

"That's if you want him to," he said. "How are you, Robbie?"

"I'm fine," Kett replied without even thinking. "Never been better."

"Sure," said Clare. "Believe me, I've been 'fine' plenty of times in my life too. You get out of it. I know you're worried about Billie. I know you're disappointed."

Disappointed didn't cut it. He could still see Raymond Figg standing in the spotlights of the sewage treatment plant, he could still hear those words tumbling from his foam-flecked lips.

Ask me how Billie knew the Pig Man. Ask me what it has to do with that Khan boy. You coppers, you think we're all Jack the Rippers, working alone. You think we don't talk to each other. But we do, we all share, we all compete, we all follow each other on fucking Facebook. You think I don't know, but I do, I know where she—

Then Lochy Percival had killed him, and whatever those words had been were locked inside the grave of his body. Forever.

"I spoke to Bingo this morning," said Clare. "I wanted to see how they were getting on, if they'd discovered anything more about this Pig Man. He's got a whole team working on it, led by your old friend DS Ridgway. They're going to find him."

Kett nodded. He knew all this, of course, because he'd spoken to Bingo too. He spoke to Bingo every single day.

Any news? he always asked. And always the same answer.

Nothing.

"They'll find her," Clare said, taking his big hand off the wheel and resting it on Kett's good shoulder. He squeezed, then let go. "They *will* find her."

The words were positive, but they still unlocked another crushing tide of darkness inside him—a weight that made him want to curl himself into a ball and slide into the footwell. He chased it away as best he could, staring out the window at the rolling scenery. The summer had gone, the fields stripped bare by the harvest. Autumn hung in the treetops and on the horizon, chasing V-shaped flocks of birds southward as it crept across the land. Autumn had always been his favourite time of year.

It had been Billie's too.

He pulled his phone from his pocket, scrolling through the numbers.

"You mind?" he asked without waiting for a reply. The phone rang, then again, then again—and for all that time his heart forgot how to beat. After what had happened to Billie, after he had called her and called her and called her on the day she'd been taken, every single ringing phone was like a hammer to his heart.

"Hello?" came the voice of the childminder, impossibly cheerful. Kett let go of the breath he'd been holding.

"It's Robbie," he said. "Mr Kett. How are the girls doing?"

"They're great," came the reply. "Moira and Evie have been playing so nicely together. Alice is... Alice is, uh."

"Alice is Alice," he said. "Don't worry, I know."

"She's really great," the childminder said. "As long as I don't try to take away her iPad."

"Oh, god, don't do that," said Kett. "It's like trying to take a jar of honey from a grizzly bear. She'll rip your limbs off. I won't keep you, I just wanted to—"

"Who's that?" asked a little voice that he knew instantly.

"It's your dad," said the childminder. "Do you want to speak with him?"

She must have nodded, because the phone rustled for a moment and then Evie started breathing into it like a stalker. He was about to ask her if she was okay when she yelled loud enough to rattle the speaker.

"I hate beans!"

The phone rustled again, clunked, and cut off. Kett held it to his ear for a moment more, frowning, then slid it back into his pocket.

"Kids okay?" Clare asked.

"Yep, apart from the beans apparently," he replied. "All three of them are with a childminder, but it's temporary. I need to figure something else out, especially if I'm coming back to work."

"Sitter?" Clare asked. "Might be able to help you there. Leave it with me. You, uh, you *are* coming back then?"

"I'm here aren't I?" he replied.

"You certainly are."

Clare punched the accelerator and the old car effortlessly hit eighty-five miles per hour. Cars *whumped* past on their left, all wide-eyed kids and panting dogs and exhausted parents.

"What's the case?" Kett asked.

"Woman in her late twenties, early thirties," said the Superintendent. "No ID. She was discovered this morning by dog walkers in a stretch of woodland just north of Beccles. They assumed she'd been killed by an animal."

"An animal?" said Kett. "I didn't think Norfolk was the kind of place where the wildlife could kill you. What kind of animal?"

"A dog," Clare said. "A big one. The victim had severe lacerations across her chest and neck, and puncture wounds too. It's nasty."

"Any sign of the dog?" Kett asked. Clare shook his head.

"And no witnesses. We do have a farmer who claimed he saw the woman with a man yesterday evening. He remembers them because they didn't have a dog of their own with them. Most people in those woods are either joggers or dog walkers. But the farmer was neck-deep in a bottle of breakfast vodka when we spoke to him, so I'm taking his story with a pinch of *go fuck yourself*."

"No sign of the man, though?" Kett said, and Clare shook his head.

The Super's foot crunched on the brake, the car slowing reluctantly. He pulled them off the main road.

"With all due respect, sir," Kett asked. "Why do you need me back for a dog attack?"

Clare swung them around a roundabout like he was trying to slingshot them out of the Earth's gravitational field.

"You're local, aren't you? I mean, you grew up here, right?"

Kett nodded. "Left Norwich when I was twelve."

"You remember the stories of Black Shuck?" Clare asked.

"The hound of East Anglia? Sure. I mean, not much,

but you don't live around here and not know about it." Kett paused, frowning. "Wait, *why*?"

"Because according to our farmer, that's what's loose in these woods. That's what he saw." Clare looked over, his frown even deeper than usual. "He saw Black Shuck, the demon dog."

THE CRIME SCENE was a good walk from the nearest road, but the fresh air was welcome.

Not that the scent of Portaloo Pine was planning on leaving Kett's nose any time soon.

Clare took the lead, his big strides carving a path through a furrowed field, his paperwork clenched beneath his arm. Kett took his time, careful not to slip on the ridged earth. To his left, the world was bright and open, drenched in golden sunlight, the air thick with crop dust. It sloped downwards, ending maybe two or three miles away in a shining silver ribbon that had to be the River Waveney. The scene was so picturesque it could have been a painting, one of Constable's landscapes.

To his right, though, was a different world entirely. The woods here were old, the impossibly tall trees clustered in tight formation, as bent and broken as wounded soldiers. Kett got the impression that they'd gathered to watch what was happening, and he felt his skin crawl. He let loose a shudder that Clare must have heard even over the bellows of his breath.

"Creepy, right?" he said over his shoulder. "It gets worse."

Kett looked past the Super to see a constable up ahead, a young man whose yellow jacket seemed to have attracted a small army of wasps. He looked decidedly miserable as he waved to them.

"This way, sir," he said, his arms wheeling around his head like he was dancing a jig while on traffic control duty. "Watch out for the little bastards."

"You mean the Suffolk lot?" said Clare with a grim smile.

"Um, no," said the PC. "The wasps."

Clare rolled his eyes as he ushered Kett through a gap between two enormous yew trees.

"Suffolk Constabulary are claiming this is theirs," he explained. "We're pretty much on the border. If it was up to me they could have it, but then it would never get solved."

Kett nodded, stepping from the day into what felt like midnight. It was as if the trees had wrapped him in a blanket of darkness and a shroud of silence, and he had to look over his shoulder to make sure the world was still there.

"Go easy now," said Clare from right behind him. "The ground is treacherous. It's not far."

It wasn't. Even from here, in the shadow of a thousand finger-like branches, Kett could see the harsh glow of field lights ahead. He set off towards them, every root grabbing at his boots, every twig pawing at his face. It was clear from the outset that the forest didn't want him here. It wanted to protect its secrets.

And its dead.

He rounded a mass of ivy-strangled trees to see the crime scene ahead. Forensics had erected a tent over the corpse, and the Major Investigation Team clustered around it, some inside, some out. Bathed in the harsh lights, it almost looked like a Renaissance painting. He paused to take a breath, nursing the ache that sat deep inside his shoulder.

"You're sure you're up for this?" asked Clare, stopping next to him.

"I'm—"

"Fine, yes, I know." The Super shook his head, and Kett knew he was wondering if he'd made the right decision. "Come on then, Kett. I assume you remember everyone."

Clare's clomping brogues announced his presence, and one by one the team turned to look. Kett nodded at DS Alison Spalding, who was hanging at the back of the group speaking quietly on her phone. She ignored him, turning away, but the grizzled face of DI Dunst was a little friendlier. The old detective tilted his head in greeting, patting his jacket pocket as he looked for a cigarette.

"Kett," he grunted. "How's that arm of yours?"

"Still attached," said Kett, reaching out with his good arm and shaking Dunst's hand. "Just."

"Robbie?"

The voice came from inside the tent and was swiftly followed by a grinning face. DI Pete Porter stepped out, his frame so huge he almost brought the entire tent with him. He took a step towards Kett then stumbled on an exposed root.

"Shitting *balls!*" he yelled.

"It's good to see you too, Pete," Kett said, shaking the man's enormous hand. Pete dragged him into a hug, clapping him on the back hard enough to make him grunt with discomfort. But it really was good to see him.

"Man, it's great to have you back," Porter said. "Even though I feel for you, being dragged out into the arse end of nowhere." He shuddered like he was five years old, scanning the shadows between the trees. "The countryside, it's *evil.*"

The tent rustled again, and PC Kate Savage appeared

in her constable's uniform. She looked a little green around the gills, but the smile she gave Kett was a warm one.

"Robbie," she said, before quickly clearing her throat. "I mean DCI Kett. Welcome back, sir."

He nodded to her, offering a smile of his own. Both Savage and Porter had visited him at hospital, and then at home, pretty much every day on his long road to recovery. Both had been welcome, of course, but Savage had been far better at making the tea.

"I thought you'd be wearing a detective's suit by now," Kett said, and Clare nodded.

"If it was up to me, she would be," he said. "But the carousel's the carousel. No short cuts even for the ones who really deserve it."

"I've got my exams coming up," Savage said as she stepped out of the tent. "Fingers crossed I'll be out of scrubs soon enough."

"Anyway," grumbled Clare, pushing to the front of the group and holding the tent flap. "Enough of the family reunion bollocks. Are you ready for this, Kett?"

The honest answer was that he wasn't sure. The black dog of his depression was still sitting inside him, growling, and out here in the cold and damp the pain in his shoulder beat like a hammer on an anvil. He found himself thinking of his girls, too, of Alice and Evie and Moira. What would they say to him if they knew he was back at work, if they knew he was falling headlong into another dangerous case?

He stared into the tent, seeing the body that lay there. More death. More darkness. What would it do to him this time?

"Robbie?" said Porter, wearing an expression of genuine concern. "There's no pressure, man, we'll be okay without you."

He looked at his friend. He looked at the other members of the team. Then he shrugged his doubts away. He was Robbie Kett, he was a detective, and right now there was a case to solve.

And the truth was that here, in the unforgiving darkness of the woods, he felt like he was finally home.

CHAPTER THREE

OF COURSE, HOME DIDN'T USUALLY INCLUDE A WOMAN who had been torn to pieces by a legendary monster.

"Jesus," said Kett as he ducked through the flap. He put a hand to his mouth, clamping his nostrils closed. The forensic tent was designed to keep foreign contaminants and passers-by away from the corpse, but it was doing a better job of keeping the stench inside. The aroma was partly death, yes, but there was something else there too, something *worse*.

"Yeah, it's bad," said Savage as she came in after him.

"We left her here for you," Porter said, hovering just outside.

"Thanks," muttered Kett. "What did Forensics say?"

"What do you think?" Porter replied.

Kett turned his attention to the dead woman—although it was hard to tell that she had once been a woman. Something had laid into her with savage force, several deep cuts running from her scalp down through her eyes and mouth, ending on her right cheek. She had been painted red, the attack deforming her into some kind of terrible Picasso.

There was no throat to speak of, just a shallow pool of blood that seemed far too bright in the artificial light. Her white coat had been pulled closed over her chest, and the prints on it—half blood, half mud—looked more animal than human. They looked like paw prints. Beneath the material he could see further injuries.

Kett ducked down beside her, taking his hand from his mouth so that he could speak.

"She was found by dog walkers?"

"Yes," said Savage, squatting beside him. She was taking small, deliberate breaths because of the smell, and if she wasn't careful she was going to hyperventilate. "Two men from the village, walking their retriever. The dog found her first."

"You know if it touched her?" Kett asked, pointing at the paw prints. Savage shook her head.

"They've taken their dog to the station. We'll compare the prints. But we have no idea how many other dogs might have been out here."

"Did they mention whether they'd touched her at all," Kett said. He pulled his pen from his pocket and tried to lift one side of the coat. It was stuck fast, the blood almost dry. "Forensics have been and gone, right?"

"Yes," Savage said. "To the Forensics, that is. No to the touching."

He tried with a little more force, gently peeling the coat away. He didn't have to look closely to see the gaping wounds across the woman's chest. He let the coat drop, standing up then instantly regretting it. The tent spun around him like it was perched on the back of some giant, lumbering forest beast that had just risen. He took a few deep breaths, scratching at the knife wound on his own chest.

"They said they didn't go anywhere near it," said Savage. "Other than to drag their dog away."

"Weird," said Kett. "If she was attacked by an animal, then why would it close up her jacket after it had chewed her to ribbons?"

"We'll know more when they take her in," Porter said from outside. "Forensics were waiting for you before they moved her. But they say the injuries are compatible with a dog attack. It was the wound in her throat that killed her, tore it right out."

"And the face?" Kett asked. "Those aren't bites."

"Claws," said Porter.

"Dogs don't attack with their paws," said Kett. "Not that I've ever seen anyway. Did the animal, you know, *consume* anything?"

"Did it eat her?" Savage asked. "Uh, yeah, we think so. Some of the..."

She paused, her breath hitching, before managing to compose herself.

"There's some flesh missing from her throat, and from her chest."

"And we found this," said Porter. Kett turned to him. The big DI was holding out an evidence bag with something small and yellow inside. Kett took it, squinting at a bloody tooth. It was curved, pointed, and almost certainly belonged to a dog.

A *big* dog.

"Shit," he said.

"Yeah," Porter agreed as he took the bag back. "That's what I said. Must have ripped into her so hard that one of its teeth snapped out of the gum."

"We've photographed the surrounding area," added

Savage. She shrugged. "There's a search team combing the paths, but it's difficult terrain."

"How far are we from the nearest village?" Kett asked, desperate for some air.

"Two and a half miles," Savage said. "Aldeby. Beccles is five miles away. There are some scattered farms and fisheries, a few isolated houses, not much else other than woods and fields."

"Yeah," said Kett. "And a demon fucking dog."

———————

"I REALLY HATE IT HERE."

Porter stood to one side of the crime scene, in one of the few puddles of sunlight that had penetrated the dense canopy overhead. He shivered, even though it wasn't particularly cold, wrapping his arms around his chest.

"Yeah," said Kett as he walked over to join him. "I remember you saying you weren't a fan of the countryside."

"It's just so big," said Porter. "And open. And old. Makes me feel small, you know?"

Kett glanced at the bulging biceps beneath Porter's designer suit, shaking his head. There wasn't much that could make Pete Porter look small.

"There's one good thing about being out here, though," said Kett. "Miles away from civilisation, no electricity in sight."

"Yeah? What's that?"

"It means there's no way you can get near a kettle."

Porter offered a scowl that was half smile. He pointed a finger at Kett.

"I'll have you know I've been practising," he said. "My tea is now the envy of the force."

"It's worse," said Savage as she emerged from the tent.

"*Worse?*" said Kett. "How can that be possible?"

"It's not worse!" Porter yelled, genuinely upset. "You traitor, Savage! You drank a cup this morning."

"I poured it out when you went to the toilet," she said. "It tasted like you'd just *been* to the toilet. In my mug."

"Lies," Porter said. "You'll see."

"You lot finished?" said Clare as he joined them. "I see a lot of chatting, not much working."

The boss still had the air of a grammar school head-teacher, like he could pull out his cane at any moment and rap your knuckles until they bled.

"What's so important anyway?" he asked.

"Porter's tea," said Savage.

"Oh Christ," said Clare, shaking his head. "It's worse, if you can believe it."

Porter muttered something beneath his breath, obviously disgusted.

"What are your thoughts?" Clare asked, looking at Kett.

"It's a weird one," Kett replied. "I've seen a few dog attacks, but never fatal ones. What always strikes me is that there are almost always defensive wounds on the arms where the victim tried to fight back. It's the first thing you do, right? You put your hands up to protect the bits you really don't want bitten. I didn't see any injuries on the victim's hands or wrists. It's like she didn't fight back."

From somewhere in the woods a flock of birds exploded from the trees. Porter loosed a squeal, and even Kett flinched. There was something about this place, something that made him feel unbearably vulnerable.

"The wounds to the head don't seem right either," he went on. "It's a slash, something dragged itself down her face. I've never seen a dog do that. Tigers, sure. But not dogs. Surely they wouldn't have the strength to leave cuts like that."

"Not unless it was huge," said Porter. He imitated a slashing motion with his hand. "A big dog on its hind legs, lunging like this, it could have been how it knocked her to the ground."

"Maybe," said Kett.

"But..." said Clare.

"But the jacket," Kett said. "Somebody covered up her chest after savaging her. Either the dog did it, or somebody else. Somebody *with* the dog."

A breeze rode through the trees, making a dozen branches creak like some hellish orchestra. It was almost, Kett thought, like the woods were agreeing with him.

"Now that would make this a very different case," said Clare after a moment. "Somebody set their dog on the victim, then tidied up the corpse afterwards. Unlikely, in my opinion, but it's worth considering. There are gangs around here, and we know they use dogs as weapons. Staffies, mainly. It's a damn shame because they're great dogs. Family dogs. I used to have two."

"This dog is no family dog," said Kett. "And it's not a Staffy either, not unless they're six-foot-tall on their hind legs."

"Great," said Clare, turning around and walking away. "That leaves us with Black Shuck, then. Porter, Kett, I need you at Beccles station, there's a witness to interview."

"Sir," said Porter, nodding.

Kett paused for a moment, listening to the wind in the trees. Then he called out to Clare.

"I'm just wondering why you brought me in for this?"

Clare looked back. Silhouetted against the halogen

lights, he looked like some kind of fairy tale monster—too tall, too thin.

"I mean, a dog attack?" Kett said when the boss didn't say anything. "It seems like an odd choice of case to call me back for."

"What's your head telling you?" Clare asked.

Kett popped his lips, flexing his shoulder to try to relieve the build-up of pain. He glanced at the tent and thought of the woman who lay there, savaged beyond recognition. They didn't know her name. They had no idea who she was. But just twenty-four hours ago she'd been a living, breathing human being with hopes and dreams and fears and sadnesses, just like anyone else.

And now, she was dead. Something had killed her. It had scratched her, it had bitten her.

It had *eaten* her.

"Kett?" said Clare.

"My head?" he said. "My head's telling me this looks like a dog attack."

And yet whatever had done that to her had covered her up with her coat, then disappeared. Kett took a deep breath, his Spidey-sense tingling.

"But my gut's telling me that a dog didn't do this. Something tells me this is the work of a man."

"And that, DCI Kett," said Clare with a grim smile, "Is why I brought you back."

CHAPTER FOUR

"Is he dead?"

DCI Kett and DI Porter stared through a sheet of one-way glass at the wiry man who sat in the interview room of the Beccles Police Station. He was in his late forties, his sunburnt face hidden by a thick, greying beard and bushy eyebrows. He wore a checked shirt and a frayed red beanie, his brown cords and boots resting on the desk in front of him. One arm lay over his stomach, the other hung by his side. His head was angled over the back of the chair, his mouth wide open.

"I'm almost certain he's dead," said Porter. "He's not breathing."

The two men craned in, squinting through the glass.

"He's moving a little bit, isn't he?" said Kett. "Look at his chest. Those are breaths, aren't they?"

"But surely his mouth can't just stay open like that. You could fit a basketball in there."

"Maybe we should check?" Kett said.

"I don't think we've got a basketball," said Porter.

"Check to see if he's *alive*," Kett said.

"Oh, right." Porter nodded. "You want tea first?"

Kett threw him a look which made his answer very clear, then opened the door. A grey-suited woman in her late thirties waited in the corridor outside, arms folded over her chest, her face taut and unfriendly. She looked Kett up and down.

"You're from the Norfolk Constab, then," she said. It wasn't a question. In fact, judging by the tone of her voice, it sounded more like an accusation.

"DCI Kett," Kett said, offering her his hand. She stared at it for a moment like he was holding a fistful of dog shit, then quickly shook it. "I'm—"

"You're not going to do anything, *sir*," she interrupted. "Not without my say so. This is Beccles, and we're south of the border here. Suffolk. The name's on the big sign outside. If you're going to use this as a base, then you answer to us."

Kett glanced at Porter, trying to fight the smile that wanted to break. Clare had warned him about the rivalry between the Norfolk and Suffolk forces, but this just seemed ridiculous. It had been the Super's idea to use Beccles station to interview anyone connected to the case. The Norfolk HQ wasn't far away—thirty minutes, give or take—but that was long enough to make coming back and forth a chore. The imposing brick building in the middle of Beccles was draughty as hell, and falling apart, but it would do the job.

"Received and understood," said Kett. "This is your palace, and I have no intention of pissing up the walls. You're welcome to sit in with us on any interviews. Uh..."

He waited for the woman to introduce herself, but she didn't respond.

"DS Helen Stuart," Porter said.

"Well, it was an absolute pleasure to meet you," said

Kett. "But if you don't mind, we've got somebody waiting for us."

"If he's not dead," added Porter.

DS Stuart frowned and opened her mouth to say something. Then she thought better of it, turning in a tight circle and walking off.

"They're a good lot," said Porter when she'd gone. He grinned at Kett. "Just not as good as us, obviously."

Kett smiled as he opened the door to the interview room, letting Porter in first. He shut the door behind them with some force, in the hope that it would wake the sleeping man. Incredibly, though, he didn't move.

"He really might be dead," said Kett.

They walked up to him, leaning over. Kett prodded him in the cheek, hard, and he loosed a sudden dragon-like snore. What followed was a series of choking noises that blasted out the smell of vodka, then a fart, then a low groan as his eyes opened. He blinked at the ceiling for a moment or two, then those bloodshot eyes swivelled around to see Kett.

"It's a miracle," said Kett. "Back from the grave."

"Uh?" said the man. He pulled his legs off the desk and wiped his face with his hands, muttering something that Kett couldn't make any sense of.

"Graham Turvey," said Porter, reading from his notepad.

"Gray," said the man.

"Gray, fine," said Porter. "I'm just going to—"

"Graham," the man said.

"What?" said Porter. The man shook his head like he was trying to chase off a mosquito.

"Gray Ham," he said.

"Well, this is going to be enlightening," said Kett, taking

a seat on the other side of the desk. "I'm just going to go ahead and call you Mr Turvey. I'm assuming it's safe for me to say you've had a drink this morning?"

"Nope," said the man. "I've had five!"

He found this immensely funny, breaking into uproarious laughter and slapping a hand on his thigh.

"Good for you," said Kett, feeling the edges of his patience start to fray. "You're aware a young woman was found dead in the woods, right?"

The man's smile slid off his face like an egg from a pan. He swayed gently from side to side, his bulging eyes locked to the desk.

"And you were the last person to see her," Kett went on.

"I didn't do it," the man said, suddenly alert. "I wouldn't never hurt a girl like that."

"Do you own a dog, Mr Turvey?" asked Porter, leaning on the desk. The man nodded.

"Three, all good little mongrels. Help me out on the farm. Got cats too."

"Have any of them ever shown signs of aggression?" Kett asked.

"Oh yes," said Turvey. "Feral little buggers. They'll take your hand off if you look at 'em the wrong way. I've got scars all over me, and they know me. You should see what they do to strangers."

"The dogs?" said Kett.

"Hell no, the cats," said the man. "Bastards that they are. But they keep the mice down. Dogs are soft as shit. They're scared of the cats n'all."

"You say you saw the woman before she died?" Kett said, changing tack. "When was that? In the woods, right?"

"Afore the woods," the man said, rubbing his lips and swallowing hard, like he had an imaginary bottle in his hands. "My farm runs along the road, all the way down to the river. I was out mending a stretch of fence yesterday, keep the fecking foxes out—not that you can ever keep them out, mind. See a fair few folk coming this way, a few people running." He barked out a laugh. "Why the feck people do that? Run? For no reason. They should get 'emselves a farm job, be as skinny as me."

Kett waited for him to continue, but he looked like a man whose batteries had just run dead.

"What time?" Kett prompted.

"Evening," was all he could offer. "Don't own a watch."

"So you saw the woman?" Kett said when he failed to continue.

"Oh, yeah, her and a fella, I remember 'em because they didn't have a dog. That's what I was gonna say, afore you broke into me there. We see runners, and dog walkers. That's it. But these two were just walkers, no dog, no running."

"Were they the only people you saw?" Porter asked.

"Sure," he said. "Always quieter after the harvest, gets colder."

"Can you describe the two people for me?" Kett asked. "The man and the woman."

"She was, like, a woman," he said, concentrating so hard it looked like his head might pop clean off his shoulders. "He was more like, I don't know, a fella."

"Right," said Kett, blowing out a long breath and tapping the table with his finger. "What about clothes?"

"Yes," Turvey said after a moment more thought.

"Specifics," Kett said, rolling his hand in the air. "If it's not too much trouble."

"Oh, right. She had this coat on, I remember that. A big white one. I thought to myself, why on earth would you go

into the woods in a coat like that? Be mussed up afore you
know it. So much bird shit and moss and all sorts."

Kett thought of the coat, the way the blood had looked
against the white fabric, the paw prints. Turvey wasn't
wrong.

"Hair colour?" he asked.

"Normal," said the man.

"Normal," Kett said, resisting the urge to pick the
farmer up and shake him. "What about him. The *fella*."

"He was shorter than her," Turvey said. "I remember
that much. Maybe a black jacket, one of those fake farmer
ones that posh pricks wear. Yeah, must have been black,
because I thought to myself they looked like a couple of
chess pieces out there, white and black. She was a queen,
and him a, what do you call them?"

"Pawn?" said Porter.

"No, don't be disgusting. A rook or whatever. But they
wasn't really walking together."

"Oh?" asked Kett. "In what way? Was he following
her?"

"No, she was following him," he said, squinting at the
memory. "And I thought to myself, I did, why was a fine
young woman like that, in her fine white coat, following a
little man? They both looked angry, too. Huffy."

"You didn't hear them talking?" Kett asked.

"No, too far away. Can't hear a fecking thing anyway to
be honest, even from up close. Didn't seem like they were
talking at all."

"That's it?" asked Porter when the room fell silent.
Turvey stared at the wall, his mouth open. He was making a
soft groaning sound, like an old computer being pushed to
its limits.

"Yup," he said after a few seconds. "That's it. They went into the woods and that was the last I saw of 'em."

"And you didn't go after them?" Kett asked, leaning forwards. "You said she was a fine young woman, a woman in distress maybe. You didn't follow them to see if you could help?"

The man blinked, and Kett was surprised to see his eyes go glossy. Turvey wiped the back of his hand over them, hitching in a breath.

"No," he said. "But I shoulda, right? I shoulda gone. Maybe nothing bad would have happened to her then. Maybe it wouldn't have got her."

"It?" asked Kett.

"The dog," said the farmer. "Old Shock, we call it. That's what got her, weren't it? Likely it ate her all up, him too."

Kett shared a look with Porter, then turned his attention back to the man in the chair.

"Did you see a dog?" he asked.

"Not last night, no. But I seen it afore. Great bastard of a thing skulking around in the dark. Took one of my sheep once, I'm sure of it. Everyone round here knows Old Shock, some even leave stuff out for it, like a... like mince pies for Santa, you know? So he doesn't kill you."

"I'm pretty sure Santa won't kill you if you don't leave him a mince pie," said Kett. "What does it look like, this dog?"

Turvey had drifted off again, his red eyes blinking at the wall. He was a grown man, a strong man, but his expression made him look like a boy.

"Just like you think it would," he said. "Looks like the devil on four legs."

GRAHAM TURVEY DIDN'T HAVE anything else to offer, other than breath you could get drunk on, so Kett sent him on his way before he could fall asleep again. He perched on the edge of the interview table, waiting for Porter to show the man out.

"You believe all that stuff about the dog?" he asked when the DI reappeared.

Porter leant on the wall, running a hand through his hair. It took him a while to shake his head.

"It's local legend," he said. "Hell, you've heard the stories."

"Remind me," said Kett.

"Well," Porter chewed his thoughts for a moment. "Let's start with the name, I guess. Black Shuck, or Old Shock, like Turvey said. Shuck comes from *scucca*, which basically means Devil. It's Old English. You impressed?"

"I'm impressed you can read a Wikipedia page," said Kett.

"Fuck off," Porter grunted. "But this dog's been seen for centuries, roaming the coastline and countryside. An omen of doom, usually. According to one account, he burst into a church and slaughtered a bunch of people. In Bungay, which is just down the road. In Fifteen-something-or-other. Left burn marks on the floor and door. It's folklore, Robbie. Folklore, fairy tales, fucking hairy old bollocks."

"So what has Turvey been seeing, out there in the dark?"

"Judging by the amount of vodka on that man's breath, I imagine he's been seeing Black Shuck, Black Beauty, maybe even Black Sabbath roaming around his farmyard. I don't trust a word that came out of his mouth. You?"

"Didn't strike me as a liar," Kett said, pushing himself up and stretching his back. "A drunk, sure, but not a liar. *In vino veritas*, as they say."

"That a disease?" Porter asked, and Kett smiled.

"Depends how you look at it," he said. "But it's definitely worth bringing up sightings of big, black dogs when we canvass the area. Listen, you—"

Kett paused when Porter's phone began to ring. The DI answered it, pacing back and forth as he listened to whoever was on the other end.

"That was the morgue," he said when he hung up. "Body's *en route*, pathology is wondering if we want to be there for the initial autopsy."

"Hell yes," said Kett, making for the door. "Wouldn't miss it for the world."

CHAPTER FIVE

It didn't matter how many times he'd seen it, it never got any easier.

Their Jane Doe lay on the central autopsy table of the pathologist's lab, as exposed as it was possible to be. No clothes, no sheet, there was only a single tattoo to cover her up—a black rose that grew over her left ribs, ending just beneath the breast. There was no dignity in death, Kett thought. No privacy. A killer didn't just rob you of your life, they robbed you of peace, too. How would anybody feel if they knew this was how they'd end up? Naked on a slab of cold steel with an audience of dour-faced police.

She'd been cleaned up, but if anything it made the wounds seem worse than before—stark and brutal against her alabaster skin. As well as the bite marks in her throat and the claw marks to her face, a hand-sized section of her chest had been opened up by her attacker. What glistened inside was almost enough to send Kett running from the room, and he had to focus on the clock above the table for a moment, counting the seconds, picturing the mechanism beneath—clinical and clean—until his head stopped roaring.

He tried not to think about it, of course, but how could he not? It could be Billie lying naked on a mortuary table. It could be his wife.

He closed his eyes for a moment, breathing steadily. Then he turned to Savage, who stood by his side—a little behind him, as if expecting to have to hide at any moment. She was holding her grandfather's lucky police whistle in her hand and was doing her best to stay composed, but he knew the stoic expression she wore was a lie. He could still remember his first autopsy like it had happened yesterday. He didn't think he'd ever be able to forget it—and god knows he'd tried.

Porter stood on the other side of him, even queasier than Savage was. He was looking everywhere except at the body, his eyes darting to the clock on the wall, to the equipment on the tray beside the table, to the floor, to the buzzing ceiling lights, to his hands, to Kett, to Savage, then back to the clock.

"She should be here any minute," Porter said. "She's a little, uh, I can't think of the word. Unusual, maybe?"

"I heard that, Porter," came a voice from behind the partition that separated the pathologist's lab from the bank of PCs and forensic equipment that made up the rest of the morgue. Kett heard the slap of a pair of rubber gloves being put on, then a young girl walked into sight. And it *was* a young girl, there was no doubt about that. She was dressed in a white lab coat, the hood pulled up over her hair. Her face was round, her cheeks red, her eyes bright, and she walked to the table with the confidence of somebody much older. "Right," she said. "Let's see what we've got."

"Um," said Kett. He looked at Porter, then back at the girl. She glanced up at him.

"Um?" she said, lifting her arms in a gesture of impatience.

"*You're* the pathologist?" he said.

"No," she shot back. "I'm a hairdresser, I'm just in the wrong room. Whoops, stupid me, I'll be off then."

Porter was smiling, but Kett was finding it difficult to see the funny side.

"DCI Kett, this is Emily Franklin," the DI said.

"Just call me *Unusual* Emily Franklin," she replied, offering Porter a withering look.

"I meant unusual in the best possible way," said Porter.

"Look, I'm just gonna go ahead and ask," said Kett. "How *old* are you?"

"How old are *you*?" she shot back, meeting his eye.

"Forty-two," Kett said. "A normal age."

"Emily's father was the pathologist here for decades," Porter explained. "He retired in the summer, and Emily's taken over from him. She's not as young as she looks, and she's very good."

"Thank you, Porter," she said dryly, turning to him. "I don't know what I'd do without you. My hero."

"Maybe we should let Miss Franklin get on with her job," said Savage, tucking the silver whistle back into her pocket. Both Porter and Kett held their hands up in surrender, and Franklin offered a genuine smile to the PC.

"I like you, Savage," she said. "Now, unless anyone else has any more questions about my age or abilities?"

"Take it away, Doogie Howser," Kett mumbled.

"Funny," said Franklin without the slightest trace of a smile. "Besides, I know who you are, *Normal-Aged* Robert Kett. It was you, after all, who sent me two corpses covered in—and full of—shit. Remember?"

How could he forget his showdown with Figg and Percival at the sewage treatment plant?

"Oh, right," he said. "Sorry about that."

"Literally, *full* of shit," she said, eyeballing him for a moment more before snapping on a face mask.

She clicked record on a Dictaphone, then took a deep breath.

"Jane Doe, dead approximately sixteen hours."

She leant over the corpse, her eyes a portrait of concentration. Using a pair of long, metal tweezers she peeled at the flesh of the victim's ruined throat.

"This was the killer strike. Throat was opened up with a series of tugging motions. It definitely corresponds with teeth, you can see the serrations here and here. I'll pull samples to check for saliva. I think there were maybe four or five separate bite-like attacks." She looked up. "By the way, the tooth you found belonged to a Rottweiler, an old one. I'm not committing to a dog attack yet, mind. One bite tore through her left carotid artery, here, another made a mess of her trachea, although it didn't quite sever it. If she hadn't bled to death, she'd have drowned in her own blood. I'll know more when I look at the lungs."

Kett took a deep breath through his mouth.

"The injuries to the face?" he asked.

"So, they look like they *could* be claw marks," Franklin said. "And most things are exactly what they appear. But not always. You remember what my dad always used to say, Porter?"

"Nothing beats a pickle sandwich," Porter replied.

"Well, yes," said Franklin. "But the *other* thing he always said was that William of Ockham was a useless piece of shit."

"Ockham's Razor," said Kett, nodding. "The simplest solution is usually the right one."

"That's the layman's version," Franklin said. "But it's close enough. I've done this job for long enough to understand that entities *should* be multiplied without necessity, because things aren't always what they seem. Look."

Kett, Porter and Savage all leaned in as Franklin picked at the skin of the victim's face.

"Four gouges, the one on the far right barely there, a scratch. The one on the other side is nasty, but not deep. It's these two in the middle that did the damage." She pushed the tweezers in, producing a steel ruler in her free hand. "They're just a couple of millimetres deep on the forehead, which makes sense because the bone would prevent further penetration. But look here, where it curves onto the cheek." She inserted the ruler, the sound of it turning Kett's stomach. "That's almost two centimetres. I've yet to meet a dog with claws sharp enough to do that kind of damage. And looking at the neatness of the wound, the absence of any tearing, I'd say it was near enough impossible for an animal to cut so cleanly with its claws."

"Even if they'd been sharpened?" Savage asked. "They do that in dog fights, sometimes."

"I'm saying no," Franklin said. "And look at the angle of the injury. It curves down from the centre of her forehead, through her eyes, angling to the right of her face. I'm not sure, but I don't think a dog would have the flexibility in its limbs to do that."

She stood straight, then mimicked an attack with her right hand, in slow motion.

"If I'm trying to gouge somebody's face then this is how I'd do it, my body would twist like this." She demonstrated, her hand straying to her left as her body pivoted. "That's the angle of the attack."

"So," Kett started, but she held up her hand. The fingertips of her glove were crimson, the blood so bright it looked like paint.

"But going back to the other injuries," she said, walking around the table so that she could access the corpse's chest. "You see the way her ribs are broken."

It wasn't clear, but Kett was happy to take her word for it.

"Pushed inwards," she said. "One of them punctured her lung. The marks here, and here, they do seem like teeth marks. I think something heavy sat on her, almost burrowed into her as it fed. It makes me think of the wildlife documentaries where you see lions with their heads right in their prey. Like, *right* inside, getting all the juicy bits."

Kett was almost certain he heard Porter gag. Franklin used her tweezers to peel back the corpse's skin like she was opening a Christmas present.

"I can't see much," she said. "But even I can tell you that something's missing. Possibly the heart."

"Missing?" said Kett.

Franklin nodded.

"I'll crack her open and have a look. But again, it just doesn't seem like the behaviour of an animal. Whatever did this, it *thought* about what it was doing."

"You're saying you think it was a man," said Kett.

"Or a woman," added Savage, earning another nod of approval from Franklin.

"Human," Kett clarified. "Maybe a human with a dog?"

"I don't know," she said. "But there was definitely a human involved somehow. I'd bet a tenner on it."

"I'll take that bet," said Porter. "I'm saying dog."

"You sound pretty sure," said Kett.

"Oh, I am," she replied. "Can somebody help me with this?"

She grabbed the corpse's shoulders, trying to lever her up. Kett took a pair of gloves from the box on the table, fumbling them on. He got his hands under the dead woman and helped turn her onto her side. Franklin gently swept the hair out of the way with the back of her hand.

"Oh," Kett said.

"Oh!" added Savage.

"Oh *shit*," said Porter.

"Oh shit, indeed," replied Franklin. "You'd better have your wallet on you, Pete."

The woman's back had been mutilated too, a deep cut running almost perfectly along her spine. But it was the injury at the base of her neck that really stood out. Something had cut deep, ragged shapes into the flesh there. Six of them, all in a row, maybe two inches high. The skin was mangled, the blood already pooling there in post-mortem lividity, but it was impossible to mistake those shapes for anything else.

They were letters.

"I've known some smart dogs in my time," said Kett. "But I've never met one that can spell."

"Indeed," said Franklin. "Made with a small blade, I think. Not as sharp as the one used on the face. It's not a skilful job, but it's not a rush job either. Whoever did this took their time."

"Was she alive?" Kett asked.

"Judging by the minimal amount of bleeding, I'd guess not." Franklin shook her head. "If I had to present a timeline, it would go slashed face, throat bitten out, dead in less than a minute, then feeding from the throat, puncture wound to the chest, ribs snapped, organs scarfed, corpse rolled, slash to the back, then the letters are the last thing. It would have taken a while."

"What does it say?" Porter asked, leaning in with one hand over his mouth. "I can't make it out. *dabbog*? What does that mean?"

"Not *dabbog*," said Savage from Kett's other side. "The letters are crooked."

The young PC looked at Kett, a shudder passing through her.

"It says *bad dog*."

CHAPTER SIX

KETT CALLED THE CHILDMINDER AS DI PORTER DROVE him and Savage back into the city in the Homicide Assessment Team car. He knew he didn't need to, but something about the woman on the mortuary slab, about the words that had been carved into her, made him suddenly anxious about his kids.

The phone beeped at him, the line engaged.

Because somebody has taken it off the hook, he thought. *Somebody who shouldn't be there, somebody who wants to hurt them.*

He forced the thoughts from his head, sliding the phone back into his pocket.

"All okay?" Porter asked, keeping the Ford at a steady sixty.

"Yeah," said Kett. "Just checking up on the girls. No answer."

"Knowing those three, they've probably burned the place to the ground," said Porter. He laughed, then saw Kett's expression. "Sorry. Bad joke. They'll be fine."

Kett let it go. The truth was he owed Porter a huge debt because the DI had been round so often in the weeks after Kett had been stabbed. He'd taken a real shine to the girls—even though he was still terrified of them—and they'd taken a shine to him, too. Mainly because they knew he'd let them get away with anything. Porter and his wife didn't have kids, but he would make one hell of a dad if he ever decided to go for it.

"We can swing by, if you like?" said Savage from the back seat. "Just to make sure? It's on the way."

Kett hesitated, then shook his head.

"I've got to collect them soon anyway," he said. "Right now, all I want to do is find out what happened to our Jane Doe in the woods."

"It's a weird case," said Porter. "I've never seen anything like it."

"Me neither," said Savage. "I've seen dogs used as weapons before, though. There was a murder over in Hemsby, where I'm from. Two years ago, maybe? It was one summer, anyway. A bunch of lads used a Pit Bull—an English one, you know, with the long nose—to take out a rival dealer. The dog tore the man's throat clean out."

Porter hit the back of a line of traffic and slowed down, drumming the wheel to a tune of his own making.

"I love dogs, don't get me wrong," Savage went on. "But I saw that dog when they tried to bring it in. It was nothing but muscle and fury. Poor thing had to be destroyed. Nobody was willing to say who it belonged to so they tried all three boys for murder with a deadly weapon. Put all three away, too."

"You wouldn't stand a chance, would you?" Porter said. "A dog like that. Pit Bulls aren't even that big. But if it wants to kill you, it will."

"Dogs don't ever want to kill you," said Kett, his breath steaming up the window. "It's always the owners."

"Agreed," said Savage. "Our suspect might have trained his dog as a weapon in the same way as those boys. He's obviously got a Rottweiler, that's where the tooth came from, right? So he's trained this dog to pounce and pin, to tear out its victim's throat. This dog kills the woman, bites her so hard one of its teeth comes out. Then the man tells it to heel or whatever and he takes over. He cuts her up a bit, carves those letters on the back of her neck. Then they leave."

"It would explain the sightings of Black Shuck," said Porter. "Big dog roaming the woods in the night, it would spook anyone."

"So we do a door to door," said Kett. "Every house. Any sign of a big dog, we grill the owner."

Porter took his chance, overtaking the van that was dawdling in front of them. Kett popped his lips.

"Say you're right, Savage," he said. "And it's one man and his dog. What happened to the guy who was with our victim? Short man, black coat, no dog. He's vanished without a trace, and there was no sign of him in the woods, right?"

"PCs did a sweep before you arrived," Savage said. "Nothing. No other bodies. It's not a big stretch of woodland."

"If he escaped, he would have called for help," Kett said. "Which means he's either dead somewhere we didn't look, or he's complicit in some way. How did Turvey describe the two? Huffy? An argument of some kind. Maybe the black coat man was working with whoever did this."

It didn't sound right; the pieces didn't click together in Kett's head.

"Or he's been taken," said Savage.

That made more sense, and Kett nodded.

"Christ, I hope this isn't another kidnapping," said Porter.

"I'd rather have a kidnapping than a murder any day," Kett said.

Even now, even though Billie's been missing for so long. Anything is better than hearing she's dead.

Porter suddenly flinched, reaching into his pocket.

"My phone's buzzing," he said, fumbling. "Never got around to setting up the Bluetooth. Can you grab it?"

"Really?" said Kett. "You really want me to go there?"

Kett pushed his hand into Porter's trousers and grabbed the phone, answering the call when he saw Clare's name on the screen.

"This is Pete Porter," he said, doing his best imitation of the DI's voice. "I make shit tea and I'm scared of trees."

"Kett?" said Clare. "Where are you?"

"Heading back to the city. We're about..." He looked at Porter, who flashed his hand twice. "Ten minutes away."

"Well turn around," Clare said. "I need you back in Beccles. We've had a call. Somebody's reported a missing woman, and from the sound of it, she's ours."

———

IT WAS WELL after noon by the time Porter pulled them to the side of the road on a residential street in Beccles, and Kett's stomach was grumbling. It wasn't so much the hunger —there was nothing like an autopsy to quell your appetite— more the fact that it had been hours now since he'd last had a cup of tea.

And he was fairly sure they weren't going to be rushing to make him one here.

"Nice part of town," said Porter as he killed the engine.

It was, the houses all detached and haughty, peeking at the street from where they hid amongst conifers and laurels. Kett climbed out of the car, flexing his shoulder and wincing at the ache that gnawed at him. He reached into his coat and pulled out a packet of Paracetamol, forcing two down his dry throat. They barely even dented the pain, but it was better than nothing.

"You okay?" Porter asked as he walked onto the pavement.

"I'm fine," said Kett.

"Better than Raymond Figg, eh?" the DI said with a smile. Kett mirrored it.

"Well, when you put it that way, it's not so bad. Number fourteen, right?"

Clare had given them the details. A call had come in at just before midday, a woman called Ivy O'Neil who was concerned about her daughter. It could turn out to be nothing, of course. These leads often did, especially mothers worrying about their children. But it didn't hurt to check.

Kett led the way to a large gate, 'Number Fourteen' painted on the beige brick wall in giant flowery type. The garden seemed not to have noticed that autumn was here, roses and buddleias and rhododendrons bursting with colour around a well-tended lawn. They'd barely passed through the gate when Kett spotted the woman standing outside the front door, her hands held out in front of her and flexing so much it looked like she was trying to solve an invisible Rubik's cube. She wore a patterned dress that was obviously expensive, but her silvery hair spilled over her shoulders, and she wasn't wearing any shoes. Kett would have put her in her seventies, although it was hard to guess. Terror made most people look older.

And this woman was nothing if not terrified.

"Mrs O'Neil?" Kett asked when he got within earshot. The woman nodded.

"Have you found her?" she asked, the words almost a scream. She looked past Kett to Savage, who stood out from the crowd in her fluorescent jacket and bowler hat. "Have you found her?"

"We just want to have a chat with you," Savage said, holding her hands up to calm the woman. She stepped past Kett and offered a friendly smile. "I don't want you to panic. We're just responding to your call. That's all this is. May we come in?"

The woman swallowed so hard that it sounded like she was choking. She looked at Kett, then Porter, then back to Savage, finally nodding.

"Thank you," said Savage as the woman turned and led them into the house. It was dark inside, the curtains half-drawn and the lights off. A wide corridor led to a kitchen at the other end of the house, and an older man busied himself there. He seemed to make a deliberate attempt not to look at the arriving police.

"Oh, you are a pain in the backside, Ivy," he shouted through. "There's absolutely nothing wrong with her. All this fuss. We don't need *them*."

The woman just waved his words away like he was a swarm of bluebottles. She peeled off to the side, entering a large living room decked predominantly in a colour that Kett could only describe as 1970s-bathroom pink.

"Wretched man," Mrs O'Neil said as she walked in. "Wretched, wretched, wretched. Oh, please take off your shoes."

Kett reluctantly agreed, grunting with pain as he bent down to untie his boots.

"Need a hand?" asked Porter, and Kett threw a scowl back at him. By the time he'd managed to pull them off Savage was already on the sofa, sitting next to Ivy O'Neil. Porter was browsing the faux walnut book cases. He picked up a framed photo and showed it to Kett as he walked into the room.

A young couple, a woman in a purple dress with blonde hair and a beaming smile, and a man, shorter than her, wearing a black coat. He couldn't tell for sure, because the victim's face had been so mutilated, but the person in the picture didn't look a million miles away from the corpse he'd just left.

Kett sighed, preparing himself for a conversation that he really didn't want to have.

"Is this your daughter?" he asked, taking the photo from Porter and holding it out to Mrs O'Neil. The old woman nodded.

"That's her," she said, putting a hand over her mouth in an attempt to hold back the sobs that were building there.

"What's her name?" said Savage.

"Oh." Mrs O'Neil frowned, like she couldn't understand what she was being asked. "Sally, of course. It's Sally."

"And you say Sally's missing?" Savage asked, her voice quiet and calm. Mrs O'Neil nodded again, breathing through her fingers. "Since when?"

"I," the woman started. She pulled her hand away, staring at it. "We were supposed to have breakfast together. Here."

"This morning?" asked Savage.

"This morning, yes, of course," Mrs O'Neil said. "But she didn't show up. It's so unlike her. It's *not* like her. In all her years she's not once missed our breakfasts. Then we heard about the body in the woods."

Kett threw a glance at Porter, who shrugged.

"How did you hear about the body?" Kett asked. "Nothing's been released yet."

"This is a small town," she replied. "Word gets around. Mrs Hill across the road said they found a girl there. A woman. Is it Sally?"

"You've tried contacting your daughter?" Savage asked.

"I called," Mrs O'Neil replied. "Seven, eight times. Her phone is off. It's *never* off. I called Roger too."

"Roger is her boyfriend?" asked Kett, holding up the photograph. "This man?"

"Bloody useless fool," came a voice from the door. The man from the kitchen walked in, his slippers scuffing the carpet. He had to be ten years older than his wife, but his rod-straight back and perfectly groomed white moustache let Kett know he was a military man through and through. He didn't sit, he just stood by the big, bay window with his hands clasped behind his back. "Wet as a duck's cock."

"*Bill!*" hissed Mrs O'Neil.

"Well, he is. One of these, what do you call them, passive-aggressive types. Never says what he wants, just sulks about it until you get so fed up with him you do it anyway."

"How long have they been together?" Kett asked.

"Too bloody long," said Mr O'Neil. "Six years."

"Seven," said Mrs O'Neil. "Eight this Christmas."

"That long?" Mr O'Neil snorted in disgust. "Ask me, she's probably buggered off just to get away from him. Always cared more about the damned dog than he did about her."

"He has a dog?" Savage asked, looking up from where she sat.

"It's dead," said Mrs O'Neil, pressing the back of her hand to her eyes.

"Good riddance to it," said her husband. "They brought the little rat here once and it shit on the carpet. Right where you're standing."

He pointed at Kett, looking at him like *he* was the turd in question.

"Never let it back in the house after that. And I wish I could have done the same with Roger."

Mrs O'Neil muttered something under her breath that sounded like *wretched man*. Kett cleared his throat, replacing the photograph on the shelf.

"We don't normally investigate missing persons until twenty-four hours have passed," he said. "Especially with adults. How old was Sa—" He almost thrust a hand in his mouth. *Is, it's always is until you're sure.* "*Was* Sally on her last birthday?"

Nobody seemed to notice him covering up his mistake.

"Thirty-four," said Mr O'Neil. "Her birthday's in October. She's too old to be mooching around the way she is. Unmarried, no children. It's not how we brought her up. It's not the kind of woman we expect her to be."

"And who can blame her?" asked his wife, glaring at him. "What kind of example have we set her? We must have put her off marriage for life."

"Like I said," Kett broke in. "We don't often investigate unless there's evidence of a crime, or of a crime that is about to be committed. Is there anything that leads you to suspect that something has happened to Sally?"

"I just know," Mrs O'Neil sobbed. "I just know. I'm her mother."

"Bloody maternal instinct, my arse," said the old man. "Sally's fine, you old coot."

"Oh *fuck off*, Bill," she spat, so much anger in her words that she half jumped up from the sofa to fire them at him. She crashed back down, exhausted, and Kett walked to Mr O'Neil.

"Why don't we have a chat in another room," he said. "My colleagues will get everything they need from your wife."

Mr O'Neil bristled, but Kett touched his elbow and firmly guided him from the room. He walked down the hallway into the kitchen, which was brighter than the rest of the house. The old man made for the table and busied himself with a stack of newspapers, lining them up so their edges were perfectly straight. He was the picture of composure, but Kett had been around men like him before. He could see the pressure cooker inside his head, a chaos of emotion that had been bottled up for so long it could take out the world if it was released.

"Does Sally live around here?" Kett said.

"She and Roger the Todger have a place over in Toft Monks," he replied, still working on his papers. "A flat. Rented, at *their* age. And it's not like we never offered them help, is it?"

"Mr O'Neil," said Kett. He licked his dry lips. "Do they ever go walking in the woods? Particularly the woods south of Aldeby, near the river."

He knew the answer in the way the old man's trembling hand scrunched the top newspaper into a ball. He knew it in the way his posture seemed to grow even stiffer than it had been before, then fall loose—like a dying animal in its final death throes. He knew the answer the same way that Mr O'Neil knew the truth about his daughter. It was written into every unspoken word, and into the heavy silence that followed.

"I'm assuming that's a yes," Kett went on. The gun had been fired, and another bullet couldn't exactly do any more damage. "May I ask, does Sally have any distinctive marks on her, any tattoos or piercings, for example?"

Mr O'Neil didn't reply, the newspaper still locked in his fist. He cleared his throat over and over, as if he'd forgotten how to breathe. Then, in stiff, jerky movements, he crossed the kitchen to an immense Ducal dresser. Nestled amongst the plates and the cups was a handful of framed photographs and he pulled one free, studying it. He showed no sign of turning around so Kett walked to his side, looking down.

He felt his heart break for the old man.

There was Sally O'Neil, standing with three other young women in what had to be a nightclub. She held a Martini glass in her hand, and the photographer had obviously caught her mid-laugh. She was wearing a long, gold dress with a split that ran from the arms to the ankles—all held together with a copper-coloured belt. You could see her side, and right there, etched on the shadows of her ribs, was a tattoo of a single, black rose.

It wasn't conclusive, of course, but Kett didn't doubt for a moment that this woman was the one who currently lay on Emily Franklin's pathology table.

"I know what you're going to say," Mr O'Neil said, his voice crumbling at the edges like a sandcastle in the wind. He was holding on to the photograph so tightly that Kett thought the glass might crack. "You don't have to say it."

"We don't know anything for certain," said Kett. "But it might help us if you, or your wife, could make an identification, positive or negative."

"I will," said the man. He seemed to regain some composure, gently placing the photograph back on its shelf, prodding it with his fingertip until the position was perfect. "Ivy won't be any good to you. The woman's a mess."

As if on cue, a fragile wail poured out of the living room door. Mr O'Neil stood there for a moment more, staring at nothing, his eyes blinking, blinking, blinking, a final stand against the charging tears.

"She was a good girl," he said. "My Sally."

He turned and walked away as his wife's cries rose in volume, but he didn't head towards her. He strolled instead to the window and stared out at the back garden, his hands once again gripped behind his back.

"I'll ask you to show yourself out," he said.

Kett nodded, even though the man wasn't looking at him. He walked to the kitchen door before turning back.

"PC Savage will take you to the mortuary," he said. "She'll wait here with you until a car arrives. May I ask, was Roger ever violent towards your daughter?"

Mr O'Neil barked out a laugh that steamed up the glass. He used his fist to clear it.

"That spineless runt couldn't hurt a crippled cat," he said. "He's pathetic. Did you speak to him?"

"We can't find him," Kett said. The old man laughed again, a dry and broken husk of sound.

"Then let's hope that useless prick's dead too."

CHAPTER SEVEN

KETT CLOSED THE DOOR SOFTLY BEHIND HIM, TAKING A deep breath of crisp Autumn air. Porter stood by his side, staring at the garden.

"She's our victim," the DI said softly. "Her mum mentioned the coat, a great big white thing. They'd got it for her birthday and she'd barely taken it off."

"Sally O'Neil had a tattoo, as well," Kett said. "Black rose on her ribs."

"Fuck," said Porter.

"Savage is going to take them over to the morgue when Franklin's finished." Kett blew out a sigh. "Though god knows how they're going to identify her with those injuries to her face."

He glanced to the side and saw Mrs O'Neil staring at them through the bay window, looking like a woman in a sinking ship. Savage appeared, steering her into the darkness of the house and giving Kett a gentle nod. He didn't envy her. She'd have to wait there with them until a car arrived to take them to the morgue, then sit with them while their world ended.

He sighed, making his way down the path. Porter unlocked the car, but Kett motioned for him to hang on. He jogged across the street, scanning the houses on the opposite side. One stood directly in front of the O'Neil place, and the net curtains in the living room were definitely twitching. He opened the gate and walked up the cobbled path, rapping on the front door. Porter ambled up beside him.

"Yes?" came a voice from the other side of the heavy door.

"You're not Mrs Hill, by any chance?" Kett asked.

"Who's asking?" she replied.

"DCI Kett of the Norfolk Constabulary."

"Well this isn't Norfolk, is it?" said the voice. "This is Suffolk."

"The 'Norfolk' part isn't the important bit," Kett said. "It's the 'Constabulary' part you really need to pay attention to. I've just spoken to your neighbours, and they mentioned that you knew about the body in the woods."

After a slight hesitation, Kett heard the sound of locks turning. A *lot* of locks. The door opened a fraction and Kett had to angle his head down to look at one of the smallest women he'd ever seen. She couldn't have stood over four foot, and it would be a miracle if she was even that. Kett put her in her mid-fifties, but she dressed like somebody three decades older.

"Aye," she said, although her accent wasn't remotely Scottish. "The body in the woods. Have you arrested 'em yet?"

"Them?" asked Kett.

"We all know who did it," the woman went on, craning her head up. She held onto the door with hands that looked more like talons, and Kett wondered if arthritis had contributed to her diminutive height. "We all know who killed that girl."

"Before we get there," said Kett. "Can I ask you how you found out?"

The woman looked behind her, then past Kett to the street beyond, licking her lips as if she was about to reveal a national secret.

"Alfie, in town, his son's a policeman. Scott told his da, Alfie told Mrs Crosby at the newsagents, who told Penelope Britton. And once Penelope knows something then the whole world knows it. Can't keep that one quiet for long. She told me and I made sure I didn't tell a soul. I'm good that way."

"You told Mrs O'Neil across the street," said Kett. The woman's cheeks darkened.

"Well, I did, but only because she asked."

"And you're telling us," said Porter.

"But you're police," she said. "I can't *not* tell you."

She fidgeted, biting her lip.

"Okay I told a few other people too, but there's not much goes on around here and what am I supposed to do if—"

Kett held up a hand.

"You haven't done anything wrong, Mrs Hill. It is Mrs Hill, isn't it?"

She nodded.

"You say you know who killed the woman?"

"Aye," she said again, speaking the word like a pirate. "No big secret that the Morton boys take their dogs in them woods. Savage, they are. Breed them to watch over their land, to fight, even take down the odd deer."

"Morton," said Kett. "Local?"

"Of course," she said. "They run a scrapyard up the

river. Farmland there too, not that they do much farming since their da died. Well, not the kind of farming you're supposed to do."

She tapped her nose, winking at Kett.

"Drugs?" he asked, and she shrugged her shoulders.

"So they say. Jeff Morton's the older of the boys, you see him in town a fair bit. Big bully of a man, but it's the little one that's dangerous. Thomas. He's only seventeen. I know for a fact they take money off the shops around here, protection money. Protection from who, though? From them! It's all a big con, but when you see Thomas you'll understand. Ask me, the poor woman, whoever she was, she came across the Mortons and saw something she shouldn't have. Then they set their dogs on her."

Kett pulled out his notepad and jotted down the details. When he looked up again Mrs Hill was smiling at him.

"But don't listen to me," she said. "I'm really not one for gossip."

———

"THANKS, SIR."

Porter pocketed his phone, reaching over to type an address into the Sat Nav. He fumbled it a few times, cursing, before getting it right.

"The farm's registered to a Mortimer Morton," he said. "Bloody stupid name, if you ask me, even for a dead man. Died this summer, kids still live there. Older one, Jeffrey Morton—he's, uh, twenty-four—has a sheet. Assault, intimidation, was put away for a couple of years for possession with intent to supply. Thomas is known to us too. They look, in my professional opinion, like a bunch of rancid bastards."

Porter looked over his shoulder, doing what Kett supposed was meant to be a three-point turn but which, thanks to the narrow street, was more like seven.

"You do have your licence, don't you Pete?" Kett asked when they bumped down from the kerb for the final time. Porter ignored him, taking a left. Kett wound down his window, grateful for the air. After six weeks off, the day had exhausted him, and it was only going to get worse when he picked the girls up. The last thing he wanted to do was go and confront a group of thugs—not to mention their dogs—but a lead was a lead, even when it was delivered by a fifty-year-old, four-foot-high gossip queen.

The traffic was light, and Porter tapped the wheel as he drove.

"Makes sense," the DI said. "Couple out walking in the woods, stumble across something bad. The old bat might be onto something."

"Maybe," said Kett. "But why would they stop to carve *Bad Dog* into her?"

"A warning, maybe?" said Porter. "Seems like a close-knit community down here, news travels fast. From the sounds of these Morton boys, they like people to know they're in charge."

"Did you get any inkling that Sally O'Neil might be into something dodgy herself?" asked Kett. Porter shook his head.

"She seemed a decent sort," he said. "Steady job—her mum told us she was an assistant manager in a care home down near Ipswich—and no criminal history. Nothing made me suspect her of anything other than being in the wrong place at the wrong time."

Kett nodded. He'd felt the same thing.

"I'm getting some vibes from the boyfriend, though," Porter said. "Her parents hated him."

"Do any parents like their son-in-law?" Kett asked. "Billie's mum was furious when she heard she'd married into the force. And didn't your mum once call Allie a—and I quote —*grocery bag full of old tits*?"

Porter barked out one of his cannon-shot laughs.

"I'd forgotten that!" he said. "That was right when we were starting to date. Christ, what a thing to say. To her *face,* as well."

"How is she, by the way?" Kett asked. "Your mum."

"Half dead," Porter said. "As much of a bitch as ever. But she's fine. In remission. Hey..."

He looked like he was about to say something, then hesitated.

"Yeah?" Kett prompted.

"Look, speaking of Allie, I was wondering if we could come over to see you one evening. For dinner."

"You're inviting yourself to my house," Kett said. "With *my* kids? Are you insane?"

"I thought it might be nice. She often asks after you."

"Pete, she hates me," said Kett. "Don't you remember the incident with the tea?"

Porter frowned, then burst into laughter again.

"That? Come on, Kett, she forgot about that years ago. You explained what happened. There was a fly in your tea, you had to tip it out in the sink. She's fine."

"It wasn't a fly," said Kett. "You know it and I know it and so does she. Your wife makes... Look, I'm just going to come out and say it. Your wife makes bad tea. It's worse than yours. It was a cup of camel piss she served me. I couldn't drink it, I tipped it out, and she never forgave me."

"I—" started Porter.

"I'm a detective, Pete," said Kett. "I know when you're lying. She's not fine. But hey, if you guys want to come over then I would love to have you. Let me get a sitter, yeah? It's bedlam when the kids are around."

"Well, actually," Pete glanced at him, almost nervously. "Look, can we have the kids there too? I'm thinking that maybe it might be good for Allie to see a family—well, you know, see the little ones. I'm thinking of trying to nudge her towards having one of our own."

Kett started to laugh, shaking his head as Porter took the roundabout that led out of town. He was conscious that ahead of them, parked in a lay-by, sat a police car.

"Pete, I literally cannot imagine a worse incentive to starting a family than spending an evening with Alice, Evie and Moira."

Porter pouted, and Kett laughed again.

"But if that's what you want, then I'm happy to oblige. Any time. You're always welcome."

Porter grinned, but Kett wasn't watching him. They'd passed the police car, and in his side mirror Kett saw it indicate out of the lay-by, its lights blazing. Porter saw it too, slowing down.

"You look nervous, Pete," said Kett. "Is there something you're not telling me?"

"No," he spluttered. "Why would I be nervous?"

"Because the police are tailing us," Kett said, suppressing a smile. "You sure you're not hiding anything?"

"It's just, I still worry when I see lights behind me," he said. "I wasn't always a good boy, as you well know."

During a night in the pub back in their Met days, the night they'd cracked their first murder together, Porter had confessed to Kett that he'd nicked a dozen or so cars when he was a teenager. He'd never been collared, but it had been close.

"The past always catches up with you," said Kett.

Porter swore, pulling the car into the next lay-by and leaving enough room for the squad car to pull in behind them. He cut the engine, both men squinting into the mirrors as a uniformed sergeant climbed out of the driver's seat. The passenger door opened too, and a woman in a grey suit appeared.

"It's your friend," said Porter. "DS Stuart."

"Joy of joys," said Kett. He buzzed down his window, working up a reluctant smile as Stuart's face loomed into view.

"Boys," she said. "Want to tell me where you're going?"

"Back to civilisation," said Porter. "Over the border, away from the smell of cow shit."

Stuart smiled, but there wasn't much warmth to it.

"A little birdie told me you're heading to the Morton farm," she said. Kett looked at Porter, mouthing *how?* Porter shrugged. Cars roared past on the main road, each shock-wave rocking the Ford. Stuart leaned in closer. "I want you to stay away from them, is that clear?"

"Why?" asked Kett. "We have reason to believe they might have something to do with our dead woman."

"That may be," she replied. "But we've been watching them for two years now. We were working a case against the father, and now that he's gone we're targeting the sons. If you march in there with your big mouths flapping then it's going to blow our investigation wide open."

Kett nodded.

"Fair enough," he said. "But if you're watching them then you might want to see where they were yesterday evening. Victim was almost certainly Sally O'Neil, lived up in Toft Monks."

"Your boss just called, filled me in," she said. "Don't worry, we're taking care of it."

"Okay," Kett said. "Whatever you do, don't take your eyes off them."

DS Stuart frowned, like she'd been expecting more of a battle.

"Okay," she said, tapping the roof of the car. "Back to Norfolk you go, sir. Try not to fuck any turnips on your way."

Despite himself, Kett laughed as the Suffolk DS walked away. The cop car gave a blast of its siren as it pulled back onto the road, and Porter honked the horn.

"We were robbed," Porter said. "I thought we were onto something there, and I can't say I'm not disappointed that we don't get to spend the afternoon busting a bunch of juvenile delinquents."

"Speak for yourself," Kett said, checking his watch. "I've got to go pick up my kids."

CHAPTER EIGHT

There was no doubt about it. It was a crime scene.

The walls were a mess, splattered with a substance that looked like blood and old brains. More of it stained the pristine, white, deep-pile carpet, even though somebody had attempted to clean it up. Sitting by the sink was a pile of razor-sharp pieces that had, presumably, once been a plate.

"Oh," said Kett. He wasn't sure what else to say.

"I left it like this," said Lisa, the childminder. "I mean, I had to at least try to get it out of the carpet, but I wanted you to see how bad it was."

Kett turned from the young woman in dungarees, her blonde hair wrapped up in a Rosie the Riveter hairband, to the girls who stood on the other side of the small, neat dining room. *His* girls, although right now he was tempted to make a break for the door while denying ever knowing them. Alice stood there with a face like fury, her skinny arms folded over her chest. Evie stood next to her, her chubby cheeks blazing. Moira had run to him as soon as he'd walked through the door and now sat in the crook of his good arm, plastering soggy kisses on his ear.

"Girls, do you have anything to say about this?" he asked them.

"I didn't do it!" Alice said, stamping her foot and shooting him a look that was almost dangerous. "I already told *her*, it was Evie."

"Evie?" said Kett, trying to keep his voice calm. He already knew she was responsible for the mess, because Alice never lied. Alice *couldn't* lie, he was fairly sure of that. She barely understood the concept.

Evie, on the other hand, could lie. She was just very, very bad at it.

"I didn't do anything," she said, her eyes swivelling to the floor, to the ceiling, to the mess, to the window, then to her hands, which she held in front of her like she'd never seen them before. "It was Moira."

"Evie," said Kett again, resorting to his growl. She stamped her foot too, mirroring her big sister.

"I didn't. It was... it just *happened*. They just fell."

"A whole bowl of beans—" said Kett.

"It was a plate," barked Alice.

"A whole plate of beans just—"

"And little bits of sausage," Alice added. "It wasn't just beans."

Kett took a deep breath to try to extinguish the spark of impatience that had taken root inside him.

"A whole plate of beans and little bits of sausage just somehow flew—"

"Fell," said Evie.

"*Flew* off the table, with some force, and hit the wall. Just like that. Like magic."

"The mermaids did it," said Evie, speaking to the floor.

"Right," said Kett. He turned to the childminder.

"I'm so sorry," he said. "She doesn't like beans."

"I gathered," said Lisa.

"She doesn't normally do this," he went on. "I'll pay to have the carpet cleaned."

Lisa held up her hands, managing a smile.

"It happens," she said. "My mum told me I was an idiot getting a white carpet, and she was right. I was more disappointed that Evie didn't tell me the truth."

They both looked at Evie, who seemed on the verge of tears. Kett put Moira on the floor and the baby grabbed hold of his trousers, instantly beginning to cry.

"Mine!" she said, trying to scale his leg like a monkey up a palm tree. "Arry."

"I'll carry you in a minute," he replied, holding out his hands to Evie. Reluctantly, she slouched towards him, still not meeting his eye. He scooped her up and she buried her head in his neck.

"What do you say to Lisa?" he asked. Her reply was too muffled to make much sense of, but it was close enough to an apology that he was willing to let it go.

"Mine!" screamed Moira, trying to grab Evie's feet.

"But while you're here, I do need to talk to you," said Lisa, looking somewhat sheepish. Kett was well aware of what was coming, and he grit his teeth in readiness. "I'm not going to be able to look after the girls anymore. I love them, don't get me wrong. They're... adorable. Mostly. But I'm starting a midwifery degree and I'm going to be too busy after this month. I'm so sorry."

"It's fine," said Kett. "You always said it was just for the summer. I appreciate everything you've done for them. They always speak very highly of you."

"She's an idiot," muttered Alice.

"Alice is just disappointed," he said, glaring at his oldest child. "If you ever find yourself looking for work during the holidays, though, you've got my number."

Lisa smiled and nodded in a way that made it perfectly clear she wouldn't be calling.

"Okay," said Kett. His shoulder was throbbing from the weight of his middle daughter so he put her down, picking up Moira instead. He turned and made for the door, only for Evie to put her arms around his legs and plant her face right in his backside.

"Daddy!" she wailed.

"Oh for fudge's sake," he said. "Evie! Alice, come on!"

Somehow, he made it out of the house, Lisa closing the door behind them with so much force it was like she was worried they were all going to run back inside. He half-expected to hear her turn the key and slide the bolt across.

"Did you have to do that?" he said to Evie, who was still clinging to his legs. He tried to wriggle free as he headed down the street to where their old, pigeon-shit-green Volvo was parked. Alice stomped along behind, kicking stones.

"I hate beans," Evie said.

"Yes, but they can't hurt you," he said. "You could have just said no."

"I'm sorry, Daddy," she said with a decidedly-not-sorry smile.

"And we don't call people idiots, do we, Alice?"

"No," she said, muttering a word that was almost certainly *idiot*. He let it go. All he wanted to do was get home, chug another couple of Paracetamol, stick the TV on for the kids, then try to work out who—or what—had killed Sally O'Neil. This was almost the worst part, getting the kids from one place to another. It was like herding cats. With Billie, it had been easy. She'd had the reflexes of a

Premier League goalkeeper. Without her, though, he was always waiting for one of the kids to walk into the road or attack a passer-by, and the experience was genuinely, panic-attack-inducingly stressful.

What he wouldn't give to have her back. What he wouldn't give to see her walking around the corner right now, that smile on her face, her hands held out to him. The thought of it was a black hole right in the centre of him, an aching, awful absence that wanted to pull the rest of him inside it and swallow him forever. If he gave into it, he knew, he'd simply vanish, right here and right now.

And his kids would be on their own.

"Where's mum?" Alice asked, as if she could read his mind. Kett counted to three—*you can do this, Robbie*—then smiled at her.

"I don't know, Alice," he said. "I'm sorry."

It was the same answer he always gave her. He didn't think she even expected anything else from him. She kicked another stone that bounced along the kerb and clacked into the door of their car.

"I want mum," said Evie. "Will she be at home?"

"Mumma!" Moira shouted into his ear. "Mine!"

They talked about her often. They talked about her every day—and he encouraged it, even though each mention of her was like a knife between his ribs—because he didn't want them to forget her. He knew that they, like him, would be losing their memories. She'd be drifting out of their heads like salt in water. The thought of it was unbearable, because if something had happened to Billie, if she genuinely wasn't ever coming home, then he and the girls were the only way of keeping some part of her alive. Without their memories, she was lost forever.

"Let's just get home," he said as he fumbled for the key.

He unlocked the car and yanked open the door on Evie's side, watching helplessly as she and Alice fought each other to be the first one in. Closing the door, he walked to Moira's side and wrestled her into the seat, the baby suddenly possessed with the strength of a Luchador. She squealed in his ear, trying to scratch his hand, and he managed to keep his curses under his breath as he clicked the belt in. By the time he'd made sure the other girls were belted up his heart was going like the clappers.

Nothing like having kids to prepare you for being a murder detective, he thought as he sat in his own seat.

"Have we got everyone?" he asked, and the girls answered with a rallying cry.

"Let's go get some dinner then."

He started the engine, laughing quietly to himself.

"Who fancies some beans?"

THEY HAD PASTA, and the girls ate it in blissful silence.

They were all knackered, content to bunch up together on the sofa in front of *Frozen* while they ate their food like zombies. The rented semi-detached house hadn't changed much in the six weeks or so that they'd been living in it. He'd not exactly been in a position to do much decorating, but he'd finally got around to unpacking the boxes that had arrived the day he'd woken up in hospital, and at least it looked a little more like home. Porter, bless him, had mounted their TV on the wall and set up Sky. Savage had washed all the curtains and hired a professional vacuum washer to tackle the crumbs and crayon and concrete-like porridge that had been trod into the carpet.

"I can't believe they rented the place to you with all this

mess," she'd said, and he'd been too embarrassed to point out that *his* girls had made that mess in the few days they'd been in the property.

On one of his physio days, she'd also mounted about fifty photographs all over the house. The PC was a dab hand with a hammer, it seemed. Kett had walked in to see his wife grinning at him from every room, and even though it had filled him with joy he'd had to fight off the tears until Savage had left and the kids had gone to bed. Only then, alone with her ghost staring down at him, had he lost it.

But it was good to have her here. And she'd appreciate it if she came back.

When she came back.

Kett checked the kids once more then walked out of the living room, heading into the kitchen. The kettle was just coming to a boil and he lifted it from its cradle, pouring water into a mug. It was just a teabag—he still hadn't managed to get back into his routine of making proper tea with loose leaves—but the smell of it instantly perked him up. He stirred it while calling Bingo on his phone. His Superintendent back in London answered after two rings, the way he always did.

"My dear boy," he said in his unmistakable baritone. "How are you? I spoke to Clare this afternoon, he told me you've got a demon dog on the loose up there in the sticks."

Kett laughed, scooping out the teabag and lobbing it at the bin. It missed, splatting on the floor.

"A demon for sure," he said. "But I don't think it's a dog. Not unless dogs have learned to carve words into their victims."

"Ouch, nasty," said Bingo. "But I have no doubt you'll catch him. If you're really back, that is?"

Kett poured a dash and a half of milk into his tea.

"I think I'm ready," he said. "I *am* ready. But the question is, should I stay up here or come back home?"

Bingo didn't reply straight away, and Kett could picture him stroking his bushy moustache. His feet would be on the desk, the way they always were, his chair tilted backwards.

"Kett," he said eventually. "You are welcome back to the Met anytime. We all miss you."

But... Kett thought.

"But your girls are settling in up there, and I worry that there are too many bad memories down here at the moment, for them and for you. It won't do any of you any good to come back. Not yet. Clare says they never would have solved the Figg case without you. Three girls would have died, maybe more victims too. You're an asset to the Norfolk team. I'd like you to stay, and I'd like to make it an official transfer."

Kett nodded, but Bingo picked up on his reluctance.

"I understand you want to be close to her," the Super said. "But I promise you, we are treating this as a priority case. I have a detective on it full time—DS Ridgway, obviously. Adam's had some promising leads, as you know, but nothing that's panned out. I trust him, and so should you."

Curls of steam rose from his mug, and he watched them caress the wall and the photograph that hung there. Billie in hospital, exhausted, a four-year-old Alice sitting on one side of the bed and grinning like the Joker, a swaddled blob in Billie's arms that they'd soon name Evie. Droplets of moisture collected on the glass and he gently smudged them away with his finger.

Don't ask, he told himself. *There's no point. Don't ask.*

"Any news?" he said, like he always knew he would.

"No," said Bingo, as patient as a saint. "But there will be. Have faith, Robbie."

Have faith.

"I'd better run," said the Super. "My bingo caller's calling is calling!"

He laughed at his own joke, then said his goodbyes, hanging up the phone. Kett kept it to his ear for a moment more, waiting for the man to jump back on and say, *I'm kidding, we found your wife!* But there was just static, then the depthless silence of the dead line. He put the phone on the counter and sipped his tea, even though it was far too hot. Then he picked the phone up again and called Superintendent Clare.

"Kett," barked Clare after a handful of rings. "You still out in the field?"

"No, home now. Needed to collect the kids."

"Fair enough. Anything new?"

"Victim's name is Sally O'Neil," Kett said as he carried the tea to their small dining table and sat down. "Lived in a flat in Tofts Wood."

"I know," said Clare. "Savage brought the father in, he made a positive ID based on the tattoo. Poor bastard. They covered up her face but he wanted to see it. Can't say I blame him, but that's not how I'd want to remember my kids. Any sign of the boyfriend? You like him for this?"

"No," said Kett. "But I'm not ruling him out. Our best lead so far is a bunch of lowlifes on the edge of Beccles, known for using their dogs as weapons."

"Ah yes," said Clare. "The Morton boys. I had a call from DS Stuart, she works for the Suffolk lot."

"I know her well," Kett sighed.

"She made herself very clear, we are not allowed to go anywhere near the Morton property." Clare paused, his heavy breaths reverberating through the handset. "But Dunst did a Land Registry check, and apparently one of their fields is north of the river. It's technically in Norfolk."

"Nice," said Kett with a smile.

"So feel free to have a nosy around," Clare said. "A peek across the river, if you will. Who knows what you might find. Remember, it's your duty as a police officer to investigate any disturbances you may hear."

Clare cleared his throat, about as far from subtle as it was possible to be.

"Or may *not* hear," the Super said. Kett could imagine him winking furiously. "Do you understand?"

"I do, sir," said Kett.

"I'm saying you should look for an excuse to investigate the property from our side," Clare went on.

"Yes, I got that," said Kett.

"But don't make it *look* like you're investigating."

"Yes, that was definitely implicit in the words that came out of your mouth."

"Good," said Clare. "So you know what I—"

"I'm going to hang up now," said Kett, doing exactly that. He took another sip of his tea, suddenly aware of the noise that was spilling out of the living room—screams, shouts, and a roar from Moira that might have been laughter or might have been a war cry.

The soundtrack of the Ketts, he thought as he pushed himself out of his chair and went to investigate.

———

IT WAS WELL after nine before he managed to get the girls to sleep. The bedtime routine had been harder than ever since he'd been in hospital. Even though he'd only been away for three nights, and Colin Clare's wife, Fiona, had been happy to step in while he was gone, the girls had taken it badly. For those three nights—in their heads at least—they'd been orphans, and they'd been as clingy as barnacles ever since.

There had been a couple of weeks, right after the paper girls case had ended, where he'd given up on getting them to sleep in their own rooms and just let them camp out together in the living room. Porter had carted all the mattresses down for him, including his, and they'd just dogpiled right there on the floor. It had taken a long time, and some serious bribes, before Alice and Evie had agreed to move back to their beds.

And Moira still hadn't.

She sat in his arms now, as heavy as a sack of potatoes. He basically had to jiggle her to sleep, and however she drifted off was how she remained for hours. Tonight, his right arm was pinned beneath her, but he had his phone in his left so he wasn't entirely helpless. The worst thing was that the remote control was out of reach, and the *Frozen* DVD was on a loop. If he had to watch Olaf the snowman sing that bloody song one more time he thought he might go on a murder spree of his own.

Kett did his best to tune it out, scrolling down the Facebook page that he had open on his phone. Roger Carver pouted back at him from a number of photos because the fool had set his privacy to Public. Pouted was the right word, too. It was clear that the man took himself way too seriously. Mr O'Neil had mentioned that Sally's boyfriend had been a classic passive-aggressive, and that poured out of every picture like a bad smell. Kett had met too many people like that, so riddled with self-doubt that they hid behind a false confidence designed to make everyone else feel inferior. He seemed the complete antithesis to Sally's outgoing charm, but then everyone knew that opposites attract.

There were surprisingly few photographs of Sally on Roger's page, and a frankly ridiculous number of photographs of a dog. At least, Kett *thought* it was a dog. It had huge, bulging eyes and a flat face that looked like it had been hit one too many times with a frying pan. Its body seemed too skinny for its head and was covered with a shaggy coat of tan fur. Its tail was a pig's tail, a little curl that sat on its back like it had been glued there.

"Maurice," read Kett, scanning the captions above the photos. Moira stirred at the sound of his voice, slapping herself in her sweaty face as she tried to brush her hair from her eyes. He jiggled his arm, shushing her, and she fell quiet again.

More photos of the dog, the poor thing clad in Christmas elf outfits or Iron Man costumes. Kett had never seen a dog look embarrassed before, but Maurice seemed to cringe out of the screen.

Then, out of the blue, a black and white photograph of the little dog.

R.I.P. buddy.

Kett clicked on the comments, scrolling down a tide of condolences until something caught his eye.

Sal make you do that?

The comment was from a man called Kavan Dunn, and Roger had replied.

Not in so many words, mate, but yeah.

He'd added a little angry face, too. Kett delved a little deeper, guessing the story from the little pieces of information there: Maurice had been old, but Sally had given him the push.

Was that enough to make you want to hurt somebody?

Was that enough to make you want to cut somebody to pieces and carve *bad dog* into their neck? Roger didn't exactly look like a killer, but then killers rarely looked the way you expected them to.

Raymond Figg, for example.

Kett flexed his neck. His right arm had gone numb, but pain throbbed out of his left shoulder and seemed to fill his entire torso. He could feel his pulse inside the wound across his chest, as if his heart had crawled its way out through his ribs. That same, awful sense of futility spread outwards from his stomach, as real as if he'd stepped into a cold, dark lake.

As real as if a black dog had curled itself around him, growling in his ear.

He brought his phone closer to his face, finding a photograph of Roger and studying it.

"Where are you?" he asked, quietly.

Dead, maybe. Or on the run, still picking his girlfriend's blood from under his nails.

Either way, if they wanted to discover what had happened to Sally, then they needed to do one thing, and they needed to do it *fast*.

They needed to find Roger Carver.

CHAPTER NINE

He woke like it was his first day on earth, like he'd been spat out of the womb into a deeper, far more dangerous darkness.

He gasped—a long, infernal, desperate sound that he wasn't even sure he'd made. Phlegm was pulled down inside his windpipe and he choked, coughing so hard that surely his lungs were going to explode out of him. It was so dark that he couldn't be sure which way was up, he didn't even know if he was standing or sitting or lying because his entire body felt numb, like it wasn't his body at all. Even when he thrust out a hand and a metallic thunk filled the air he couldn't be sure if he'd made contact with anything or not. It was as if every nerve had been burned out of him, as if his skull had been hollowed and stuffed with cotton wool.

He loosed another moan, trying to reach inside himself to look for a memory, something to anchor him. His thoughts were a churning ocean, too dark and too deep to penetrate. But there were things there beneath the surface, big things, dangerous things. He searched for anything of himself there, but all he found was a storm that screamed back at him, *which screamed and screamed and screamed and wouldn't let him think.*

He put a hand to his head, realised that he could feel again. The blood was returning to him like an electric current, the pins and needles unbearable. He cried out, trying to shape a word, but his tongue was a lump of dead flesh inside the cavern of his mouth, it wouldn't do what he asked of it.

Reaching, he found a wall right in front of him, so cold that it could only be metal. He followed it with his fingers, working up until it hit a new plane right above his head—a lid, he thought. And suddenly he knew where he was, he knew what had happened. He had suffered some kind of stroke, and this was his coffin.

No! *he tried to scream, but his mouth only grunted.*

I'm not dead! *he attempted to say.*

"Ungh ugh ugh!"

The panic was a hurricane inside him, but he felt detached from it, as if he was experiencing it from a million miles away. He had a sudden thought that his soul had been trapped inside him, that he was stuck half in and half out of the shell of his body. Then this thought, too, slipped out of his head like his mind had been greased. He found himself reaching for it on the floor of his coffin, finding only wetness there, and filth.

What are you doing? *he demanded of himself, only to lose the answer before losing the question, too, the words whipped away by the fury of the storm inside his skull.*

He fell back in a sudden bout of vertigo, felt for a minute like he was being picked up and twirled around. It seemed to take an age to settle. An eternity. Sitting, now, he discovered another wall behind him, metal like the others. This place was too big to be a coffin, too wide. It was more like a crate.

Or a cage.

Help, *he wanted to say, but his idiot mouth lolled open, producing nothing but spit that dribbled down his chin and dropped onto his chest. He ran his fingers through it, understanding that he was naked.*

Help, *but his voice betrayed him, whining like a dog's.*

I'm not a dog, *he thought. But in the chaos of his thoughts, he couldn't even be sure of that. He felt his legs, felt his stomach, felt his face. What was he?*

Who *was he?*

Because that was the other thing he couldn't find inside him. His name.

He thumped the walls of his cage as if it might dislodge some fragment of himself. But all it succeeded in doing was making his ears ring, like he was sitting inside a cathedral bell. He clamped his hands to his head, groaning, the world careening around him in demented, grinning circles. The ringing went on, and on, nothing to do with him, he was sure of it.

It was coming from outside, like somebody smashing a hammer into a pipe. Louder. Louder. Louder.

A blade of light pushed out of the dark and slid into his head. He screamed, his hands moving from his ears to his eyes. But even through his fingers, the light was too much, as if the world was burning.

Darkness again, and when he looked he saw that it was because somebody stood above him, filling the open hatch of his cage, so big that they blocked all but a trickle of light. He tried to stand, he held out a hand as though this person might pull him to safety. But his legs didn't work, they were made of rubber, and it was as if somebody else controlled his arm, spinning it impotently back and forth, back and forth. He felt the strength go from his back, his body flopping against the wall once again. He slipped down, drowning in the dark while that figure watched him.

Please, *he tried to say.*

"Unnng," was what he heard, a baby's mewl.

Something fell to the floor in front of him, a clang of metal, a spray of something cold and wet on his exposed skin. The stench of meat clawed its way inside his nostrils and he gagged.

"Eat," came a growl from the monstrous silhouette overhead. "Eat."

No, he wouldn't. But past the drowsy fear, past the awful absence where his panic should have been, he felt something else.

Hunger, huge and desperate.

"Eat."

He wouldn't, but he did, scooping up whatever mess sat between his legs, shovelling it into his mouth—great chunks of meat and jelly, and something else there too, crunchy, almost bitter. He ate, and he thought he might be crying as he did so. But how could he tell? All there was of him was the guttural noises that spilled from his mouth, and the terrible, aching hunger that sat in his belly.

"Good," said the voice, followed by a low chuckle. "Good dog."

A hand on his head, grabbing a fistful of his hair.

"Good dog."

The meat had filled him, and his thoughts were settling. He felt a calmness, now, a wave of peace that was almost euphoric.

Good dog, *he thought, and he laughed.* That's right, I am a good dog.

He reached up and touched the hand that rested on him.

"No!" roared the sky. Whatever held his hair shoved him,

his head hitting the back of the cage. The world filled with fireworks and he curled himself into a ball, whimpering. It was only when the flashing pain had stopped that he noticed he was in the dark again, face-down in the filth.

"No!" came the voice again from outside. "No!"

That ringing again—clangclangclangclangclangclang —so loud it might destroy him.

And above it all, the same voice, screaming.

"Bad dog! Bad dog! Bad dog!"

CHAPTER TEN

Saturday

KETT WOKE TO THE SOUND OF THE MEXICAN HAT Dance and a finger up his nose.

He peeled open his eyes, grabbing at his own face to find that it wasn't a finger at all. It was a toe. Evie burst into hysterical laughter, and so did Moira, the pair of them rolling around in his bed like this was the funniest thing they'd ever seen.

"Daddy had a toe in his nose!" Evie yelled between fits of giggles.

"Toe!" Moira parroted. "Toe! Nose!"

It was all a little much for his waking mind, and Kett grumbled as he sat up. His phone was blaring out that awful tune—the one that Alice had installed, and which he hadn't been able to change.

"Daddy!" Evie said, launching herself at him and gathering him in a hug. Moira did the same, and he had to fight to get his hand free in order to grab the phone.

"Morning, girls," he said. He slid his thumb across the screen to answer the call. "Kett."

"Daddy had a toe in his nose!" Evie practically screamed at the phone.

"That sounds... painful," said the voice of PC Savage.

"Not so much painful as confusing," said Kett, pulling his other hand free to wipe the spit from the corners of his mouth. He glanced at the window to see a finger of weak, cold light. It couldn't be much past six. "Evie, give me a second."

He rolled them off him as gently as he could and clambered out of bed. Evie burrowed herself into his warm patch, pulling the blankets over her head, and Moira started screaming at the injustice of it.

"Sorry," said Kett. "It's the kids."

"Oh, right," said Savage. "Thanks for explaining. For a second I thought you were at the zoo."

"It's not far off." He checked his phone, saw that he'd been right. It was three minutes past six. "What's with the wake-up call?"

"Clare asked me, sorry," Savage said. "He wants everybody in early."

"That might be tricky," said Kett. "Unless he wants the kids as well?"

"He says he's sending you reinforcements," Savage said. "They should be with you by half-past."

"Please tell me he doesn't mean Porter," Kett said. "Or even worse, Dunst. The girls will eat him alive."

Savage laughed.

"He didn't say."

Kett thanked her and threw the phone onto the bed.

Moira had managed to worm her way beneath the duvet and the pair of them thrashed around like a lake full of alligators. He picked up his phone again and took a photo—not for him but for Billie, when she came home. He didn't want her to miss any of these moments, not a single one.

"Come on, you pair of pillocks," he said, lifting the duvet to see two sweaty faces grinning up at him. "Let's go get Alice."

It was like waking a hibernating bear—only more dangerous—but twenty minutes later the four of them were sitting at the kitchen table while Kett made toast. He was burning his fingers for the second time, the same way Billie used to do every single morning, when the doorbell rang.

"Wait here," he told them as he walked out of the kitchen and down the hall. He may as well have been speaking Russian, because Alice and Evie were out of their chairs in a heartbeat, racing past him.

"Someone's at the door!" screamed Alice.

"Monsters!" added Evie in a guttural roar that made her sound possessed.

"Out the way," Kett ordered, opening the door to see a young woman there—a girl, really. For a second he was confused, then he noticed the curly brown hair, the height, and the frown that she wore on her face.

"You're Clare's daughter, aren't you?" Kett guessed. She nodded, the frown becoming a smile when she spotted Alice and Evie there.

"Clarissa," she said.

"Clarissa Clare," Kett said. She turned her smile to him.

"Yep, that's my dad for you. No imagination. Could be worse, though, he could have called me Claire."

Kett laughed, standing to one side.

"Come in, if you can."

Alice and Evie were all over her as she walked through the door. Alice ran her hand over the girl's crocheted handbag, fawning.

"I like your bag," she said.

"I made it," said Clarissa. "I can show you how, if you like?"

"Can you?" said Alice, wide-eyed.

"You're the backup?" Kett asked as he closed the door, shivering in the cool air that had crept around his ankles.

"Dad said you needed a babysitter," she replied, kicking off her shoes. "I've done plenty, don't worry."

"My kids are..." Kett wasn't sure how to say it, but in all honesty they were presenting a pretty clear picture. Evie was on the floor by Clarissa's feet, her backside in the air as she tried to demonstrate a roly-poly. Alice had opened the girl's bag and was rummaging around inside. And the screams coming from the kitchen as Moira tried to escape her high chair were like something from a horror film.

"Don't worry, Mr Kett," Clarissa said. "I babysit my three little sisters all the time. Triplets. They make yours look like cherubs."

"I find that very hard to believe," said Kett as Evie tumbled over sideways and clonked into the wall. "And call me Robbie."

"Stupid wall!" Evie yelled, slapping the plaster.

"Can I have some money?" Alice said as she tea-leafed the girl's purse.

"You're sure you'll be okay?" Kett asked, but Clarissa handed Alice a twenty-pence piece before scooping Evie up and carrying her into the kitchen.

"Right," she said. "Who's the boss around here?"

"Me!" screamed all three girls in unison. Clarissa laughed, and it seemed utterly genuine.

"Then I need to talk to you all about how much fun we're going to have today."

———

IT HAD BEEN six weeks since he'd last been here, but the bullpen of the Norfolk Constabulary CID hadn't changed at all. The place was a hive of activity, the large Incident Room full of detectives from across the county—and beyond. The walls were a gallery of horror, photographs of Sally O'Neil mounted everywhere, both living and dead. Kett wasn't sure which were more terrifying, the images of the savaged corpse, or those of the bright-eyed young woman she had been before her murder—a woman who would never again laugh, or smile, or dance with her friends, or feel the cold, autumn sun on her face as she walked across the harvested fields.

The thought of it woke the black dog inside him again, a quiet, overwhelming feeling of despair that made him hang his head and close his eyes. How many times would he stand in a room like this? How many times would he promise the victim that he would find out who killed them? However much good he did, however many bad men he put away, there would always be more—grinning faces that slipped from the dark and crept through the night and swallowed their innocent victims whole.

There would always be more.

He knew, too, that there was a room in London just like this, only it was Billie who gazed down from the walls, who silently pleaded to be found. To be *saved*. He felt as if he had to physically restrain himself from running out of the room, getting in his car, and heading south to do just that.

"You okay, sir?" asked Savage. Kett opened his eyes to

see her approaching him from the other side of the room. She looked worried, and he did his best to smile at her.

"I'm fine," he said. "Tired."

"That's what you get when you sleep with toes in your nose," she replied. "Kettle's on. Boss wants to see you."

"Where's Porter?" asked Kett, partly for professional reasons, and partly to make sure the DI was nowhere near the tea station.

"Already in with Clare," she said.

Kett nodded his thanks then walked out of the room, heading down the corridor to Clare's office. The door was open, but he knocked anyway. Clare was on one side of the desk, scribbling something on a sheet of paper. Porter sat opposite, staring into space. They both looked up, Porter smiling at Kett, Clare grunting.

"Clarissa get to you?" the Super said. Kett nodded. "She's a good'un. Probably the only one of mine I'd let loose. She'll take good care of the girls."

"Thank you, sir," said Kett. And he meant it. There were very few people he would ever entrust his children to —especially strangers—but he knew enough about Colin Clare and his family to know that he could trust them.

"Sit down," Clare said.

Kett did as he was told, yawning as he took in the room. It, too, was exactly the same as he remembered, like he'd been away for hours rather than weeks.

Except for one thing.

Kett leaned forward, studying the giant mug on Clare's desk. It was angled away from him, so he couldn't be sure, but it almost looked like it said *MY TOSSING MUG*. Kett glanced at Porter, nudging his head at the mug. It was Clare, though, who saw him.

"Don't even think about it, Kett," he said. "That's my mug."

"Does it say..." Kett started, and Clare turned the mug to face him.

"My Tossing Mug," the boss said with a grim smile. "Clever, isn't it?"

"Uh..." said Kett, looking once again at Porter. The big DI had his hand to his lips and was obviously trying not to laugh. "I'm not sure what it's trying to say. It's your *tossing* mug?"

"Fiona got it for me, for my birthday," he said. "She had it made."

"Your *tossing* mug," said Kett.

"*My* tossing mug," Clare shot back, glaring at him. "You're not allowed to use it. Nobody is. It's mine."

"I... I have no intention of putting your tossing mug anywhere near my mouth," said Kett. Porter was sniggering now, and Clare looked back and forth between them, evidently confused.

"Oh fuck you," the boss growled. "Both of you. You're just jealous."

He shoved the piece of paper he'd been writing on across the desk.

"All the properties in the area surrounding the woods where our victim was found," he said. "There aren't many. Porter, I want you and Dunst to take everything east of the woods—if Keith ever gets his fat arse out of bed, that is. Spalding's working something else for me, so Kett, I want you to take Savage. She's got a good head for this. Look quick, but look hard. I get the feeling that whatever killed Sally hasn't gone far. Kett, the scrap of Morton territory I mentioned yesterday is in your grid. Like I said, I want you to investigate it."

He winked.

"I get it," said Kett.

"But not first. I don't want the Suffolk lot getting wind that we're chasing their leads. So, you know, drop into another few places on the way. Don't make yourself too obvious. Okay?"

"Sure," said Kett. "I do understand."

"Don't, under any circumstances, cross the river," Clare went on. He winked again. "Unless those circumstances demand immediate action. Am I making myself clear?"

"Yes," said Kett. "Crystal."

"So you—"

"I'm leaving now," said Kett, standing up. He followed Porter to the door, then turned back, looking at the mug.

"I just don't think tossing means what you think it does, sir," Kett said.

Clare's growl of annoyance, and a lobbed pencil, chased him from the room.

CHAPTER ELEVEN

THE COUNTRYSIDE WAS BITTER, AND IT WASN'T JUST the temperature. It was unseasonably cold, the thermometer reading seven degrees, and Kett left the Volvo's engine running just to keep the heat on. But there was something else, too. The sky was more grey than blue, the colour leeching from the trees, from the fields. It was as if he was looking at the world through a dirty lens, and this made him think of Sally O'Neil and all the other dead folk he'd witnessed. Was this how they saw the world after they'd gone? Was this all that was left when their eyes clouded over?

"Steaming up a little," said Savage, leaning forwards and smearing her cuff over the fogged-up windshield. Through the little porthole she'd made, Kett could see the end of the driveway on which they were currently parked. One corner of a large brick farmhouse peeked back at them past a bank of trees, like it was trying to figure out who they were.

Savage checked her phone, shaking it as if it might improve the signal.

"It's getting there," she said. "Here. This was Number four, wasn't it?"

Kett nodded, rubbing his hands together to stop them from going numb. Half of him was listening to Savage, the other half was wondering whether he should call home and make sure the kids were okay.

"Okay, so Land Registry says it's owned by a husband and wife, Eden Howarth—that's the man—and Pollyanna Craft. Registered for equestrian use. It's pretty huge actually, almost twenty acres."

"So it borders the woods where Sally was murdered?" Kett asked.

"I think it *includes* part of that woodland," Savage said, squinting at the screen. "To the south and west is the Morton land. East is the farm that belongs to Graham Turvey. At one point this was a riding school, but they don't seem to still be trading. Looks like Howarth was made bankrupt in 2014, in his late forties. He had a few High Court rulings against him. Been pretty quiet ever since. He's claimed disability for years now, for mobility problems."

"And her?" Kett asked.

"Uh... not much. Fifty-three. She's listed as a shareholder on the defunct business. Can't find much more, not with the coverage out here, anyway."

"Then I guess we should go ask them in person," said Kett.

He put the car in drive and bumped down the last stretch of the potholed track, the pair of them bouncing in their seats like marionettes. As they rounded the trees he saw the house open up in front of them, far bigger than it had looked from the main road. In fact, it was less a farmhouse than a Regency home, three stories of big windows and a forest of chimneys. The place was in a sorry state, though, some of the windows were covered with plywood and the bricks were in desperate need of repointing. One side of the faded red double door had been knocked partly off its hinges and sat there like a loose tooth.

The track kept going after the house, curving around to the side where a cluster of sad-looking outbuildings sat in their master's shadow. A huge wooden garage held what looked like an ancient red Land Rover and a cart that could have been used as a prop in a Jane Austen novel if it still had its wheels. The whole place looked drab, like something had sucked the life right out of it.

Kett killed the engine and climbed out of the Volvo. After the heat of the car, the outside felt colder than ever and he wished he'd brought an overcoat. He pulled the lapels of his jacket tight to his chest and walked briskly to the front door.

"I'll let you do the honours," he said to Savage. "Your knock's a hell of a lot more impressive than mine."

Savage skipped up the handful of stone steps and pounded on the door so hard that Kett heard the echo of it inside. He peered through the gap where it had come loose, seeing a small hall and another set of doors with mullioned windows. Everything beyond that was drenched in darkness.

The PC knocked again, even louder this time.

"Nobody home," she said.

"Nobody who wants to talk to us, at least," said Kett.

He stood back to take in the few windows that hadn't been covered, seeing nothing there but shadows. Then he set off along the front of the house, his feet slipping in the damp earth. Weeds pushed their way out of their graves in their thousands, and giant trunks of red-tinged ivy stretched up the crumbling brick, fanning out like peacock tails.

"You hear that, sir?" asked Savage.

Kett held his breath, slowing his steps. There, a soft snort, a brittle cry. Savage popped the studs for her extendable baton, staying close to Kett's side as they reached the far end of the building. It was only when they rounded the corner that the noises made sense, and Savage laughed quietly as she clipped the holster shut.

Ahead, in a wide courtyard between the side of the house and a set of stables, a woman led a horse by a rope. Kett took in the horse first. He'd never much liked the creatures, but this beast was as handsome as they came. The colour of warm fudge, it stood maybe six feet tall, its pale mane decorated with ribbons, its tail beautifully braided. It trotted in expert circles around the woman, its head held high and its feet lifting well clear of the ground with every step. Every now and again it would shake its head, blasting great, billowing clouds of steam into the air.

The woman was the exact opposite of the horse. Her hair was short and grey, so tangled at the back that Kett made out a couple of dreadlocks there. She was large, but most of that bulk was in what she was wearing—layer upon layer of seemingly random cloth topped with a leopard-print dressing gown, her skirts hanging down to her Wellington boots. Her face was pinched and drawn, so gaunt she looked like a Halloween decoration, a witch.

She studied the horse intently—so intently, in fact, that it took a moment before she realised she was being watched. She jumped, almost leaving the ground entirely, her mouth shaping a perfect O. The horse caught wind of her panic, its front legs rising, hooves scuffing the weed-strewn cobbles. It turned to them, its dark eyes wide with panic.

"Sorry," said Kett, lifting both hands. "I didn't mean to scare you."

It looked as if she was about to ask Kett who he was, then she turned her attention to Savage in her constable's uniform and seemed to relax. She walked to the horse, coaxing it, patting its steaming flanks until it settled. It pressed its velvet lips to her face and she whispered something, stroking the stripe on its nose.

"Just give me a second," she said without looking back. "He's antsy around strangers."

"Take all the time you need," said Kett. He watched the woman lead the horse away into the stables. "Beautiful creature."

"You're not wrong," said Savage. "Palomino. He's healthy. They obviously look after their horses better than their house."

"And better than themselves," Kett said.

He stamped some feeling back into his cold feet, counting the seconds until the woman reappeared. She walked with some difficulty, her back bent and one leg dragging behind her. The pain of every step was etched in her expression, and Kett walked swiftly across the courtyard to meet her.

"Take your time," he said. "We're in no hurry, and you're in no trouble."

The woman smiled, although it obviously wasn't easy.

"I'm in a lot of trouble, m'boy," she said as she came to a stop. "But maybe not the kind of trouble you're used to." She gestured to herself, flapping her layers of clothes like wings. "Came off a horse. Broke my back in two places and dislocated my hip. Fifteen years ago, nearly, and it gets worse every day. How can I help you?"

"Mrs Craft?" asked Savage. The woman waved her away.

"Polly," she said. "I've never been Mrs Craft, not even in my teaching days. Not Pollyanna neither. Just Polly."

"How many horses do you have?" Savage asked, genuinely interested.

"You like them?" Polly replied. "I've only got three, now, and two are so old they barely poke their noses out the door. Like me, really." She snorted a soft, horse-like laugh. "The pally there I took as a favour to an old student who couldn't keep him. He's beautiful, but a handful. Too much for me, really, but I haven't the heart to let him go."

"It's just you here, then?" Kett asked.

She laughed again, but there was a bitterness to it this time.

"I bloody wish it was," she said. "Eden's around some-where, the useless bugger. See that?"

She nodded up at the house.

"Looked exactly the same when we bought the place. It's how we could afford it. *We'll do it up ourselves*, he told me. *It will be a palace*. A palace for old folk and fools. Not one room looks any different now to what it did twenty years ago. The old hound's as worthless as they come, he needs a good beating to do anything. I don't even live in it any more, I stay in the cottage up the way. Got fed up rattling around like old bones."

"We'd like to speak with Eden, too, if he's here?" Kett said.

"Well, he'll no doubt show up at some point," she said, scanning the far end of the courtyard. "No phones here, the uh, what do you call them? Portable ones. But there isn't much he doesn't stick his muzzle into. He's worse off than I am, takes him half an hour to get down the stairs."

She turned back to Kett.

"What's this about, anyway? All my licences are in place, as far as I know."

"It's not about you," said Savage. "We're speaking to everyone in the area. I'm afraid I have to let you know that a young woman was killed in the woods by the river, on Thursday evening."

Polly frowned as she took in the news, tilting her broken body in a way that made Kett think she was going to fall. He rushed to her, taking her arm, and although she held onto him she made a series of tutting noises that didn't seem all that grateful.

"Stronger than I look, m'boy," she said.

"We can go inside, if it's easier," Kett said. She shook her head, patting his hand as she pulled herself free.

"I'm too ashamed to let you see it," she said. "Eden was doing the downstairs facilities and none of the toilets even have toilets. The smell of it's unthinkable. Raw sewage. Enough to give you nightmares. He never finished anything, that man."

Kett knew those nightmares all too well. Sometimes he woke up and he could still smell the stench of the treatment plant like he was back there with Percival and Figg, like it was him who had drowned in it.

"Ask me what you need to. Let's do it as we walk, though. Eden always liked the barn, we'll see if we can catch him there."

She led the way, Kett by her side and Savage following.

"Do you ever go down that way?" Kett asked. "The woods? As far as I can tell part of it belongs to you."

"I think you're right," she said. "I lose track. It's all written down somewhere. Eden sold off a few acres of woodland to help pay for repairs, although I never saw him repair a damned thing. Can't build on the forests, though, can't cut the trees down, so we never got much. I always said he should try to shift some of the farmland, but who wants to be a farmer these days? Easier ways to be miserable."

They reached the end of the stable block, a barn appearing to the side. It was huge, but it, too, was falling apart. One end of the roof had caved in like somebody had struck it with a giant club.

"Eden!" Polly shouted. "Get your crippled arse out here, we've got company."

If he was in there, he didn't respond. The only answer was a soft, distant pop, almost like a firework going off. Kett scanned the horizon, trying to figure out what it might have been.

"Eden!" Polly yelled down the path. She shook her head. "Sorry. I need to chain the old bastard up."

"Do you ever visit the woods?" Kett asked again, scanning the open fields to either side of the buildings. From the look of it they hadn't been used for crops for years—a roiling sea of tangled grass and bramble that was almost waist-high. There were a couple of patches of bare earth where somebody had tried to dig beds, but taming the land seemed like an impossible task. Polly continued to walk towards the barn, her limp growing worse with every passing second. She put one hand to her back, waving the question away with her other.

"Nothing there," she said. "You've seen one tree you've seen them all. I used to go to the river, but I'd drive there and there's no road goes near them woods. Now I don't drive either, too painful. Don't walk, don't drive, don't ride. Almost everything I do happens within a hundred metres of that damned house. I'm a prisoner."

"What about your husband?" asked Kett. They'd reached the barn now and Polly wrestled with the large, sliding door. Kett tried to help her but once again she shooed him away.

"Eden?" she called inside. The only thing to reply was a pigeon, which made a break for the rafters. There was enough light coming through the ceiling to reveal that the barn contained not much of anything—a heap of old mechanical equipment on the far side, and a deserted work-bench by the door. Polly cursed beneath her breath. "May have gone walking—as much as you can call what he does walking. He used to disappear for hours sometimes. He may visit the woods, I don't know."

Kett shared a look with Savage, both of them filing the information away for future use. Kett reached into his jacket and pulled out one of the photos of Sally O'Neil and Roger Carver he'd printed just before leaving the HQ. The tech team had pulled it from Facebook—a shot of them smiling at the camera at what might have been a wedding. He held it out to Mrs Craft.

"Polly, have you seen either of these two people before?"

She sighed as she took the photograph, patting several pockets in her various dresses before finding a pair of wire-frame glasses. They were so bent that she didn't put them on, pinning them to her nose with one finger instead. She frowned, then shook her head.

"Sorry," she said. "We don't get many visitors here. I mean who on earth would want to come and see us?"

She offered the photo back but Kett shook his head.

"Can you show it to your husband when he reappears?" he asked.

"I'll try," she said, tucking the photograph away with her glasses. She flapped her arms, ushering them out of the barn door while she closed it.

"Have you seen anyone else around the area acting suspiciously?" Kett asked. "Strangers, maybe. Anyone acting out of sorts."

Polly put both her hands on the small of her back and arched backwards, wincing. Two more pops thumped out from somewhere far away, and Kett squinted towards the horizon again.

"You hear them?" Polly asked.

"Yeah," said Kett. "Gunshots?"

"Shotguns," said Savage. "It's not quite pheasant season yet, but it's close enough."

Polly hissed a laugh through her nose.

"Those arseholes aren't shooting pheasants," she said. "They're doing it to annoy their neighbours."

She looked at Kett.

"You're asking me if I've seen anyone acting up around here, and the answer is yes. Across the river, bunch of hooligans, and worse."

"The Mortons," said Kett, and she pulled a face to confirm it. "It's funny you should mention them. They're our next stop."

Pop pop pop. A cluster of distant shots that sounded like fireworks.

"Won't be the first time that family's been in trouble," Polly said.

"So I've heard," said Kett. "Thank you for your time, Polly."

He nodded to the woman and turned to leave, Savage by his side as they made their way back to the house. They hadn't gone far before Polly called them back.

"Detective," she said. "How did she die?"

Kett turned back.

"We're not sure," he said. "We thought an animal attack,

but there are signs it may be something more. Some of the locals think it's Black Shuck."

He smiled wearily, but she didn't.

"You know the legend?" he asked.

"Of course," she said. "Everyone around here does. And you should be careful, Detective."

"Why?" he asked.

"Because some legends are real." She looked past the house, out into the woods, gathering her dresses around her as if they were armour. "Some legends can kill you."

CHAPTER TWELVE

It took less than five minutes to drive from the crumbling riding school to the northernmost corner of the Morton's land. The neighbouring properties were separated by a line of sickly trees and a barbed wire fence that had seen better days. According to the map that Savage had saved on her phone, the triangle of land jutted out from the river like a sail, measuring just less than three acres.

"I think they've forgotten about it," said Savage as Kett pulled the car over by an old metal gate.

There was a good chance she was right. The land was even more neglected than the fields around the Howarth house, the triangle of marsh overrun with tall grass and brambles. It was so wild that from here Kett couldn't even see the river, just the tops of the trees that edged it.

"Shall we get a closer look?" Kett said. Savage nodded, climbing out of the car.

The sun had finally decided to wake up, shrugging off the grey sheets of cloud and casting a golden light on the countryside. The dew steamed off the ground, turning this untamed farmland into something mysterious, beautiful, and almost ethereal.

"Watch out for the cow shit," said Savage as she walked up to the gate.

Kett smelled it before he saw it, staying well clear.

"I had a friend back by the coast," Savage said as she tested the gate. One side was padlocked, the chain orange with rust. "His family owned a couple of shotguns, for rats and rabbits. You ever fired one?"

"Once," said Kett. "We did a firearms training day. Nasty bastards, shotguns. Left me with a bruise on my shoulder that took days to go away."

"Probably because you weren't holding it right," said Savage, putting one foot on the bottom bar and propelling herself over.

"Whatever you say, Annie Oakley," Kett shot back, following her over far more carefully. Even then, his wet boots slipped, almost depositing him on his arse in another steaming pile of shit.

"You and gates don't really get on, do you?" she said, flashing him a smile. He scowled at her. "Anyway, he took me out a few times, with the guns. Malcolm, his name is. Taught me that the best thing to shoot with a shotgun, if you're not hunting for your dinner, is a cowpat."

"Nice," said Kett.

"It erupts," she went on. "I kid you not. Goes for miles. Like a shit volcano."

She imitated it with her hands, in slow motion.

"It's magnificent."

As if on cue, another flurry of shots thumped through the morning air. They sounded a lot closer than they had at the Howarth house. Savage's smile fell away.

"In all seriousness, we need to be very careful," she said,

craning her neck to try to see over the vegetation. "I'll be okay, they'll see this jacket from a mile off. But they might mistake you for a rabbit."

"You'd better go first, then," said Kett.

"What a gentleman."

She set off, struggling on the uneven turf. It really wasn't easy, the ground seemed designed to trip them up and catch them off guard. Lumps of rock hid beneath the moss, sending their boots sliding into pools of green water. Some of the mounds were five-foot-tall and crowned with thorns, and every now and again pheasants would burst up from the bushes with clapping wings and cries like sirens.

But they persevered, and after a few minutes the ground began to slope down again. Ahead of them the river appeared, its waters dark in the shade of the trees that lined its bank. The land on the other side of the water was the stark opposite, an industrial wasteland that seemed to have no place out here. Stacks of compacted scrap cars towered higher than the trees. Dozens of wing mirrors and shards of steel and aluminium caught the harsh light, leaving glowing spots on Kett's retinas. Smoke drifted skywards from three or four fires. Above it all rose a crane, tipped with a magnet. It rotated lazily, the silhouetted figure inside the cab shielded by more reflected sunlight.

"We should have approached from the east," said Savage, holding her hand to her brow. "If this was a battle we'd be screwed."

Kett squinted, making out more figures walking between the stacks and past a barricade of shipping containers.

There were dogs, too, chained in the shade. Big ones.

"See them?" Kett said, nodding.

"Look like Rottweilers," said Savage. "Hard to be sure from here. Three of them."

"Two more over there," said Kett, pointing to the base of the crane. They didn't exactly look scary now, basking in the sun, but he'd been around plenty of dogs in London that had tried to take his hands off. And Rottweilers were as fierce as they came.

Fierce enough to kill a young woman in the woods, for sure.

"How far are we from where Sally O'Neil was killed?" Kett asked. Savage scanned the horizon, pointing behind her to her left.

"That's it over there," she said, gesturing to a strip of woodland maybe two miles away. "They'd have had to cross the river, but it's not far."

"Not far at all," said Kett.

A quiet burst of laughter drifted over the river and up the hill, followed by two more gunshots. Kett couldn't see anyone armed with a shotgun, but there was definitely something going on down there.

"How do you want to handle this?" asked Savage. "Suffolk Con made it pretty clear we had to leave this place alone, right?"

"Right," said Kett. "But here we are, just strolling through the *Norfolk* countryside, on a beautiful morning *Norfolk* walk, and what do we hear? Gunshots and dog barks and shouts."

He did his best Dorothy impression.

"Oh my!"

"Sir..." said Savage, giving him a look that he was very familiar with. He just smiled at her as he set off towards the river.

"Don't worry, Savage," he shouted back over his shoulder. "You can just blame me."

"I always do," she shot back, trudging after him. "I always do."

Kett slipped and slid down the last section of hill before pushing into a tangle of bushes that seemed designed to stop him. Brambles caught on his suit, scratching his skin.

"Little fuckers," he grumbled.

"You need the stick?" Savage asked, patting her telescopic baton. He shook his head, growling through the last of the foliage and finding himself on a brick pontoon. Another jutted from the bank on the far side of the river, maybe ten metres away, and midway between them was a platform that at one time might have supported a bridge. The bridge was gone, but there was a wooden rowing boat moored to the pontoon beneath him, one that looked like it hadn't been used in decades.

From here, Kett could make out less of the salvage yard —just the tops of the stacks and the towering crane. Four rusting shipping containers ran along the river, almost touching. Occasionally somebody would pass one of the gaps, and Kett was close enough to catch snatches of conversation and more laughter. He saw dogs, too, three of them fighting over a lump of meat and bone that could only have come from a cow.

A shotgun barked to the left of where he was standing, and Kett noticed a small explosion in the air. Fragments of clay rained down on the river and shot scattered like hail across the wet soil further up the hill.

"Please tell me we don't have to get in that boat," said Savage as she burst free of the thorns. "It's got more water inside it than there is outside."

"Isn't this *Swallows and Amazons* territory?" he asked. "You don't fancy a marine incursion?"

"No," she said. "And no. The Broads are further north."

"Fair enough," said Kett. "Let's just do this the old-fashioned way, then."

He opened his mouth, took a breath, then paused.

"You're absolutely sure this side of the river is Norfolk?"

"I'm positive, sir," said Savage. "Why?"

He didn't answer, he just roared at the top of his lungs.

"Jeffrey Morton, Thomas Morton, can you hear me?"

A second of shocked silence, then it was like somebody had thrown a bone into a kennel, a serenade of barks and howls rising up over the noise of the scrapyard. One of the giant Rottweilers pushed itself between the shipping containers, running to the river so fast that Kett was convinced it was about to throw itself in. He had to force himself not to take a step back as the dog skidded to a halt, every cell inside him ordering him to retreat.

Another dog appeared, then two more, all four of them standing on the riverbank barking so loud that great gobs of spit erupted from their muzzles. They were big dogs, practically solid muscle, and Kett would bet that each of them weighed as much as he did. If there hadn't been ten metres of water between them, he was fairly sure they would have taken his head clean off.

Or maybe bitten out his throat.

"Easy," he shouted, although he honestly wasn't sure if he was giving the order to them or to himself.

"I hope those things can't swim," said Savage. She had her baton in her hand, just in case, and her entire body was rigid with panic.

"Hold your ground," said Kett. "Don't let them see you're scared."

"It's a bit late for that, sir," said Savage.

Somebody appeared in one of the gaps between the containers, just the flash of a greasy, unkind face beneath a blue hat. He locked eyes with Kett for the briefest of seconds before vanishing. Somebody else took his place, somebody taller and broader who squeezed his wide frame onto the narrow stretch of riverbank. The man must have been in his early twenties, his head shaved and covered with tattoos. He wore a dirty white Adidas T-shirt and baggy basketball shorts, flipflops on his feet. Taking a deep drag of his cigarette, he walked to the nearest dog and stroked its head. If anything, though, it seemed to make the animal even wilder. The whites of its eyes—and its teeth—were the brightest thing in sight.

"Shut it!" he roared, and the dogs obeyed, their barks dropping into low growls. He spoke with an accent that wasn't local at all—it was broad Brummie. "Who the fuck are you?" he said to Kett, before turning to Savage. "You're too fit to be a cop. Stripper? You're on the wrong side of the river, love."

He laughed at his own joke, and Savage muttered something under her breath.

"I'm DCI Robert Kett."

The full force of his words carried over the soft rush of water. If the man was intimidated, though, he didn't show it. He hawked up a ball of yellow phlegm and spat it into the middle of the river. The dogs stood by his side, their lips pulled back to reveal their teeth. The growl they were making was like a B52 flying overhead.

"DCI?" said the man. "What's that stand for? Dick Caressing Arsehole?"

"You got it," said Kett. "I'm going to take a wild stab in the dark and guess that you're Jeffrey Morton."

For a second, the man's face creased into a frown. Then he grinned—a gold tooth flashing—and wiped the back of his hand over his nose.

"What gave it away?" he said. "My good looks?"

"More the fact you don't know your alphabet," said Kett.

"Know it well enough to spell F-U-C-K O-F-F," the man said. "You know that's our fucking land you're standing on. Got every right to set the dogs on you. Rotties can swim, you know that?"

"Not well enough," said Kett. "Big dogs sink fast. I wouldn't try it."

Morton shrugged.

"Got plenty more where these came from. What the fuck do you want anyway? Police usually show up at the front door. Knock it down half the time. Why you skanking around in the shit over there?"

"You shooting something?" Kett asked.

"Well that ain't fireworks you can hear," said Morton. "Why don't you come on over and have a look?"

He pretended to lunge, and the movement set the dogs off again. Each bark was so loud it felt like a physical pulse of sound against Kett's ears.

"Thought as much," the man said, grinning. He smacked the nearest dog on the head with the flat of his hand. "Shut it, you twat."

The animals fell quiet, their dark eyes never leaving the intruders on the other side of the river.

"Believe me," said Kett in a growl of his own. "If I wanted to come over there, I would. Can you tell me where you were the day before yesterday? Between five p.m. and midnight."

Morton narrowed his eyes, chewing on the question.

"Why?" he asked after a moment.

"A young woman was killed in the woods on Thursday evening," said Kett. "The woods right next to your land. Looks like she was attacked by a dog. A big dog."

Morton sniffed, spitting again.

"Nuffink to do with me, mate," he said.

"What about your brother?" Kett asked. He turned to the shipping containers and shouted. "Thomas? I know you're there."

Jeffrey Morton looked back, then shook his head.

"Guess you're wrong about that, too," he said.

"Greasy face, blue hat, he's there." Kett stood to his full height, meeting the man's eye. "He either comes out, or I come over. I'm not fucking around here, Jeff."

Morton seemed ready to call his bluff, but in the end he must have decided it wasn't worth the risk.

"Tommy," he said, speaking over his shoulder. "Come talk to this twat, will you?"

A few seconds ticked by, then the same face Kett had seen before emerged from between the shipping containers. Thomas Morton was everything his brother was not. He was younger, still in his teens, and as skinny as a rake. He was short, but he walked with the self-conscious stoop of somebody much taller. His blue cap—Birmingham City FC written on it in white—was pulled low over his eyes, and tufts of lank, mousy hair poked out the sides. Like his brother, he wore an Adidas T-shirt, but he had tracksuit trousers instead of shorts—grey and plastered with dirt—and a pair of brand-new Nike trainers.

Jeffrey threw a hand around his little brother's shoulders, pulling him close in a way that made Kett think he was about to noogie him. He didn't, but he did slap him gently on the cheek a couple of times. Kett was more interested in the reaction of the dogs, the way they skittered out of Thomas's path, their back ends drooping. The boy's presence seemed to make them forget all about Kett and Savage. The Rottweilers respected the older brother, that was clear.

But they were terrified of Thomas.

"The man wants to know if you killed someone," Jeffrey said. "A woman in the woods."

Thomas muttered something that sounded like *fuck off*. He pushed himself free of his brother and bounced on his toes like he was about to try boxing Kett's ears from ten metres away.

"Ain't killed nobody," he said in the same Brummie accent, the last word rising in pitch like an airplane taking off. "Don't know what the fuck you're talking about."

"Was it you shooting the guns?" Kett asked. Thomas shrugged his bony shoulders.

"So what? Ain't no laws against shooting guns at shit."

"I'm pretty sure there are," said Kett. "But I honestly don't care. I just want to know where you both were on Thursday evening, let's say between dinner time and midnight."

The look that the brothers shared was subtle but unmistakable. They were hiding something.

"Fucking here, wasn't we?" said Jeffrey. "Just pissing about."

Thomas nodded.

"You didn't go for a walk in the woods, then?" asked Kett.

"Just said it, didn't I?" the older brother replied.

"There was a man, too," said Kett, brushing a fly from his face. "With the dead woman. In his thirties, black jacket. Have you seen anyone around here who you haven't seen before? Any new faces?"

"Just your ugly mug," said Jeffrey with a grin. He winked at Savage. "And your pretty one."

Savage made a noise that sounded like she was throwing up in her mouth, quiet enough for only Kett to hear.

"Do you ever go walking in those woods?" Kett asked. "The ones just downriver from here, on the border with your neighbours."

Thomas's smile was sharp and dangerous, and Jeffrey laughed, smacking his brother on the shoulder at whatever private joke they were sharing.

"Don't go anywhere near that bitch's house," Jeffrey Morton said. "They're fucking crazy, her and those bloody horses. And the husband does nuffink but complain. We stay well clear, which means we don't go to the woods. Happy?"

Kett was a long way from happy. He glanced past the two brothers, over the shipping containers to where the crane swept in a slow arc. The crunch and crash of metal, and the hum of the machinery, was like an orchestral warm-up before a concert.

"Oi, mate, I asked if you were happy?" Jeffrey went on. "In other words, can you please fuck off now?"

One of the dogs huffed quietly, but Thomas's presence seemed to be keeping them quiet. Kett nodded, turning to go.

"Bye-bye, Mr Policeman," Thomas said. His laughter was as cold as the water that ran between them. "Couple of bitches."

Kett had to resist the urge to climb in the boat, paddle to the other side of the river, and knock the boy's head from his shoulders—dogs or no dogs. But he didn't, because at that moment the wind seemed to shift, toying with the hair on the back of his neck. It carried all the noise of the scrapyard with it—the rumble of the trucks, the bleep of a reversing forklift, more barks from further away. There was something else, too, something so quiet that Kett wasn't even sure he'd heard it. Then it came again, just a trace of sound on the wind.

It sounded almost like somebody shouting.

Somebody shouting for help.

Kett turned back and studied the brothers. Jeffrey had Thomas under his arm again, almost in a headlock. He shrugged at Kett.

"What?"

"I just want you to know that I'm coming back," Kett said.

He pushed his way into the bushes.

And sooner than you think.

CHAPTER THIRTEEN

"We can't do it, Kett. It's just not up to us."

Kett leaned against the side of the Volvo, watching Savage as she knocked on the front door of the first of a line of small, terraced houses. They seemed ridiculously out of place here in the middle of the countryside, surrounded by vast stubbled fields. It was as if the rest of the world had been obliterated, leaving these four little houses standing shoulder to shoulder. Savage knocked again, the boom of it audible even from back here on the road. But if anyone was home, they weren't interested in talking to her.

"Kett?" Superintendent Clare's voice crackled through the phone. "You still there?"

"Yes, sir," Kett said. "I just think it's worth investigating, and urgently."

"How sure are you?" the boss asked.

Kett popped his lips. Maybe the sound of shouting had been the breeze, or the whine of a distant dog, or just the scrapyard workers messing about. It was so faint it could have been anything.

It could have been somebody in trouble.

"I heard it," he said.

"And it's not just because I *asked* you to hear it?" he said.

"I heard it," Kett said.

Clare sighed.

"I can't let you go in," the boss said. "And believe me, I tried. Suffolk really doesn't want us to. And I can't very well let them know we heard somebody calling for help, because then they'll know we were there. But I'll put in an anonymous call, get some officers round from south of the river. They can at least check it out."

They wouldn't, Kett knew. Not if there was an ongoing investigation. With the guns and the dogs, any raid of the Morton site was going to be a major operation. There would have to be undeniable evidence of a crime taking place—not just whispers carried on the wind.

"But you did your job," said Clare. "Now we know something's going on. The presence of Rottweilers on site, and the fact that Jeffrey Morton has a criminal record, means we can build a pretty significant case against them in the O'Neil murder. All we need now is the path report to come back with some DNA and we're well on our way. Anything else going on out there?"

Savage was at the second house now, speaking to a young woman in a dressing gown who was gesticulating wildly about something with one hand and using the other to keep her robe closed.

"There's not much out here, to be honest," Kett said. "Half the houses are empty, and the people who are home seem to have lost their minds."

"That's the sticks for you," Clare said. "Bleak out there. Keep searching, and let me know if you find anything. I'll see what I can do about the Mortons. Right now what I need from you is patience."

"Not my strong suit," said Kett. "But I'll try."

He hung up, sliding the phone back into his pocket. He pushed himself off the car and walked down the path to where the woman was still chatting to Savage.

"... and then they take them into the woods, just like you say, and they kill them."

"*What?*" exclaimed Kett as he reached Savage's side. He offered his hand, but the woman retreated into the darkness beyond her door.

"Uh, this is Miss Murphy," Savage said. "She was telling me about the, uh, aliens."

"The aliens?" said Kett.

"Yeah, the aliens," said the woman, her eyes wide. "Seen 'em up there over the trees, bloody great big things they are. They'll drag you into the woods and kill you."

"Right," said Kett. "I'll be sure to make a note of it."

He nodded a thank you and walked back the way he'd come, making his way to the fourth house along, while Savage tried the door of the third. As soon as he knocked he was greeted with a fusillade of wild barks from the side of the house. Poking his head around the corner, he saw a minuscule wooden kennel with a mesh door. The white Staffordshire Terrier inside could barely stand, and it pressed its nose to the metal as it blasted out its harsh warning.

"Hey," Kett said, approaching carefully. "Hey, you're okay."

The dog stopped barking but kept snarling, its ears flat and its teeth bared. The box it was in was less like a cage and more like a coffin, so small the dog would struggle to turn around. It stank as well, the floor crusted with shit. The

Staffy snuffled, its big nose sniffing the air as Kett advanced. There was a big scar running across its snout, close to its eyes, and both of its ears had been mangled.

Kett got down on his haunches, offering a hand. The dog didn't exactly relax, but it did stop growling. It rocked from side to side, the closest it could come to prowling. He couldn't be sure, but he thought it might be female.

"Good girl," said Kett. "Good dog. Don't have much room in there, do you?"

He extended his fingers a little further and the dog sniffed him. Its demeanour seemed to change instantly, its face becoming alert, its tongue poking through the mesh as it tried to lick Kett's fingers.

"That's some gift," said Savage, advancing slowly.

"They've always liked me, for some reason," Kett said. "Kids and dogs."

"You have a kind face," she said, crouching down beside him. "It helps."

"I do not have a kind face," Kett said. "I have a mean, angry,   I'm-gonna-beat-your-door-down-and-kick-your-arse face, thank you very much."

"Sure," said Savage, holding out her own hand. The dog sniffed her fingers, its tail wagging so hard that its backside was bumping off the walls of its crate. "Hey, you're gorgeous."

"Well, sure," said Kett. "But that's nothing to do with having a kind face."

"I was talking to the dog," Savage said.

The dog took the compliment well, its big tongue flashing against the mesh.

"Poor thing," Savage went on. "I wonder how long it's been kept in there for. You'd lose your mind, wouldn't you? Caged like that. You'd go insane."

Kett nodded. He stood up, walking around the back of the house and hammering on the door he found there.

"This is the police," he roared. "Open up."

Something thumped inside the house, followed by an angry shout. Kett heard footsteps, then a huge shape appeared in the frosted glass.

"What do you want?" a man yelled back.

"It's the police," Kett said again. "I need to talk to you about your dog."

More angry mutters, then the door opened to reveal a guy in his fifties who was easily the size of the Michelin Man. He was dressed in a grey wife-beater vest and a pair of boxers that looked like they might be older than he was. He had a can of beer in his hand even though it wasn't even mid-morning, and he took a swig with a look on his heavily stubbled face that said *what are you gonna do about it?*

"What's the little bitch done now?" he said.

"Absolutely nothing," said Kett, trying to put a lid on the rage that was boiling inside him. "What's your name?"

Kett took a step towards the man as he spoke, filling the doorway. The intimidation did the trick because the man lowered his beer to his side, his eyes widening.

"Al," he said.

"Al, my name is DCI Kett. Can you tell me how long your dog has been caged this morning?"

The man shrugged.

"I put her in there yesterday," he said. "She had a run around in the morning, long enough to take a shit. She's a snappy bitch so she deserves to be locked away. Wish I'd never taken her."

Kett loosened the fist he'd made, flexing his fingers.

"You're aware of the welfare act?" Savage said, appearing by his side. "A dog must have adequate space to move around, it must have suitable living quarters, it should receive a healthy diet and be kept with other animals. Most importantly, it should be protected from pain, injury, disease and suffering."

"That dog looks like it's suffering, Al," said Kett. "What's her name?"

"Name?" he said, laughing like it was the most ridiculous question he'd ever been asked. "Why the fuck would I give it a name?"

"So you fight it, then?" Kett asked.

The man opened his mouth to answer, but he must have sensed the rage spilling over in the two police at his door. He shook his head, everything jiggling.

"I never did the dog fights, not for a long time," he said, unaware of the contradiction in his own words. "She's retired, I took her in out of mercy. I never fought her."

"Breeding dog, then?" Savage asked.

"Never," he said, nodding.

"Maybe you should tell your brain and your mouth to work together next time," Kett said. "You'll be more convincing that way. But listen to me, Al. I need you to listen to me very carefully. I'm going to be back out here every day. If I see your dog in that shitty little box one more time then I swear to god I'll put you in a cell of your own. Understood? It'll be smaller than that."

Al nodded again, dumbstruck.

"And if I ever hear that you used that dog for a fight, then I'll make *you* fight it, with your hands tied behind your back. Is that clear?"

It was clear enough for the man's bottom lip to start wobbling, his eyes to go wet. Kett eyeballed him for a moment more, just to make sure he got the message. Then he turned to walk away.

"Oh," he said, suddenly remembering why he was there in the first place. "Have you seen anyone new in the area? Anyone you don't recognise? Or any big dogs?"

The man shook his head.

"Be sure to let us know if you do," said Kett.

He left Savage to hand him a contact card, walking back the way he'd come. The Staffy had its scarred and pitted face pressed to the mesh, waiting for them to appear, and it started whining when it saw them. It pawed at the door, its eyes bright in the darkness.

"I'll be back," said Kett. "Don't you worry."

It hurt his heart to walk away, but he kept going, letting Savage out of the gate before him.

"Good job," she said. "I know it's not exactly related to the case, but it's nice to know we've made a difference to one living thing, at least. Dogs shouldn't be chained up like that. Caged. It's awful."

Kett nodded. For the briefest of seconds, a single thread of thought unravelled itself from the darkness at the back of his mind—there for a second before it was pulled away again. He grasped for it, something about Sally's murder, something about a chained dog, something he couldn't quite catch.

"Sir?" asked Savage.

He ignored her, walking back to the Volvo and climbing into the driver's seat. Savage hopped in next to him, clipping herself in and putting her bowler hat in her lap. From here, Kett couldn't see the dog in its crate, so he started the engine and crawled forward until the side of the fourth house came into view. Al was out there already, his arse crack the size of the Grand Canyon as he unlocked the crate. The dog was out like a shot, running in crazed circles around the crate.

"Go on," Kett willed. "Bite him in the bollocks."

Savage laughed, then pulled a face.

"It would be funny, but you'd probably end up having to dress the wound while we waited for the ambulance."

"Good point," Kett said, shuddering.

The dog wasn't interested in biting anything. It was practically gallivanting around the small garden pissing and sniffing and barking with joy. Al looked back, and Kett put two fingers to his eyes before pointing them at the fat man.

I'm watching you.

Then he floored it.

CHAPTER FOURTEEN

"So," said Superintendent Clare, pacing back and forth along one wall of the Incident Room, a clipboard gripped in his giant hand. "Where are we?"

The place was packed, two dozen detectives and uniforms fighting over chairs as they settled down. Kett had only just walked through the door, Savage still with him, and he hovered at the back of the room as the team fell quiet. Well, *almost* quiet. At the front, Emily Franklin, the young pathologist, was chatting loudly to DS Spalding. Clare tutted at them, banging the clipboard against his hand.

"Is there something you'd like to share with the rest of the class?" he yelled, loud enough to make Franklin jump. She stood up, red-faced as she glared at the Super.

"Jeez," she muttered. "Don't have an aneurism."

She turned to the room, putting both hands on the back of her chair. In her stripy tank top and beige cords she looked like a Sixth Form student.

"Uh, yeah, so I've finished a full autopsy on Sally O'Neil. The words on the back of her neck were carved there by a right-handed person, and handwriting analysis—as much as you *can* analyse something carved into human flesh—tells us this was probably a man. It's just as I said before, the injury to her throat is what killed her. The cuts to her face were made by a blade, not claws. And yes, her heart was missing. But there is something new. There are impressions of teeth in the wounds in the victim's throat, but they're not dog teeth, they're *human* teeth."

"Oh Jesus," Savage whispered, and from the swell of quiet noise around the room, most of the other police were saying something similar.

"Yep," said Franklin. "Whoever killed our girl took a few good bites out of her too. There's no sign of regurgitated flesh, so he swallowed it. He *consumed* the victim."

"Right," said Clare. It might have been the LEDs in the windowless room, but he looked about three shades paler than he had five minutes ago.

"Bloodwork has come back from the crime scene," Franklin went on. "Every sample of blood we found there belongs to the victim. Nothing from the killer, or from Roger Carver, the boyfriend. No semen. The saliva from the wounds is human, it's being tested as we speak. There was a trace of saliva from a dog, but I tested the dog who discovered the body and it's a match. Pawprints too. As far as I can tell, there was no animal at the scene during the crime. I can't explain where the Rottweiler tooth came from, I can only assume it was being carried by either the victim or the killer."

She practically spoke the whole thing in one breath, slumping into her seat as soon as she'd finished.

"Anyone have anything else?" asked Clare.

Porter put his hand up like he needed to go to the bathroom. Clare nodded at him.

"Dunst and I interviewed everyone in a ten-mile radius east of where Sally's body was found," he said. "No real leads, but two of the people we spoke to said they'd seen a big dog in the woods, just like Graham Turvey did."

"How big?" asked Clare.

"Big enough for them to notice," said Porter. "One of them actually reported it to the RSPCA, thought it might have been injured because of the way it was walking. We're waiting to hear back from them to see if they ever investigated."

Dunst cleared his throat as he flicked through his notebook.

"The exact description, and I quote, was 'a big bastard dog with a short snout and long tail. Uh, walked like every bone in its body was broken. Still moved fast, didn't see much more because I was too busy getting the fuck out of there.'"

"When was this?" asked Clare.

"The night before our victim died," said Porter.

"No mention of a human with it?" asked Kett. Porter looked back and shook his head.

"Kett?" asked Clare.

"Almost everyone we spoke to mentioned the Morton family," he said. "They have a scrapyard just south of the river. Savage and I paid them a visit." Clare shot him a warning look. "A *subtle* visit," Kett went on. "Because we heard gunshots. It's a little wild there, Jeffrey and his brother are both basically still kids, they've got guns and big dogs, Rottweilers. Something's going on there."

"But it's not our turf," said Clare, a little too quickly. "I've passed it all on to Suffolk Con, we'll let them take the lead on the Mortons. The Rottweiler tooth we found gives us an advantage. What's your gut tell you, Kett?"

Kett chewed it over.

"I don't know," he said. "It's a solid theory: Sally and Roger go walking in the woods. The Mortons are already there, maybe doing something they shouldn't be. A drug deal, perhaps. They kill Sally, maybe Roger too, mutilate the bodies to make it look like a dog attack or a crazed killer, then leave. But..."

Everyone watched him, waiting.

"It seems a little elaborate. We spoke to the brothers, and there isn't a brain cell between them. They don't seem the sort to perform an elaborate cover-up. Except..."

More silence. Kett glanced at Savage.

"What was your take on the younger brother, Thomas?"

"Nuts," she said without hesitation. "Seriously unhinged. He had that look, the same one that Christian Stillwater had. Cocky, incredibly sure of himself, ice-cold, like he could slit your throat and not think twice about it."

Kett nodded.

"That's more plausible," he said. "Thomas Morton sees Sally and Roger walking into the woods, he follows them, maybe had one of his Rottweilers with him. Those dogs are well trained, they're fierce. If somebody's faced with a dog like that, they won't run, they'll do as they're told. Maybe Thomas incapacitates Roger—he probably didn't kill him, because we would have found some evidence of it—then goes to work on Sally. Afterwards, he takes Roger away somewhere. And yet..."

Kett shook his head.

"Again, that little shit doesn't seem capable of so much foresight. He was greasy, sloppy. It doesn't seem like the sort of crime he would commit, especially not without sustaining some kind of injury himself. And more than that, his dogs were almost scared of him. Wary, certainly. I don't think he'd have the same control over them that his brother does. If we can get a DNA sample, we can at least rule him out."

"We don't have his DNA," said Clare. "But his brother was arrested before. We may have a sample from him. Franklin?"

"That could work," she said. "Siblings should expect to share around 3,500 centimorgans with each other."

She was met by a room full of blank stares.

"It's a lot. Enough to pursue, if not to convict."

"Get on it," Clare barked at her. He scuffed the floor with his brown brogues, frowning so deeply that his forehead looked like an accordion. "Anything else?"

There were a few mutters, but nobody said anything.

"Then keep working the case," said Clare. "Word's out that we've got a dead woman, a missing man, and a monster. I need this to be over before the nationals get wind of it. The whole tossing paper girls story was awful enough, we don't need another psycho killer on the loose, dog or not."

He paused, looking at each and every person in the room like they'd pulled down their trousers and taken a shit right there on the floor.

"Go on then!" he roared.

Everyone jumped to attention as Clare stomped away. Kett fought the exodus of people as he made his way to Porter.

"You alright, Robbie?" the big DI said. "This one's a nightmare."

"It doesn't make a lot of sense," Kett replied. "But they never do, not straight away. It will, though, in time."

"Amen to that," Porter said, scooping up some paperwork.

"I'm going to do some more digging on the Mortons,"

Kett said. "Can you do me a favour and pull up Jeffrey's criminal record."

"I can do that, sir," said Savage. "Clare's assigned me to the case. 'Detective in all but name,' he said."

"Thanks," said Kett. He paused, thinking about the Staffy in the crate, the scar on its nose. "Actually, Savage, can you find out about dogfighting in the area? See if there's anything going on there, something the Mortons might be involved with."

"I know there is," said Savage. "We got called out to a fight maybe a year ago. Near Dereham. It was... it was disgusting. Poor things. When we got there one dog was dead, another had to be put down because it had been torn open so bad. Three more dogs were rescued, but... But it's not like they're ever saved. They can't be adopted. They're usually put to sleep. Maybe it's better that way, better than having to fight."

"Bastards," said Porter. "Punishment for dogfighting should be making the arseholes who do it fight to the death."

Savage nodded in agreement.

"What is the punishment?" asked Kett. "A fine, right, and jail?"

"Up to twelve months and £20,000," Savage said.

"That's enough of an incentive to murder somebody who witnessed a fight," Kett said. "Maybe that's what Sally and Roger stumbled into, the Morton boys fighting their dogs."

"But there's no way of finding out, because it's not our jurisdiction," said Savage.

"I'm working on that," said Kett. "And the murder still took place north of the river."

He turned to leave, but Porter called him back. The DI's expression had brightened.

"Oh, by the way, Allie said yes," he said. Kett shook his head, mystified. "To dinner. With the kids."

"Oh, great..." said Kett, hoping the lie wouldn't show. "I'll try to work something out for some time next month—"

"She said tonight works great."

"*Tonight?*"

"Yeah, tonight." Porter grinned. "It's Saturday, no work tomorrow. Come on, Robbie, you owe me."

"Owe you for *what?*" Kett spluttered.

"For all the amazing tea."

Kett managed a smile, shaking his head.

"Porter, if you promise me you'll never make me another cup of tea for as long as I live, then you can have dinner with us *every* night."

Porter grinned, offering his hand. Kett shook it.

"Deal."

CHAPTER FIFTEEN

It wasn't a promise that lasted.

Kett sat back in his chair, arching his aching back and checking his watch. The little hand was already sliding towards four, the afternoon a blur of police reports, newspaper archives, and family trees. He sniffed the air, suddenly aware that he could smell tea. Looking over his shoulder, he saw Porter walking across the Incident Room with a steaming mug in his hand. Dunst followed, scratching at his grey stubble and grinning like an idiot.

"Oh for fuck's sake," Kett muttered.

"Wait," said Porter. "I just wanted to prove to you that it's better than it used to be. Give it a chance. Before you say anything, just try it."

"You promised me, Pete. You promised me no more shit tea."

"It's good, I swear on it."

It wasn't good. Kett could tell that the moment the mug landed on his desk—leaving an instant ring mark on Jeffrey Morton's criminal record. Kett lifted the mug and placed it on the empty Norfolk Constabulary coaster that sat about three inches away. It looked positively anaemic, a cup of hot milk with a strange yellow tinge that was as far from tea as it was possible to be.

Porter smiled at him like a kid presenting a macaroni art project to his parents.

"Ah, what do you want me to say, Pete. It's not tea."

"You haven't tried it," Pete said.

"He's right," goaded Dunst. "You should try it."

"It looks a little hot," said Kett, scanning the room for an unlucky pot plant where he might be able to pour it once the DI had left the room. "I'll get around to it."

"I added extra milk to cool it down," said Pete.

"Extra milk on top of all the other extra milk?" Kett asked. "Brave move. Did you, uh, did you forget the teabag."

"I did not," said Pete. "In fact, just to prove to you that I can make a proper cup of tea, I left the teabag in."

"In the cup?" said Kett. He fished a pen from his pocket and dunked it into the mug. Sure enough, a teabag floated to the surface like a corpse in a canal. "Oh god."

"You mean, *Oh god, this looks amazing*?" Porter asked. Kett sighed. He jabbed the pen at the teabag a couple more times in the hope he might extract some kind of flavour. Then he picked the mug up.

"One sip and you go away, okay?"

Porter nodded. Kett took a sip, managing to choke it down. It was like downing a shot of UHT milk that had been sitting in somebody's locker for a month or two.

"It's great," he croaked, wincing.

"See!" Porter said. "All that fuss for nothing." He thrust his hands up to Dunst. "See, we're not all philistines."

Dunst was trying not to laugh, but he was finding it impossible. He thumped his wheezing chest as he descended into a coughing fit.

"See!" said Porter, speaking to the rest of the room.

Kett pushed the mug away with his finger, then used the same digit to tap on the Jeffrey Morton file in the hope it might distract Porter from asking him to finish the drink.

"The Morton family moved to Norfolk in 1992," he said. "Mortimer Morton was a conman who narrowly evaded prison in Birmingham. Narrowly evaded being executed by another crime family too, for embezzling from somebody he shouldn't have. He smuggled his ill-gotten gains south, bought the land on the cheap, ditched his wife for a local girl and had his two boys. Jeff in 1995, Thomas in 2001. He built the scrapyard, had a couple of close calls with the police—affray, one charge of domestic battery that was dropped, about six drink-driving arrests, although he never went away for it. Rumours of drugs, reports that he was using the outhouses to manufacture meth and the fields to grow marijuana. Several raids over the years but no evidence of anything other than personal use. When Morty died, the boys inherited everything. Jeffrey was already an adult so he formally adopted his little brother."

Kett scanned the rest of the files, trying to remember what he'd been about to say.

"Oh, yeah, known associates include a royal bunch of parasites, two of whom have been arrested for dogfighting. Another is doing time for assaulting a police officer, glassed her during a barroom brawl. Kenny Fields."

"Arsehole," said Porter. "I remember it. She left the force right after."

"Jeffrey Morton did his two years for possession down in Cookham Wood, the YOI. He was too young for Wayland. Records were quashed when he turned eighteen, which is how he was able to adopt Thomas. He's been in trouble since then, but nothing we can arrest him for.

Closest it came was when he thumped some old boy in the local pub. The guy didn't want to press charges and the CPS declined it in the end."

"Fits what I found," said Porter. "They're a menace, the brothers and their entourage. There are complaints against the family going back nearly three decades, sometimes several every week. Considering they're in the middle of nowhere, they get on a lot of people's tits."

"Can I take a look?" asked Kett.

Porter handed him a sheaf of documents, dense with printed text. Kett flicked through them, seeing words like *threatening behaviour, noise complaint, dangerous driving, gunshots, intimidation, littering, dog waste,* over and over and over.

"Most are from the neighbours," Porter said. "The Mortons treat the whole region like it's their own backyard, and they shit all over the place. There are complaints from Beccles, and Bungay, and some of the smaller towns. Sounds like Jeff and Thomas were trying to set up a protection racket. Give them money and they'll protect your shop, don't pay up and they'll trash it. But again, there was never enough there to convict, and I think they got bored of it."

Kett was half listening, and half scanning the documents. He stopped when he saw a familiar name.

"Eden Howarth," he said. "Complained that the Mortons were using his land and threatening him and his wife. Said it was affecting their riding school."

"Yeah," said Porter, leaning over. "He complained like clockwork. Every week, sometimes every day. There are hundreds of them. He claimed that's why they went out of business, that's why he went bankrupt, because people were scared of the idiots on the next plot over."

Porter wasn't exaggerating. Most of the official police

complaints were Eden's, and they went on right up until 2014. Kett reached the end then looked up.

"This is it?" he asked.

"Yeah, I figured he just got bored of it, or maybe they finally scared him into silence. Haven't heard a peep from him for the last five years."

Kett instinctively reached for his tea, then recoiled when he remembered who'd made it. He covered his retreat by pretending to stretch his arm out. Something was niggling at him, another nebulous thought that he couldn't quite put his finger on. He pushed his chair back and stood up.

"I think I'm going to pay another visit to the Howarth house," he said.

"Now?" asked Porter. "What about your tea?"

"I'll drink it when I come back," Kett said, making swiftly for the door. "It can't exactly taste any worse for being cold."

Porter's unmistakable gasp of betrayal followed him out of the room.

THIRTY MINUTES LATER, Kett turned off the main road and pulled the muddy Volvo onto the track that led to Eden and Polly's house. He'd looked for Savage before he'd left the station, wanting to take the young PC with him, but Clare had already assigned her to a task and she was nowhere to be seen. It seemed too quiet out here without her.

He slowed as he rounded the end of the driveway, crawling past the broken front door and parking in view of the courtyard between the house and the stables. There was nobody there now, but the cobblestones were covered in piles of horse shit. He could smell it as he clambered out—not an unpleasant odour, like most other kinds of shit, just *countryside* smell.

He shut the door and buttoned his suit jacket, stepping carefully over the slippery ground. In all honesty, he wasn't sure why he was here, just that something was fluttering around his head like a bat in a belfry—a suspicion that not everything in this place was entirely right.

"Mrs Craft?" he called out, his voice echoing off the side of the house like a panicked horse. From somewhere inside the stables he heard a snort, the clop of a hoof. "It's DCI Kett, from Norfolk Police. I need to speak with you."

Nothing. Kett made his way towards the house. Most of the big windows were too high to reach without something to stand on, but near the back of the property was a small staircase leading down to a door—probably a servant's entrance. Kett grabbed the iron railing and stepped into a pool of shadow, cupping his hand to the glass window in the door. He couldn't make much sense of the darkness there, other than the fact there were mountains of old boxes. He tried the handle, finding the door locked, then he pounded on it.

"Polly?" he called.

Trying the door once again, just to be sure, he walked back up the steps and took the path that led down to the barn. The overgrown gardens and fields appeared on either side of him, a few tenacious flowers doing their best to survive the cold snap. There were more buildings here than he'd noticed earlier, small brick workshops and kit rooms and sheds and what might have been an outhouse. They were all in danger of being lost to nature, thick-veined limbs of ivy trying to wrestle them into the ground and bird nests cluttering the gutters. Creatures skittered in the under-growth, and Kett couldn't stop the shudder passing through him as he imagined all the dark eyes that watched him go. If he wasn't careful, he was going to end up as afraid of the countryside as Porter was.

He upped his pace, reaching the barn and calling Polly's name again. Only a handful of blackbirds replied, their calls like a car alarm. Kett walked down the side of the building, seeing nothing. More neglected fields lay ahead, and past them—some way away—sat the woods where Sally O'Neil had been murdered, the trees peeking back at him over the horizon. He stood there for a moment, his hands on his hips, soaking up the sun from an unexpected break in the clouds.

Then he heard it. Somebody talking. It was coming from the other side of the barn, and he followed the sound of the voice. Whoever was speaking was doing so quietly, their hushed whispers almost lost beneath the gentle wind. Kett reached the end of the barn and poked his head around to see a patch of weed-thick land pocked with murky pools of water. On the other side of it, maybe twenty yards away, was a small, dilapidated building.

Pollyanna Craft knelt by the door, her hands clasped in her lap as she rocked back and forth, back and forth. She had a daisy tucked behind her ear, a white one that was almost lost in the dreadlocked mess of her hair. Her layers of clothes spilled out beneath her in a way that made Kett think of the famous painting of *Hamlet's* Ophelia floating dead on the water—although he couldn't for the life of him think why that image had washed into his head. She was still whispering, her tone now harsh and urgent, and as Kett crept forward he could make out the occasional word.

"... belong here, and I... can't do it by myself, it's too much... never imagined it to be..."

Kett stopped, not wanting to get any closer for fear of scaring the woman to death. She continued rocking, plucking the flower from her hair and laying it at the foot of the door. A gust of wind tore over the fields, the little shack rattling with the force of it. For a second Kett thought the whole thing might come down.

"… for you, my dear. Forgive me."

Kett cleared his throat, too quietly for Polly to hear. He did it again, and her head jerked in his direction, her face creased with panic.

"Oh!" she said. "Oh, oh my." She clamped a hand to her chest, massaging it. "Oh, twice in one day. You really shouldn't sneak up on an old woman."

"I'm sorry," Kett said. "I was calling you, I thought you'd heard me."

"I was miles away," she said. "I can get lost back here."

She grabbed the door frame of the shack and struggled to put one foot in front of her. Kett moved to help her but she waved him away, grunting and grimacing for a full minute before she was upright. She rested her hand on the building a moment more before steering the broken boat of her body around to face him.

"What can I help you with? Uh, I'm sorry, I've forgotten your name."

"DCI Kett," he replied. "You can call me Robbie."

This, at least, brought a smile to her face.

"I had a nephew called Robbie," she said as she lumbered towards him, wincing with every step. "He was the best thing that happened to our family. I always wanted kids, but Eden never did. He always told me to wait until the right time, and I did, year after year after year, and then it was too late."

She came to a halt, her whole body heaving as she tried

to claw in a breath. She was so stooped that she looked in danger of keeling over at any moment. She had to crane her head back to look up at him.

"Do you have children, Robbie?" she asked, her eyes bright.

"Three," he said. "Three girls, in fact. Seven, three, and one."

"Then I understand why you're all the way out here," she said, laughing quietly. "It must get noisy at home. How does your wife cope?"

Kett frowned, automatically feeling for the ring on his wedding finger. Only now did he notice how long it had been since he'd last thought of Billie, *hours*, and he missed her. She returned to his head, all smiles, all golden light, and he had to take a long, sudden breath through his nose to stop the wheeling rush of panic and adrenaline she brought with her.

"She was amazing," he said. "*Is* amazing. She just isn't around right now."

"I'm sorry," the woman said, flustered. "I didn't mean to... Tell me their names."

"The kids?" Kett smiled. "Alice is the oldest. Then Evie. Moira's the baby, even though she's really not a baby anymore."

"They make you human, don't they?" she said. "They make life worth living. Without them, what are we? I always thought that, spent my whole life thinking that. What am I, without them?"

She frowned, as if her own words were confusing her.

"Look, Polly," said Kett. "I hope you don't mind me asking. Is Eden here? I really need to talk to him."

"Sure," she said without hesitating. "He's around. I think he was in the barn just a moment ago. I'll check."

She started to walk but Kett held up his hand, stopping her in her tracks.

"I need you to be honest with me, Polly. If something has happened, if something isn't right, then you need to tell me."

Polly seemed to grow even smaller, one hand grasping in her hair for the flower that was no longer there. Kett looked past her to the crumbling building she had been kneeling beside, its peaked roof cracked like a skeletal ribcage. The daisy sat in the open doorway, a flash of white against the darkness inside. For some reason the set-up made him think of a church or an altar.

"Who were you talking to just now?" Kett asked, his tone gentle but firm. "Was it Eden?"

Polly didn't reply. She didn't meet his eye. Kett took a breath, then bit the bullet.

"He's dead, isn't he?"

It was like he'd yanked the spine right out of her. Polly started to fall and he rushed to catch her. Her weight caught him by surprise, almost pulling him over too as he lowered her carefully to the ground. She sat on her backside, an engine of sadness roaring to life inside her. Great, heaving sobs shook her until, just like that, she managed to contain them. Polly pinched her nose, her shoulders shaking as her red eyes rolled up to meet his.

"I'm so sorry," she said. "I'm so, so sorry. I knew it wouldn't be forever, but I just didn't know what to do, and I couldn't live without him, and..."

"It's okay," said Kett, crouching beside her. "Take a moment, then tell me what happened."

She sucked in a shuddering breath, then another, then she pulled her hand from her face and seemed to calm down. Past the grief, there was almost a sense of relief in her expression, in the way the lines seemed to fade from her brow.

"He was a bastard," she said. "Oh they always are, aren't they? The ones you love. And I did love him. I *do* love him. How did you know?"

"It was a hunch," said Kett. "When we were speaking to you earlier you referred to him in the past tense, just once or twice. Then we noticed that his complaints against your neighbours, the Morton family, suddenly stopped back in 2014. I wasn't sure, but I suspected. Something in the way you were, the way you talked about him."

"You know it too, don't you?" she said. "Loss. Did your wife die?"

"It's more complicated than that," said Kett. "She's missing."

"I'm sorry," said Polly, manoeuvring her body to try to get comfortable.

"We can go inside?" Kett suggested, but she shook her head.

"If it's all the same to you, I'm of a mind to get this done now." She looked back at the little building. "And within earshot, too. Eden'll be rolling around down there, for good or ill."

"You buried him?" Kett asked. "May I?"

Polly gestured towards the shack with a shaking hand, and Kett got to his feet. A smell greeted him as he lowered his head to the door, earthy and old. There was something else past it, something sharper, almost acidic, that he couldn't put his finger on. He pulled out his phone and turned on the torch, the cold beam of light revealing a bare dirt floor covered with flowers. Some were fresh, but others looked like they'd been here for years. The smell came from them, he thought, the smell of rotting petals.

"He had a heart attack," said Polly from behind him. "He literally just dropped like a stone. It was like somebody had... had thrown a switch. Dead before he hit the ground, like they say."

"When was this?"

"Five years ago now," she said, shaking her head. "It feels like five minutes. It feels like an eternity. I don't know."

"You saw it?" Kett asked, switching off the light and walking back to the woman.

"I was there, yes," she said, slapping the ground with a dirty hand. "It was my fault. We were arguing about that stupid house. He was screaming at me, really screaming, and he just went."

She wiped another tear from her puffy eye, sniffing hard.

"I think it might have been my fault, Robbie. I was scared what people might say, of what the police might do. I wanted him to die, I think I even said it to him, right before it happened. I think I said *just die, Eden, just... just go away and die*. And he did."

"That doesn't sound like a crime to me," said Kett. "But unfortunately, not declaring his death certainly is."

Polly hung her head, sobbing almost silently now. Kett felt a sudden wave of sympathy for her, living out here all by herself with that terrible weight of guilt resting on her. No wonder she was so bent, so broken. He crouched beside her again and rested his hand on her shoulder.

"Nobody is going to think badly of you, Polly," he said. "I can understand why you did what you did."

"I wanted him close," she said. "I couldn't bear the thought of him leaving me here by myself, of him being buried somewhere else. And I needed the money, I really did. His money, the sickness benefits. I have nothing,

Robbie, he cleaned us out when the business went under. Me, the horses, Eden's money is all we have."

Kett sighed.

"Here's what's going to happen," he said. "I'm going to call this in, and we'll get somebody out here to remove Eden's remains."

Polly lifted her head, panicked, but Kett squeezed her shoulder gently through her layers of cloth.

"They'll do it respectfully, I promise. They'll take a look, they'll make an official record of his death, then we can talk about ways to bring him back here. Okay? If you'd like this to be his official resting place then we can make that happen."

Polly sucked in another breath, wiping the spit from her lips. Eventually, she nodded.

"I don't want to lose him," she said, looking back at the shack. "I don't ever want to let him go. He was mine, always. It's what he promised."

Kett gave her another reassuring squeeze, then stood up. He, too, looked back at the little building, thinking about the body that lay there beneath its shroud of flowers and dirt. And maybe it was just the immense silence that hung over the farm, or the unfathomable darkness inside the building —maybe it was simply his own hammered nerves—but it almost felt like Eden Howarth was staring right back at him.

CHAPTER SIXTEEN

The black dog followed Kett all the way back to Norwich.

It climbed into the car with him, sitting on his lap, the stench of it unthinkable and the weight of it unbearable. It was so bad that it was hard to breathe, and twice Kett pulled over to the side of the winding country lanes to open his window and gulp down air before the howl of panic inside him grew too big to control.

The depression was hounding him because of Billie, he knew. He couldn't help but feel guilty for forgetting her, for letting her slip out of his thoughts like she was slipping from a rope into a cold, dark lake. He'd forgotten her, he'd abandoned her. It had only been for a few hours, sure, but that was just the beginning. Maybe next time she'd vanish for a whole day. Then a week. She'd be lost.

It couldn't happen again. He wouldn't let it.

"I'm sorry, Billie," he said aloud. "I won't forget."

He used the Bluetooth to call Bingo as he drove onto the main road, the phone ringing twice before it was answered by his old Super in the Met. It was the most futile question in the world, he knew. Utterly pointless. And yet, he couldn't stop himself. He literally could not stop those two awful words from spilling out of his mouth.

"Any news?"

A sigh, the sound of Bingo stroking his moustache.

"I love you for trying, Robbie," Bingo said. "But no, no news."

Kett hung up, slamming a hand on the wheel and almost nudging the old Volvo off the road. For a second—less than a second, just the smallest increment of time—he wondered if doing that would solve his problems, if maybe in death he would find Billie there, waiting for him.

Then Alice ran into his thoughts, smiling the same smile her mother had worn. Evie was there too, hanging onto her sister's coattails, Moira toddling along behind. And he hated himself for ever thinking it, for ever thinking about leaving them alone.

He called home, the house phone ringing, and ringing, filling him with the same sense of dread he always felt when he heard that infernal noise. Then it clicked, and somebody breathed into the line.

"Evie?" he said.

"Mine!" came Moira's voice, followed by Evie's.

"Give it to me, I answered it, it's mine."

"Mine!" screamed Moira, then the phone clattered to the floor.

It made Kett smile, the way hearing their voices always made him smile—even when they were driving him to desperation. The black dog padded off his lap and slunk into the back seat of the car, still there but much quieter.

"Girls?" he said. He heard a clunk.

"Daddy?" said Alice. He heard her running, knew that

she was trying to escape her sisters. "Are you coming home?"

"Very soon," he said. "Everything okay? Is Clarissa okay?"

"She's nice," said Alice. "We made bags. Mine's purple. Evie didn't do it because she's stupid."

"Is Clarissa there?" Kett asked. "Can I have a quick word?"

"Yeah," said Alice.

There was a bleep, and the phone went dead.

"Alice?"

Kett gave up on them, calling Superintendent Clare instead. When the boss didn't answer, Kett left a message on his voicemail detailing everything he'd learned at Polly's house.

"She's in shock, I think," he said towards the end of the call. "She refused help, but it might be a good idea to send somebody out there to check on her. Or I can do it in the morning. We should contact her next of kin, Eden's too, and let them know. I can't see her surviving out there for much longer."

He indicated, taking the exit.

"I'm heading home for the kids, sir. But I'm here if you need me."

He killed the call, making it halfway across town when he remembered that Porter and his wife had invited themselves for dinner.

"Bollocks," he muttered, ready to dial Porter's number and cancel the whole thing. But he hesitated, chewing it over for a moment before deciding against it. He wasn't exactly great company at the moment, and maybe having guests over would be a welcome relief for the kids.

Besides, there was something else he needed Pete and Allie Porter for this evening.

He stopped at the Co-op for a pack of pasta and some sauce in a jar, grabbing a random bottle of wine from the shelf. He was so focussed on getting back in the car that it took him a moment to realise where he was. Just down the road sat the little parade of shops that included David Walker's Newsagents. The windows were boarded up and covered with fly posters, and somebody had painted a big, black N over the L in Walker's. Kett felt a pang of sympathy for the little man, wondering if he'd even survived the incident with his newspaper girls. He'd been old, and frail, and the public hadn't exactly been kind—even though he'd had nothing to do with it in the end.

Kett climbed into the Volvo, fighting the traffic for another fifteen minutes before he pulled into his street. For once, there was a parking space right outside his house, and he took a few moments to appreciate the peace before cutting the engine and walking to the door.

"I'm home," he said as he opened it. He gritted his teeth against the inevitable rush of screeching children, but nobody appeared. Closing the door behind him, he peeked into the living room to see that it was empty, *Ice Age* playing on the TV with the volume off. "Clarissa? Alice?"

It was there before he could stop it, the tiniest worm of dread burrowing into his chest. Then he stepped into the kitchen and saw them there, all four of them sitting at the table with crayons gripped in their hands. They all looked up momentarily, but it was as if he wasn't even there. Clarissa sat beside the high chair, helping Moira colour in a picture of Elsa and Olaf. She looked up, laughing at Kett's expression.

"My dad calls that catching flies," she said.

Kett snapped his mouth shut, walking to the table and gently kissing Moira's head. She smelled of shampoo, and he suddenly realised that all of them were in fresh pyjamas.

"Who are these people?" he asked. "And what have you done with my children?"

Clarissa laughed, her cheeks blazing.

"They've been amazing," she said. "As good as gold. We've watched some films, eaten plenty of fruit. Alice and I made some bags."

"I'll show you mine later," said Alice, busy scribbling. "I'm busy."

"Busy!" echoed Moira. Evie was concentrating on her picture so much that her tongue was poking out between her lips.

"I hope you don't mind, I gave them all a bath. We popped into the garden and got a little dirty. Clothes are in the machine, I ran a prewash to get the stains out. They've been so calm. The only time they even came close to causing a fuss was when you called."

"My god," said Kett, throwing the girl a bemused smile. "You're a saint."

"That's what dad always tells me. He says that's why I should charge you a thousand pounds." She laughed, putting a hand to her mouth self-consciously. "But I won't. Ten pounds an hour is fine by me."

Kett patted his wallet, cursing himself for forgetting to take out cash at the shop.

"I'll pay you fifteen an hour," he said. "You're worth it. But I'll have to give it to you tomorrow. If you're happy to come back tomorrow, that is?"

"I'd be delighted," she said. "Same time?"

"Yeah, thank you. We're having dinner soon, if you want to join us? Pete Porter is coming, and his wife."

Clarissa pulled a face.

"I'll be going, then. Before he offers to make me a hot chocolate."

"Hot chocolate too?" said Kett, laughing. "That man should be arrested for crimes against hot drinks. His tea is the worst."

"No, his *wife's* is the worst," Clarissa said. She got out of her chair and, as one, all three kids burst into a series of protests. "I'll be back tomorrow," she shouted over them, giving them a sweet little wave. "I'll bring my old Duplo; I've got boxes of it."

"You okay to get home?" Kett asked, and she nodded, practically skipping down the corridor towards the front door. "Byeeee!"

"I don't want her to go!" yelled Alice, climbing from her chair and chasing her. Kett held out a hand, rooting her in place. She was stronger than ever, grabbing at his arms to try to pull him out of the way. "No! I want her to stay!"

"I'm here now," Kett said.

"You're a butthead," said Alice. "You never make anything with me."

The door closed, and Kett released his oldest daughter like a greyhound out of its cage. Moira was barking out a series of angry cries, wrestling with her high chair. She grabbed Evie's drawing and crumpled it up, and within a split-second Evie was screaming at her little sister.

"No! That was mine! No!"

She threw the crayon she was holding at Moira, and Moira threw it right back, and before Kett could stop it a tornado of colour was blasting across the kitchen table.

"Come back!" Alice sobbed through the letterbox behind him. "Clarissa, come back!"

"I hate you!" shouted Evie, clambering down from her chair.

"Butt-ed!" screamed Moira.

Kett breathed out a sigh.

"Great," he said, wishing he had some of Clarissa's magic. Some of *Billie's* magic. "Welcome home, dad."

———

DI PETE PORTER knocked on the door just over an hour later. The clocks had almost hit seven, and the world outside was starting to slip into shadow. The girls had finally calmed down, Moira's eyes drooping as she sat on the sofa watching *Cbeebies*. He'd bribed them into silence with a handful of Milky Bar buttons each, asking them to try to remain calm and polite while their guests were there.

But as soon as the doorbell went, of course, the three of them shot off the sofa like they'd been catapulted, running into the hallway so fast that Moira tripped over Evie's legs and went sprawling.

"There's someone at the door!" screeched Alice. "Monsters!"

"Monsters!" wailed Evie, running around in circles.

"It's not monsters," said Kett, scooping up Moira as she cried and bucked like a bronco. "I told you who it is."

He fought his way past Alice and opened the door.

"Evening," started Porter. "It's good—"

"Pete!" yelled Alice, grabbing the big man in a stomach-high bear-hug. "Guess who looked after us today? Clarissa. And guess what we made? Can I show you?"

"Can we let them in first?" Kett asked, gently prising Alice away with his free hand. Moira was in danger of splitting his skull open with her furious screams. "Sorry, Pete."

"It's nice to be wanted," he said, smiling at Moira. "Oh dear, what happened to this one? Has she not had enough raspberries today?"

He stuck out his tongue and blew a giant raspberry right in Kett's face.

"Thanks, Pete," Kett said dryly as he wiped the spit from his forehead. But it did the trick. Moira's screaming stopped dead and she stared at Pete wide-eyed. After a moment she stuck out her hands and the big man whisked her away.

"How's my little warrior?" he asked, booping Moira on the nose. "How's my little Moiry-woiry?"

"Um, hello?" came a voice from the doorstep. "Have you forgotten me?"

Allie Porter poked her head into the house, and she didn't look particularly impressed. She glared at her husband, who stood there sheepishly before making a token effort to open the door a little wider.

"Of course not!" he said. "Come in, come in. Robbie, you remember Allie, right?"

It had been a long, long time since Kett and Porter had worked together in the Met. Even though they'd come up the ranks alongside one another, they'd not always socialised, and other than being a guest at their wedding, Kett had only met Allie a handful of times. Shortly after they'd married, she'd landed a teaching job outside of the city and Pete had dutifully followed her. In all the times the DI had visited the house during the last six weeks, he'd never once brought Allie with him. That was partly to do with her job, Kett knew. She was a deputy head at a high school in the suburbs, and it didn't leave her with a lot of free time. But it was probably also to do with the fact that, as far as Kett could remember, she wasn't actually very nice.

She was striking, though. You couldn't argue with that. Her hair was dyed platinum blonde and styled to perfection. She wore a full face of makeup, and her dress looked expensive. Twenty years ago, Pete happily boasted that Allie turned heads wherever she went, and Kett didn't doubt for a second that it was still true. But she was the opposite of Billie in so many ways. Billie had never had an expensive haircut. She'd barely ever worn makeup, either. Her beauty had been something else, something that shone from inside her.

"Hello?" said Allie, snapping her fingers in Kett's face. "Robbie? Remember me?"

"Sorry, Allie," Kett said, leaning in and giving her an awkward hug. "It's been a long day."

"We can go, if you like?" she replied, raising an eyebrow.

"No, don't be silly," Kett said, closing the door behind her. "Come on in. I'll get the pasta on the boil."

"Don't," said Porter, trying to dodge Moira's sticky finger as she jabbed it at his nose. "I've had your cooking one too many times. I ordered Chinese, it'll be here soon. My treat."

He kicked off his shoes and walked into the living room. Allie followed, handing Kett a bottle of wine. Alice and Evie were already in there, both of them pounding the sofa into dust as they jumped up and down on it. Kett frowned as he followed them in.

"What the hell is wrong with my cooking?"

CHAPTER SEVENTEEN

"I'll grind your bones to make my bread!"

Porter roared, sending the girls scuttling to safety—Moira's eyes bulging with genuine terror. Their screams were like scalpels in Kett's brain and he winced, then grunted as Evie threw herself onto him, planting her knee right in his crotch. Pain detonated inside him, settling as a dull ache in his stomach.

"Okay, okay," he groaned, turning her around so she was sitting on his lap. "That's maybe enough now. It's way past your bedtime, young lady."

Evie pulled a face of genuine irritation.

"I was talking to Pete," Kett said.

"Aw," pouted Pete, sitting on the sofa next to Allie. He slung a hand around her shoulder and she leant into him, scrolling through something on her phone. She hadn't really been paying attention, but it was impossible to deny how good Porter was with children, especially now that he'd had a little practice. Kett thought back to just a few weeks ago when the idea of managing all three of them in the hospital had almost driven the man insane. Now, he looked like a seasoned pro.

He was beat, though.

"I don't know how you do it," he said, wiggling a finger in his tie to loosen it. "They never stop."

As if to prove his point, Moira came waddling out from behind the sofa and slapped Pete's leg before screaming hysterically back to her hiding place. Evie was trying to wiggle free to go on the attack again, but Kett held her tight. Alice, who always seemed to find imaginative games hard, had run up the stairs to her bedroom an hour or so ago and was playing *Minecraft* on the iPad, delighting in the fact that she was allowed to stay up so late.

"Five minutes," said Kett. "Then I'm going to put you to bed."

"I'm still hungry," said Evie.

"Evie, I literally just sat and watched you eat a whole bag of spring rolls," Kett said. "A whole bag. I think there were twenty of them."

She wiggled some more.

"I need a poo," she said.

"Now that I *can* believe," Kett replied. "You must have a ball of Chinese food in there denser than a neutron star."

"Gross," said Allie, staring at her phone.

"They are gross," said Kett, smoothing down Evie's hair. "But we wouldn't have it any other way, would we?"

"See," said Porter, squeezing his wife. The smile he gave her was the smile of somebody who desperately wanted her to look up and pay attention to what was happening around her, and it almost broke Kett's heart when she just leaned even closer to her phone. "They're lovely, really. Can't you just see a few of these running around at home?"

Moira giggled her way out from her hiding place once

again, making it halfway to Porter before stopping. She wobbled, taking a huge breath.

"You are knackered, mate," said Porter, letting go of his wife and holding his hands out to her. She thought about it, then made for Kett instead, climbing up on the sofa beside him and slouching there like a sullen teenager. "Oh I see," Porter said. "Dump me like that why don't you, what a cheek."

He stuck his tongue out at her, but she was too tired to care.

"Come on, Evie," Kett said, giving his daughter a gentle pat on the backside. "Let's get your teeth brushed and put you to bed."

She looked like she was about to argue, but her words were swallowed by a yawn.

"Story?" she said.

"No chance," replied Kett. "Say goodnight."

Evie waved to Porter.

"Night night, Uncle Pete," she said. She frowned at Allie. "Night night, uh, *woman*."

Kett pulled her to his chest then struggled out of the sofa. Moira tried to get up too but he walked swiftly to the door. "Stay here for a moment, sweetie, while I get your sister in bed."

She made a noise like a whistling V2 rocket, and Kett closed the door before she could detonate.

"Sorry, Pete!" he yelled.

Evie slung her arms around his neck as they made their way upstairs, and he took her straight to her bed, bringing her toothbrush in and doing as good a job as he was able. He handed her a favourite bunny then tucked her in, kissing her on the forehead.

"Thank you for being amazing," he said. "I love you. I'll

come and check on you in ten minutes."

But she was asleep before he reached the door. He pulled it almost closed, then poked his head into Alice's room. The iPad lay on her lap, *YouTube Kids* blaring, but she was already fast asleep. Kett smiled as he took the tablet away and eased her down beneath her covers. He kissed her, too, smoothing back her hair. She frowned, grumpy even when she was unconscious.

"Thank you for being you," he whispered. "Love you, Alice."

Clicking off her light, he checked Evie once again then made his way downstairs.

"Right," he said as he walked back into the living room. "Now for the..."

He clamped his mouth shut, his eyebrows shooting up in surprise. Pete and Allie sat side by side where they'd been before, but Allie now cradled Moira in her arms. The baby was, incredibly, fast asleep, her face pushed into Allie's chest, one chubby arm resting on her neck. Her legs trailed over Allie's lap and onto Pete's, making her look ridiculously long. Allie just stared at Moira, her expression unreadable and yet somehow full of affection, and surprise. She was biting her lip, her free hand brushing the blonde curls out of Moira's eyes. Pete was grinning, and he turned that beaming smile to Kett.

Kett nodded, then walked out of the room to give them some peace. He checked his watch as he made his way into the kitchen—almost nine-thirty—filling the kettle and quietly putting three mugs on the counter. He was exhausted, but he knew the night was a long way from being over.

There was something he needed to do.

He was pouring water into the mugs when he heard the creak of the living room door. Porter tiptoed into the kitchen, still smiling. He gave a double thumbs up to Kett.

"I have literally never seen her holding a baby like that," he whispered. "Moira went straight to her, put her head down, and *boom*, she was asleep."

Kett nodded, counting the seconds with his watch as he let the tea steep.

"I mean, it's way too early to say," said Porter. "And she has so many issues with kids, from her mum I think. But maybe, just maybe, this might change her mind."

He was standing there with both sets of fingers crossed.

"I hope so," said Kett. "I really do. You deserve to be happy."

"So does she," said Porter. "This would be so good for her."

"You can always take one of mine," said Kett. "Borrow them for a day. Or a year."

Porter laughed, then frowned as Kett added the milk to the cups.

"What are you doing?" the DI asked. Kett looked up at him, frowning. Porter pointed at the milk. "Milk first, then tea, then water. Then more milk."

"*What?*" said Kett.

"Milk, tea, water, milk," said Porter. "It's how you make tea."

"What fudging planet were you born on, Pete?" asked Kett, shaking his head in disgust. He put the milk back in the fridge then handed Porter his mug. It was too hot for him, and he winced as he placed it on the table, sucking his fingers.

"The boss said you solved at least one mystery today," the DI said, scraping back a chair and sitting down. He pushed an empty takeaway container away with his finger. "Eden Howarth is dead?"

"Yeah, it's a sad story. We met his wife this morning, she blamed herself for him having a heart attack. Buried him in the garden, been living with it for five years."

"Shit," said Porter, and Kett threw him a warning look. "What?" he said. "The kids aren't here!"

"Fair enough," said Kett, sitting next to his friend. "Anything else happen when I was gone?"

"Suffolk Con are refusing to budge on their investigation," Porter said. "Mortons are off-limits. Other than that, the board is empty. No new leads, no sign of Roger Carver, no idea who, or what, killed Sally O'Neil. This is a bad case."

"Which is partly why I let you come round tonight," said Kett. "Look, Pete, would you mind doing me a favour. A *huge* favour."

"Anything," said Pete.

"I need you and Allie to watch the kids for me, just for a few hours."

"Now?" said Porter. "Where are you going?"

"It's probably better you don't know," said Kett. He mulled it over for a moment, then shook his head. "Actually, scratch that. It's probably better you *do* know, just in case something happens."

"Robbie?" said Porter, drawing his name out. "You're scaring me."

"I'll be fine," Kett said. "But this is something I have to do."

He took a sip of his tea, the taste blasting away some of

the tiredness. Pete looked at him with a grimace of horrified expectation.

"I'm heading back to the Morton place," Kett said. "And I'm going to find out what those dickheads are up to."

CHAPTER EIGHTEEN

HE SHOULD HAVE BEEN EXHAUSTED—AND HE *WAS* exhausted, a cloud of white noise buzzing inside his skull, his limbs leaden—but the adrenaline was doing a good job of keeping him sharp.

He stopped the car a quarter of a mile from where he and Savage had parked earlier that day, just up from the border where the Howarth house met the northernmost scrap of Morton land. He'd have got closer, but the Volvo didn't let you turn the lights off—the damned safety-obsessed Swedes—and he couldn't risk being seen. What he was about to do went *way* past official police business. If he was caught out here, if the brass got wind of what he was up to, then he could lose his job.

Of course, if the trigger-happy Morton brothers caught him snooping then there was a chance he could lose his life, too.

That wasn't going to happen. All he was going to do was cross the river, have a quick sweep of the scrapyard, and find whoever had been calling for help. He still wasn't sure if he'd heard what he thought he'd heard. It might have been the wind, or the whine of gears, maybe even the distant barking of a dog.

But it could have been Roger Carver.

There was only one way to find out.

He exited the car, shutting the door quietly. The night had fallen more aggressively here than it had in town, the sky as thick and dark as a coffin lid over his head. Inky clouds cut out all but a dull halo of light from the moon, spitting a miserable drizzle of rain on the countryside. The quiet out here was strangely deafening, almost oppressive, and once again he couldn't shake the idea that something out there was watching him. It was easy to see how the locals could believe in Black Shuck, the demon dog.

Kett shuddered, wishing he'd brought some painkillers with him. His shoulder was throbbing in the damp air, and the scar on his chest stung like a bastard. His brain was aching too, the wrecking ball of a migraine starting to swing itself into action.

Fishing his phone from his pocket, he flicked on the flashlight. It did little to chase away the night, but it was enough to make out the road ahead. He set off at a pace, hunkered against the rain, searching the banks and the ditches beside the road until he saw the gate up ahead. He took his time clambering over it, each squeak and clank surely loud enough to wake the dead. The ground on the other side seemed even more treacherous than before, and at one point his leg plunged into one pool of stagnant water and his phone skittered into another. He dug it out, swearing beneath his breath as he dried it on his jacket. The torch still worked, and he used it to navigate his way to the top of the hillock.

There, he turned it off, sliding the phone back into his trousers. He wouldn't need it up ahead, because the scrapyard lights were blazing. Surrounded by an ocean of darkness, the place looked like a football stadium—or maybe some giant tanker ship floating on the water. He squatted for a moment, cocking his head as he tried to discern any noise from inside.

Sure enough, a bark—muffled, though, as if coming from inside a building. Two more followed, then the site fell silent again. Kett thought of those dogs, wondering what kind of damage they might do to him if they caught him prowling around. He patted his jacket pocket, reassuring himself that he had a weapon with him just in case. Then he made his way down the hill.

It was harder than it had been earlier that day, as if the bushes and brambles had grown. They seemed to want to stop him going any further, but he fought them quietly until the last of the vegetation gave way and the river opened up before him. The little boat was still there, and he winced as he put a foot in it—freezing water spilling over his boots as he untied the rope. There was no paddle, but he was only five feet or so away from the middle stack and one good shove away from the bank took him there.

He grabbed the algae-slick bricks, bumping his way around to the other side before shoving himself off again. The boat rippled, water splashing up the sides as if trying to work out who he was. It spun awkwardly, the current dragging him past the pontoon, but he managed to lean over and grab a fistful of rushes, hauling himself in. It wasn't exactly a graceful exit, and he was glad nobody was watching as he almost roly-polied onto the muddy bank. But the boat had done its job. He was here.

Shivering, Kett crept up the bank, running quietly to the nearest of the four huge shipping containers. It gave off a hollow *bong* as he put a hand to it, the noise echoed by another distant bark. He paused there again, his pulse like a drumbeat inside his skull, so loud that at first he didn't hear it.

Somebody shouting.

He closed his eyes and held his breath, listening. The wind whipped around his ears, toying with him, delivering scraps of sound so faint they were almost ghostly.

There, another shout, a man's cry full of distress and loaded with panic.

Kett squeezed through the gap between the shipping containers, shrouding himself in the shadows that had gathered there. Ahead was a wide track going from left to right, and past that was a mountain of scrap cars, their bodies flattened and their windows shattered. A huge halogen spotlight sat above him, connected to the crane which sat there like a sleeping dragon. Another light blazed to the right, halfway up the path.

A bark, this one closer—echoed by another from somewhere further away. Kett could still make out that awful shout, the voice muffled as if whoever was making it was trapped. It was coming from somewhere to the right and Kett ran that way, staying low and keeping to the side of the shipping container. His boots drummed the compacted gravel path, stones pinging into the wrecked cars like a kid whacking a glockenspiel. To his right was a chain fence, topped with barbed wire, and ahead the path veered to the left, away from the river. He crossed over as he neared the junction, using the cars as cover, peeking around the corner to see a dog right ahead.

Fuck.

The Rottweiler stood in the middle of another path that led towards a group of buildings. It was eating something on the ground, trying to pin it down with its paw while it gnawed at it. A spotlight further up the path cast the dog's shadow all the way to where Kett was hiding.

He ducked behind a mangled Warrior truck, inhaling the stench of rubber and oil. From here the calls for help were clearer, sharper. The man was almost screaming, and Kett could make out words there:

"No! No! Please stop!"

What the hell were they doing to him?

He patted his pocket, feeling his phone there. Surely this was enough of a reason to call it in? To get a squad of police officers out here? But if they knew he'd been on-site without a warrant then it didn't matter, the case could be dismissed. He pulled the phone out anyway, opening the voice recorder. He could always say he was walking by and he heard the screams. At least this way he'd have evidence if they challenged him.

He pressed record, held the phone up, only to notice the sudden, throbbing growl from beside him.

Oh shit.

He turned his head slowly, the Rottweiler ten feet away. It was staring right at him, its lips pulled back to reveal the rows of big, lethal teeth inside, the hair along its back puffed up to make it look even bigger than it already did. Kett felt his insides liquefy in a rush of cold terror, and as slowly as he dared, he raised a hand.

"Easy," he said. He knew enough about dogs not to make eye contact, keeping his gaze on the ground as he reached into his jacket pocket. "Easy, boy, nothing to worry about here."

The dog growled some more, then unleashed a bark that made Kett's ears ring. Every muscle in its body was quivering, steam billowing out of its open mouth. Kett knew that if he made the wrong move now, if he spoke the wrong word, then the dog would go right for his throat. He couldn't help but think of Sally O'Neil, how quickly those teeth would have opened her up.

"Easy," Kett said, pulling out the only weapon he had with him. The bag of deep-fried chicken balls was cold and greasy, but they still smelled delicious. "You hungry?"

The dog barked again, spit soaring. Kett reached into the bag and grabbed a chicken ball, holding it out.

"Come on, boy," he said. "You want one?"

The dog's head cocked, a big tongue flashing. It seemed a little confused as to what to do next, little whines and growls spilling from it. Kett tossed the chicken ball at its feet and its body language changed instantly, its backside thumping from side to side as it scarfed the unexpected treat. It turned in circles, sniffing the ground, before looking back at Kett.

"You want another one?" Kett asked, holding it out. "You'll have to come get it."

The dog obeyed instantly, padding to Kett.

"You're a good lad, aren't you," Kett said, offering his empty hand first. The dog sniffed it, then woofed gently. Kett scratched it behind the ear as he offered the second chicken ball, which vanished inside its dripping maw. The dog licked his hand, then pushed its muzzle against his face, snorting.

"That's gross," Kett said quietly. He tried to put the bag of chicken balls back in his pocket but the dog butted it with its heavy head and they scattered. It began hoovering them up, the gulping noises it was making louder than the cries for help that were still echoing through the stacks. "Ah crap," said Kett as he watched the last of them disappear. "You were supposed to share them with your friends."

The dog snorted again, its arse smacking Kett in the face as it surveyed the ground for more treats.

"You're welcome," he muttered. He prayed he wouldn't meet any other dogs, partly because he was out of treats, and partly because he now stank like a giant, greasy chicken ball.

He set off again, staying low as he neared the buildings ahead. He knew enough about the layout of the scrapyard from Google Maps to be sure this wasn't the main house. That lay on the other side of the compound, an ugly bungalow which had been extended so many times it looked like some kind of mutant. Ahead were two large, square buildings made out of corrugated iron, possibly warehouses or equipment stores. Behind them was a gang of wooden utility sheds and three or four newer cars parked haphazardly between the clusters of overgrown vegetation. Another pile of scrap metal sat to the side, so tall that Kett felt like he was walking into a canyon.

"No! No! Please stop!"

The voice was louder now, so desperate that Kett felt the hair at the back of his neck rise to attention. It was a futile cry for help, though. There wasn't another home for miles, just woods and water and wasteland.

Kett checked behind him, seeing the Rottweiler still snuffling for scraps of chicken. He could hear another dog barking somewhere else on site, but it didn't sound close enough to worry about. He crept forwards, breaking into a run as he crossed the path into the shadow of the first warehouse. Only here, past the thunder of his heartbeat, could he make out the sound of other voices. Men, laughing.

And that same awful cry. "No! No! Please stop!"

Kett scanned the pile of scrap behind him, spotting a three-foot scaffolding pole with a knuckled joint on the end. He lifted it, testing its weight. It was hollow, but heavy enough to do damage. He rested it on his shoulder as he walked around the back of the warehouse, spotting the door on the other side. A weak light spilled out of it.

"No! No! Please stop!"

"Get him, Tank!" came another voice, followed by more laughter. Kett heard a furious bark, muffled, like the dog had something in its mouth. A scream rose up, the noise of somebody being mauled to death.

No time to call for backup. No time to wait. Kett gripped the bar and flexed his aching shoulder. Then he burst through the door.

CHAPTER NINETEEN

"Police!"

Kett tore into the warehouse, taking in as much information as he could in the split second before the people inside could react. The space looked huge, lit by a yellow light that hung from the ceiling. The floor was dirt, and a circular pit had been dug into the centre of it—maybe five metres across and ringed by a short fence. It was drenched with blood, old and new, and right now a man lay in the middle of it, curled into a ball, while a dog tore out his throat.

There were two other men in the warehouse, both of whom were staring at him in shock. The closest was Jeffrey Morton, and his face twisted almost instantly from surprise to anger. The other was Jeffrey's little brother Thomas, who was standing at the edge of the pit, his hands on the metal gate. The screams from the man below had reached a terrible crescendo.

"Don't fucking move!" Kett ordered, pointing the scaffolding pole at the older brother. Jeffrey didn't listen, glancing towards a table that sat on the far side of the warehouse. Too late Kett noticed the double-barrelled shotgun that lay there, breached.

"Fucking shoot him!" Thomas screeched.

Jeffrey was going to do just that. The big man turned, stumbling into a run, his flip-flops slapping. Kett bolted after him, but he was too slow. Jeffrey grabbed the gun, trying to snap it closed as he twisted back around.

One of the cartridges was loose, jamming the mechanism.

"Fuck!" yelled Jeffrey, ripping it out. He snapped it shut, lifted it.

Kett roared as he swung the pole, the knuckled tip hitting Jeffrey's face so hard that the man's feet actually left the ground. He tumbled back onto the table, snapping it in half and thumping to the ground. The shotgun clattered to his feet and Kett picked it up, lobbing it into the pit where it couldn't do any harm. The man inside was still crying for help—"No! No! Please stop!"—although Kett had no idea how he was still alive.

"Fucker!" Thomas Morton said, fiddling desperately with the metal gate that opened into the pit. He looked back over his shoulder.

"Get on the ground," Kett said, his voice like thunder. "Now, Thomas, or I'll drop you like I did your brother."

He started towards the scrawny teenager, hefting the scaffolding pole like a baseball bat and wincing as a pain like an electric charge ripped through his injured shoulder.

"*Now*, Thomas. I'm warning you."

There was a click, then Thomas jumped back—a smile on his face.

"Tank, go on boy, rip his fucking head off."

A ball of solid muscle thumped out of the pit like streak lightning, almost flying. Kett didn't even have time to swear before the dog was on him. He thrust the scaffolding pole out, some miracle causing the dog's teeth to lock around the end of that instead of his arm. The force of the collision knocked him onto his back, the heavy dog scrabbling onto his legs.

Thomas was on the run, but Kett couldn't do a thing about it. The dog's teeth gnawed on the pole, its eyes boiling with fury, its claws gouging through Kett's trousers and into his skin. He grunted, grabbing the pole with both hands and forcing the dog back. It was an English Pit Bull, dense and dangerous—clever, too, because it let go of the scaffolding pole and then sank its teeth into Kett's right arm.

Kett sucked in air, choking on spit, the pain burning through him. He managed to get a leg up, driving his boot into the dog's back legs. But its jaw was locked. It thrashed, tugging so hard that it dragged Kett across the floor. It was going to rip his arm off.

Then it was going to kill him.

"No!" he grunted. "Fuck!"

A dark shadow came out of nowhere, rushing to his side. Something landed on the dog, covering its face, and it squealed, letting go of Kett in order to twist around. A pair of arms grabbed it, and there was a groan of effort as a figure in black wrestled the dog over to the pit and dropped it inside. It bounced right back onto its feet, shrugging free of the black cloth before hurling itself up again. The figure slammed the wire gate shut, trapping it inside.

Kett rolled onto his front, then pushed himself to his feet. He clamped his injured arm to his chest, conscious of the blood that poured out of his jacket sleeve. The stranger turned around, and beneath a black Nike cap he saw that it wasn't a stranger at all.

"Savage?" he said, swaying with a sudden bout of vertigo.

"You just can't bloody help yourself, can you?" she said.

"Where the hell did you come from?"

"Porter called me," she said. He noticed that her clothes were soaking wet. "Told me you were about to do something stupid, pointed me in the right direction. I found your car, the rest was pretty obvious. Good job that river isn't deep. You okay?"

"Better for seeing you," Kett said, nodding to the pit. "And better than him."

The man was still screaming—probably because Savage had just thrown the dog back onto him. Kett staggered to the side of the pit, ready to climb down and help. But Savage put a hand on his arm.

"You might want to pause for a moment, sir," she said.

Kett wiped his eyes again, looking down into the pit as the man loosed another volley of shrieks.

"That's not Roger Carver," said Kett after a moment.

"Not unless Roger Carver is a shoulder of mutton wrapped in a T-shirt," said Savage.

That's exactly what he was looking at. A bloody slab of raw meat had been wrapped tight in a faded Meatloaf T-shirt, the whole thing held together with parcel tape. Fixed to the top was a deflated football with a photograph of a man's face attached to it—Kett couldn't be sure, but it looked like Nigel Farage. The Pit Bull was tearing into the dummy again, ripping out great chunks of flesh.

"No! No! Please stop!" screamed the man.

Except the noises weren't coming from the man, they were coming from a portable speaker that had been left inside the pit, inbuilt disco lights flashing.

"*What?*" Kett said. Savage was rolling up his jacket

sleeve, exposing the puncture wounds in his forearm. There were three of them on the top, and one underneath—thankfully nowhere near the blue threads of his veins.

"They're training it to kill," Savage said.

She scanned the room, spotting the collapsed table that Jeffrey Morton was still lying on. She ran to it, taking a moment to check the older brother's throat for a pulse before grabbing a roll of parcel tape from the mess. Kett held up his sleeve as she rolled the thick tape seven times around his arm.

"I've seen it before, with dogs. They record the sound of something in distress, make up a dummy, it teaches the attacking dog to keep going, to keep mauling and biting. It's sick." She split the tape with her teeth. "That should hold, but you're going to need serious work on that arm."

"It will have to wait," said Kett, pushing past Savage and making for the warehouse door. "Morton Junior's on the run."

"I saw him," Savage said. "Was going to go after him, then I figured you might need me more."

"You figured right," said Kett as they stepped into the night. Some twist of fortune meant that nobody had heard the fight. The dogs must have been well used to shouts of anger and cries of distress. Savage pointed into the dark that led past the mountain of scrap towards the edge of the yard and the countryside beyond.

"He went that way."

Everything ached, but Kett broke into a run, finding his rhythm. Savage bounced along by his side, her face taut with worry as she searched for their prey. Her wet boots squeaked and sloshed as she ran. There were fewer lights out here, and every shadow seemed to be a grinning Thomas Morton, armed with a shotgun and ready to kill.

"How did you get it to let go of me, by the way?" asked Kett.

"You don't want to know," Savage replied. "But let's just say I once heard the only way to get a dog to let go of a person is to stick a finger up its arse. And now I know it's true."

Kett had no idea what to say to that.

"We never, ever speak of it again," Savage added.

They kept running, searching the dark, waiting for Thomas to break cover.

Clank.

"Over there," said Savage, pointing to the noise. They were almost at the perimeter fence now, Kett could make out the shape of it up ahead. Beyond it was the marshy land that followed the river. Kett heard another clank, then a yelp and a wet thud, like somebody falling.

"He's over the fence," said Kett.

They were far enough away from the heart of the compound for Kett to risk using his phone's torch. He flicked it on, sweeping the feeble beam back and forth.

"Two o'clock," said Savage. Sure enough, there was a point where the chain fence sagged as if it had been climbed over a hundred times, the barbed wire at the top had snapped and was drooping like willow. "Can you manage?"

"I can try," said Kett. He passed the torch to Savage and threw himself onto the fence. It bowed beneath his weight, letting him scale it easily. His arm was still burning, and his right hand had gone worryingly numb. He tumbled off the other side, just about managing to keep his feet on the slippery marshland. Savage practically vaulted the fence in one go, landing like a gymnast. She handed his phone back and he shone the torch into the night.

Thomas Morton was a flailing shape, stumbling towards the woods.

"Thomas!" Kett boomed, no longer caring about the scrapyard dogs. "Stop! You're under arrest, you little shit."

If Thomas heard them over his own frantic whimpers, he made no show of obeying.

"For fuck's sake," Kett grumbled, his feet almost slipping out from beneath him as he ran through a boggy patch. Savage was already a dozen yards ahead of him, her arms pumping like pistons. Ahead, Thomas was halfway to the woods. If he reached them, the chances were they'd lose him in the dark. The boy looked back, his arms wheeling as he fought to stay upright.

Kett's head was spinning, his pulse pounding in the injuries in his arm and shoulder. His stomach churned, and he knew that if he pushed himself much further he was going to vomit up the Chinese food he'd had that evening. But he kept going, fighting the exhaustion and the pain.

"Police!" Savage shouted. "Stop now!"

She was almost on him, and he was almost in the trees.

Go on, Kett silently ordered her. *Get him.*

It was too much. The edges of his head were already lost to a pulsing darkness and he slowed to a halt, putting his hands to his knees and clawing in a breath. They were still south of the river, Suffolk territory, but he lifted his phone anyway and prepared to call for reinforcements—medical aid, too, for Jeffrey Morton. As he did so, the beam of torchlight flashed across the marshy land, glinting back at him from the pools of stagnant water.

And from the eyes of something standing on the other side of the field.

At first, Kett thought it was a fox, then he turned the beam of light back and saw that it was way too big for that.

Its bulky outline was an inky shadow against the night, down on all fours, hulking and dangerous. It was too far away for Kett to make out properly, but those eyes shone back at him like they belonged to the devil himself.

Then it moved, breaking into an ugly, shambling run.

Heading right for where Thomas Morton and Savage were vanishing between the trees.

"Shit," Kett said. "Shit shit shit."

He started running again, tripping, slipping. He tried to keep the phone out in front of him but the effort was too much and it dropped to his side, everything suddenly vanishing like he'd been struck blind.

"Hey!" he yelled. "Savage, there's something else out there!"

She was too far away to hear him. He lifted the phone again, the finger of cold light picking out the ridges, the pools—and there, the dog-thing that chuffed its way towards the woods.

That rose slowly onto its back legs and began to run.

"Savage!" Kett roared. "Dammit, hey, you, stop! Police!"

Thomas vanished, sucked into the trees like they'd eaten him alive. Then Savage was gone too, as though she'd never been there. Kett could just about see the outline of whatever chased them as it powered towards the woods, impossibly fast. He opened the phone as he ran, calling 999.

"This is DCI Robert Kett," he said breathlessly when it connected. "I'm in pursuit of a dangerous suspect, south-west of the Morton scrapyard in Suffolk, entering wood-land. Officers in danger."

He didn't wait for a reply, just killed the call and aimed the torch ahead of him. The creature was nowhere to be seen, pulled into the darkness between the ancient trunks.

"Savage?" he called out. "There's something in there with you. Be careful."

It seemed to take him an age to reach the first line of gnarled trunks. This wasn't the same woods where Sally O'Neil had died, but it would be hard to tell the difference between them. These trees, too, looked old and diseased, a leprous colony of giants that fought Kett back with their twisted fingers. He ran between two enormous trunks, branches scratching at his face, at the wounds in his arm. There was no light here at all other than the glow from his torch, and he swung it wildly from side to side. Shadows leapt and danced back and forth so wildly that it made him seasick.

"Savage?" he called. "Kate?"

Nothing. He stopped, gasping, listening.

A soft cry, the crack of a branch. Kett called Savage's name again, ploughing through the vegetation, percussive snaps exploding with every step.

Then another noise, the piercing note of an old-fashioned police whistle. It was Savage's lucky whistle, the one her grandfather had given her. It sounded too far away, like she'd been in here for hours rather than seconds.

"Kate? Where are you?"

He was answered not by her, but by a noise he couldn't place—a wicked, guttural cry that could have come from a human or from an animal. It was close, and the sound of it filled Kett with a fear that could have been ice water. It came again, almost laughter now, like a hyena. Kett's head rang with panic. He hadn't felt like this since he was a child, since he'd believed in monsters.

The police whistle again, closer now. He followed the sound.

"I'm coming," Kett shouted, the trees swallowing his words like he'd whispered them.

"I've lost Morton," Savage called back.

"Forget him, there's something else here. Watch out, it could be anywhere."

It could be right behind him, a sudden rush of sound. Kett whirled around, his torch catching the swaying branches overhead, the rustling leaves. More noises to the left of him, something big bolting across the damp earth.

A scream tore through the night, loud enough to rip the world in two.

"Fuck," Kett said, breaking into a run again, tripping on an exposed root. He landed hard, his injured arm catching on a rock. The world flashed white like a percussion grenade had gone off right in front of him. He clawed in a breath as he got back up, using the trees to keep him on his feet.

Another scream, weaker now.

"Kate?" Kett called. Where the hell was she?

He pushed on, desperate now, calling Savage's name until he heard her.

"Robbie?"

A shape to his side. He shone the light at it, seeing Savage with her hand in front of her face, the whistle glinting.

"Ow," she said, and he realised he'd blinded her. He lowered the beam to the ground, stumbling towards her. Her free hand found his and she held it tight. He could feel her body trembling—partly from the cold, he guessed, but mainly from fear. He was shaking too, after all.

"You okay?" he asked, moving the torch in a circle around them like it had the power to ward off evil. "I wasn't sure if you were screaming."

"Not me," she said. "I think it's the boy."

As if to confirm it, another cry rose into the night—mournful, desperate, and on the edge of death.

"Help me, help me, help—"

"You armed?" Kett asked. It was a stupid question, Savage snapping out her telescopic baton as she took the lead.

"What did you see?" she asked.

"I thought it was a dog," he replied, following behind her. "But it stood on its back legs. I think it's a man. I think it's whoever killed Sally O'Neil."

He wasn't sure how he knew, but he did. His gut knew. Some ancient part of him that had, over millennia, been taught to recognise a predator, just *knew*.

"Help me," said Thomas Morton, just a whisper.

A shrill whine, a soft bark, then a noise like somebody stamping on a melon.

"Thomas?" Kett yelled. "Where are you?"

Snuffling from up ahead, ripping sounds. Was that a swallow? A wet purr? Then something running. The sounds turned Kett's stomach and he had to force one foot in front of the other, step after step after step, until they pushed past the skirts of a giant conifer to see Thomas Morton on the ground.

What was left of him, anyway.

Just like Sally, his throat had been ripped out, his neck a puddle of blood that looked as black as tar until Kett angled his torch at it. It bubbled, his body twitching like a broken puppet. There was a stench in the air—not just blood but something else, something bestial.

Savage ran for the dying man, skidding to her knees in front of him and putting her hands to his throat in a futile attempt to stop the blood. Thomas's fingers groped for her, his eyes big and bright even in the dark. He was losing strength by the second.

"Kett!" she said. "I need some help here."

Kett ran to her, but then he stopped. Something big moved behind the trees, a flash of heavy darkness that bounded away. Kett stumbled past Savage, grabbing a low branch to steady himself while he stared into the awful nothingness between the trunks. It was as if the world stopped here, as if walking any further would send him spinning into the vast, aching absence of space.

And yet wasn't that something right there? Two points of distant light that gleamed back at him like a wolf's eyes. He lifted his torch, too many sweeping shadows to make sense of, and one shadow that didn't move, that stood upright behind a tree and coughed out a senseless, idiot noise.

"Kett!" shouted Savage. "I'm losing him!"

Or maybe the noise it was making wasn't senseless. Even as it turned and ran again, dry wood cracking beneath it, Kett wondered if he'd heard a word in its cry. *Two* words, over and over.

"Robbie, hurry! Please!"

He turned and ran back to Savage, kneeling beside her as she fought to keep the dying boy alive. And behind them, those same two words were barked into the night like gunshots.

"*Bad dog. Bad dog. Bad dog.*"

CHAPTER TWENTY

IT WAS ALMOST AN HOUR LATER THAT KETT SAW THE
flashlights cutting through the woods.

He sat against a tree, his backside numb and his arm
clamped to his chest. Savage sat beside him, shivering in her
wet clothes. Her head rested on his shoulder, and she was
quiet enough that she might have drifted off. Only Kett
knew she wasn't asleep, because her breaths were deep,
unsteady sighs, and she kept rubbing her bloodied hands on
her trousers and scratching at her fingers.

Thomas Morton lay dead in front of them. Savage had tried
to close his eyes, but one had peeled open and was peering at the
swaying canopy overhead like he was trying to find something.
His throat was a ruin, the gaping wound more obvious now that
the blood had dried. The youngest Morton brother had been a
kid, and he looked younger than ever in death. Criminal or not,
he hadn't deserved what had happened to him. He hadn't
deserved to be ripped to shreds by a monster in the woods.

A *monster*.

There had been enough time for Kett to try to digest

what he'd seen, but he still couldn't make sense of it. Not really. He knew it had been a man—there surely couldn't be any doubt about that—but the way it had moved on all fours, the way its eyes had shone through the night, the noises it had made. Kett was a devout sceptic, he always had been, but in this ancient place, this altar of the night, he could easily believe in devils.

Somebody called out, the lights rising up over the hill like dawn.

"Kate," Kett said quietly. "They're here."

Savage lifted her head from his shoulder, shivering.

"Took them bloody long enough," she said.

"Over here," Kett yelled.

"Here!" Savage joined in.

She got to her feet first, helping him up with her sticky hands.

"Hello?" came a voice. "Where are you?"

A beam of torchlight caught Kett right in the eyes, the pattern of his retinas exploding. He lifted his good hand to cover his face, hearing the sound of feet pounding towards him.

"Jesus Christ!" said the voice, one that Kett half recognised. "What the hell is going on?"

Kett dropped his arm, blinking spots of light from his vision to see DS Helen Stuart from the Suffolk Constabulary. She stood next to another detective, an older man, and five uniformed officers who continued to spread out to search the woodland. It wasn't exactly the cavalry he'd been hoping for.

"What the fuck are you two up to?" Stuart said. She nodded at the corpse. "Thomas Morton?"

"Yeah," said Kett.

"Fuck me," she said. "I told you, I *told* you not to go near him."

"Who are you?" asked the man. He was lean, fit, his grey hair styled in a crew cut—probably ex-army—and he made no attempt to offer his hand.

"DCI Robert Kett," said Kett. "This is PC Kate Savage."

"You're a long way from home," said the man. "Mind telling me why you're here, and why *you're* out of uniform?"

"We were searching the woodland north of the river," said Kett. "We had a report of a creature in the woods. Then we heard screaming, somebody calling for help. We breached the Morton compound and found the brothers and their dogs. They attacked, Thomas fled, we pursued."

It was almost the truth, and he and Savage had rehearsed it long enough for it to sound convincing.

"Jeffrey Morton's in one of his warehouses at the yard," he went on. "He might need medical assistance."

"You think?" said Stuart. "His fucking jaw's broken."

"He had a gun," Savage chimed in. "He was going to open fire."

"You haven't answered my question, young lady," said the other detective, glaring at Savage. "Why are you out of uniform?"

"I'm off duty, sir," she said. "But I wanted to help. This case has got us all spooked and we need it resolved—whether that happens north or south of the river. I did my best to save his life, but his injuries were too severe."

"And what, exactly, did that to him?" the man asked.

"The same thing that killed Sally O'Neil," Kett replied. He checked himself. "The same *man*, I mean."

"You saw him?" Stuart asked. Both Kett and Savage nodded.

"It was hard to get a good look in the dark," Kett said.

"He's obviously disturbed, he moved like a dog, made noises like one. Dressed like one too, maybe. He was wearing old clothes, rags, maybe furs, and he was filthy. We lost sight of Thomas for a few minutes."

He looked at Savage and she nodded.

"Less than that," she said. "I lost him for just over a minute, in the trees."

"And in that time the killer found Morton and opened his throat," Kett said. "No hesitation, no motivation. We got to him too late. Our priority was saving the victim's life, and by the time we called it there was no sign of his attacker."

DS Stuart shook her head, obviously disgusted. But the other copper nodded, his posture relaxing.

"You're injured," he said, nodding to Kett's arm. He glanced at Savage. "You too?"

"Not my blood, sir," she said. "But the boss here's been bitten pretty bad."

"By a person?" asked the man.

"Dog," said Kett.

"I'll have one of my officers show you out of the woods," the man said. "There's an ambulance there. Get yourself sorted, get home, but we'll need a full report on this tomorrow morning. First thing."

"Sir," Stuart protested. He held up a hand, silencing her.

"What's done is done. We're not enemies, as much as you seem to think we are, Detective Sergeant, and we all want to see this creep behind bars. Get home, talk to us tomorrow. Scott?"

A constable appeared, holding a massive torch. Kett nodded his thanks to the detective as he followed the constable into the trees. His entire body ached, and he could feel his thoughts slipping from side to side inside his skull. He was so dizzy he almost fell, and it was Savage who stopped him—taking his arm and holding him up.

The policeman escorted them along a different route, as far as Kett could tell, and when they finally emerged from the woods it was onto a road lit up by rain-flecked head-lights. Kett stumbled onto it like a man who'd found land after years at sea, making for the ambulance that sat a dozen yards down, parked in a passing place with its engine running.

"Oh shit, look at this," said the paramedic who sat in the passenger seat—a woman in her fifties who barely looked taller than Alice. She hopped down. "Nasty."

"I want to say the dog came off worse," Kett said, offering his arm. "But that would be a lie."

"Who on earth wrapped this?" the paramedic said as she unwound Savage's parcel tape. "Feels like Christmas morning."

At least they managed to laugh. Savage climbed into the back of the ambulance with the other paramedic while the woman set about cleaning Kett's wounds.

"You're lucky," she said, dabbing antiseptic in the cuts before fishing around in them with a cotton swab. "They're not deep. This one's the worst, it might need stitches. The others will heal by themselves. You up for a visit to the hospital? You might need a rabies shot if the dog looked infected."

"It wasn't rabid, just well trained," said Kett, shaking his head. "I'll be fine at home."

"Why am I surprised?" the woman said as she mummi-fied his arm in bandages. "You cops never want to go to the hospital."

"Spent more than enough time there recently," he said.

"Well, keep an eye on it. Change the dressing every day, plenty of napalm to keep the germs away. You'll be fine."

Savage hopped down to the road, sucking something.

"All good?" Kett asked. She nodded.

"All great, and I got a sweetie."

"Hey, where's mine?" Kett said, and the paramedic handed him a packet of pills instead.

"Just Paracetamol, I'm afraid," she said. "Anyone else on their way?"

"Yeah," said Kett, swallowing two and pocketing the rest. "But there's no helping him, I'm afraid."

The paramedic sighed, nodding in understanding.

"The boss asked me to take you home, if you need a ride," said the PC, who had been waiting patiently beside the ambulance. "We're parked over the way there."

"We'll be fine," said Kett. "But do me a favour and run us back over the river to my car?"

The cop nodded, illuminating the road behind the ambulance with his torch. There was no sign of life at all, other than them, as if everything was in hiding. As if everything knew what else was out there, prowling the night. Was it there now? Was it watching them with those silver eyes?

He, Kett forced himself to think. *It's just a man. Just a man.*

"And when you're done with us, come back and keep an eye on those paramedics," he said to the constable as they made their way up the lane. "It's not safe out here."

Not safe at all.

KETT SLID the key into the lock and opened the door as quietly as he could, pushing it shut behind him. He dropped his keys on the sideboard and almost dropped himself right there on the mat, the exhaustion like a lead blanket around his shoulders. The drive back had seemed to take forever, even though the roads had been clear. He'd been alone—Savage had parked her little green Punto behind his and was happy enough to make her own way back to the city—and twice he'd had to jolt himself awake.

He heard quiet voices coming from the living room, and the door opened to reveal DI Porter there. The big man opened his mouth, then saw Kett's face, then saw his arm, and finally snapped his mouth shut again.

"Yeah," Kett said quietly. "It's been one of those nights."

Porter eased the living room door closed, steering Kett into the kitchen.

"Did Savage get to you? I called her."

"Yeah," said Kett. "Thank you. She saved my arse, again. She saved my *life*. Everyone okay?"

"Everyone is fine," he replied. "Except for Allie, who is, once again, not your greatest fan. Moira's still asleep on her, can you believe that? Hasn't made a peep. Evie needed a poo about an hour ago but she settled fine."

He pulled a face.

"What?" Kett asked.

"Do you always have to do that?" he asked. "Wipe their arses? It's pretty gross."

"Only until they're in high school," he replied, laughing at Porter's expression.

He dragged out a chair and slumped into it, flexing his arm. The pills the paramedic had given him were as effective as a pair of cheap earplugs against an air raid siren, the pain crackling beneath his skin like there was a fire burning there. But it was still better than that awful numbness he'd felt in the woods.

"Clare called," said Porter, leaning against the counter. "He heard the alert from Suffolk. He's kinda pissed. What happened out there?"

"The Mortons didn't kill Sally O'Neil," Kett said.

"Yeah?" Porter said. "How do you know?"

"Because Jeffrey Morton's unconscious and Thomas is dead, and the bastard's still out there."

"*What*?" Porter exclaimed, moving to the table and sitting opposite Kett.

"I'll fill you in in the morning," Kett said. "But I saw it. Saw *him*. The man that killed Sally. He's fucked up, Pete. There's something very, very wrong here."

Porter was about to reply, but he was interrupted by a soft cry from the living room.

"The Kraken is awake," said Kett, sighing.

Allie appeared, Moira in her arms. The baby was rubbing her eyes, searching for a familiar face.

"Mumma," she said, her first word, still, even after all this time. "Mumma."

"Hey, beautiful," said Kett, holding out his hands. He was a poor consolation prize, he knew, but this was all he could offer.

"Sorry," said Allie. "I had to move, my back was killing me."

She handed the baby over, Moira pressing her sweaty face into Kett's neck, her hands patting him on the cheek.

"No, I'm sorry," Kett said. "I shouldn't have left you like that."

"We'll head off," said Porter, taking his wife's hand. She held him tight, but she was watching Moira with that same enigmatic smile. "You gonna be okay?"

"I'll live," said Kett. "I'll fill you in tomorrow."

"Get some sleep while you can," Porter replied as he walked into the hall and grabbed his shoes. "Clare wants us in at six for a full debrief. Because he's a fudging winker."

"He certainly is," Kett said. "Thanks Pete, thanks Allie."

"I had fun," she said with a nervous shrug. She walked off and Porter looked at Kett in amazement, mouthing, *She had fun!*

Kett smiled as he watched them go, but it burned away almost instantly. All he could think about was the man in the woods, those bestial noises, those flashing eyes—and the smell he'd left behind him. He'd torn Thomas Morton's throat out in a single blow, and that hadn't even been the worst of it. Kett could still hear those awful, wet, gulping noises.

The sound of one man *eating* another.

"Dadda," said Moira, fully awake now. She leaned back, pointing into the hallway. "Shoes."

"No, lovely," he said. "It's bedtime."

"No," she pouted, straining to get away. "Shoes on."

"Okay, okay," he said, too tired to argue. "Shoes on, then bed. Deal?"

She didn't reply, she just manoeuvred herself off his lap and waddled out of the kitchen. It didn't matter. As exhausted as Kett was, he didn't think he'd be getting a lot of sleep tonight—not with the devil haunting his dreams.

Not the devil, he had to keep reminding himself. *Not the devil.*

But if it wasn't the devil or the demon dog, then what the hell was it?

CHAPTER TWENTY-ONE

WHAT THE HELL WAS IT?

It prowled back and forth in its cage, the space too small to stand up in—not that it was allowed to stand up without feeling the stick—and too small to turn around. But it could rock from side to side, it could take half a step to the left, half a step to the right, its hands—no, they were paws, it had no hands—filthy with the muck that covered the floor. It could make noise, but only some. It had used words once, it was sure of it, but now every time it spoke its master appeared, and it felt the stick—whack, whack, whack—sometimes on its rump, on its legs, mostly on its nose. It hurt so bad, so bad. But the other noises were okay. The whines. The barks.

It whined now, pressing its mouth to the bars of its cage. There was no light out there, but it could hear other noises, other barks and other whines and the movement of heavy bodies in cages just like this one. It called to them, but only quietly, because if the master heard it then it would get the stick.

What was it? What was it? It couldn't remember. It was

*only ever called two things. Good dog, if it behaved itself.
And if it didn't?*

Bad dog! Bad dog! Bad dog!

Whack.

*It flinched at the memory of sound, of pain. Those were
the only memories it had, there was nothing else inside its
head but the master and the stick. It knew there should be
more there, because it had a memory of memories, even
though it couldn't recall what any of those memories were.
Something had happened to it, something had opened its
skull like the lid of a box and scooped out everything inside,
then stitched it all shut again. And now it was just* it.

Just bad dog. Bad dog.

*Hungry dog. It was that too. Its stomach felt as hollow
and as empty as its head. It thought that if something was to
pick it up now, it would weigh nothing at all, just a husk of
dry leaves and powdered bones. How long since it had eaten?
A pointless question, because how long had it been since it
had seen the sun, seen the moon, seen the sky, felt the rain?
All that was left of the world was this cage, and the cold, dark
space beyond. All that was left of it was its hunger. Perhaps
that was all there had ever been.*

Perhaps this was all it *had ever been.*

*A bark, then another—not loud, but excited. The other
dogs had better hearing. They always heard the master
coming long before it did. Its stomach growled, its mouth
filling with saliva. It wanted to wipe it away but it knew it
did not have hands, only paws, and paws were not for
wiping. Only masters had hands. It barked, its throat
aching, its mouth dry. It pushed its head against the bars
until it hurt, listening into the dark, waiting half in fear,
because the master was unpredictable and cruel, but half in
excitement, too, because the master brought food and the*

master could sometimes be kind and that kindness was wond—

Snap. The sound of the door, then a thunder of barks. Its calls were there too, deep and desperate. It thumped its head against the bars, again, again, until the lights came on, blinding it, forcing it to retreat inside its cage.

A rustling sound, then an explosion of something incredible, something delicious, inside its head. The smell drove it wild and it threw itself at the door. It could hear the cages being unlocked. It knew that if it didn't get out soon then the other dogs would finish the food. It barked wildly, trying to be the loudest, trying to get the master to hear it.

A shadow outside the bars. It dropped its head, because it knew that meeting the master's eyes meant the stick, meant another day without food. It splayed its paws, it pressed its face to the filth and stuck its tongue out.

Please, it thought

"Whine," it said.

And all the while it could hear the other dogs feeding, it knew there would not be much left.

Please. Please. Please.

It pressed itself lower, it pushed out another wretched, mewling whine.

"Good dog," the master said. The lock snapped back and it moved before the door was fully open, scampering on all fours to where the other dogs fought and jostled. Two of them —the big, black ones—were fighting over a dripping slab of meat. It wanted it so bad, but it was scared of the bigger dogs and their bigger teeth. There were scraps, though, three more dogs wolfing them down, their dark eyes wide and wary.

It moved to the pile of food and licked a ribbon of meat into its mouth. It was too tough to chew so it worked it down in great choking gulps. Another lay ahead but a dog beat it to it. There, another piece, and this time it reached for it with its hands.

It understood its mistake too late.

"Bad dog!"

The crack of the stick across its backside. It rolled into a ball, the other dogs still feeding, sating themselves. The stick dropped again, landing on its knuckles, and the pain was a too-bright light it could feel in every part of it. It struggled back to all fours, it splayed its front legs and pushed its face to the ground. The master was a giant, the master loomed above it. The master raised its stick, but it did not strike.

Instead, there was a morsel of meat in the master's fingers, held to its nose. It sniffed, suspicious, but when the meat did not move it took it gently with its teeth, chewing, swallowing. There was a hand behind its ear, scratching at the scabs there. The touch was beautiful, wonderful.

"More?" the master asked. It did not speak, it did not nod. It pretended not to understand, and took the meat when it was offered. "Are you my good dog?"

It could not know the words, it only licked its master's fingers.

"Good dog," said the master. "Now back in your cage."

It could not bear the thought, it wanted to cry, but dogs did not cry any more than they spoke. Slowly, mournfully, it crawled back into the stinking darkness of its cage. It whined, it nuzzled the master's hands, but it did no good. The door closed, the lock snapped shut. The master walked across the room and opened the big door—enough for it to see the moonlight outside, to feel a sudden, silky touch of air. The dogs bounded to freedom, as they always did, one of the big ones dragging its meal along with it.

It pawed the door. Why could it never join them? Why

could it never go outside? It would be a good dog, it promised. It would not run away.

"Not yet," said the master, who stood by the door. "I can't trust you. What are you?"

A good dog, *it pleaded wordlessly, worthlessly.* A good dog. Always.

It felt sleepy, like it always did after the master fed it. Its mind was too cluttered, an empty nest of dog hair and old bones inside its skull.

A good dog, I promise, *it thought. But it was too late. The master turned off the light, the big door closed, and once again there was only silence, and darkness.*

CHAPTER TWENTY-TWO

Sunday

KETT WOKE TO THE SOUND OF SOMEBODY HAMMERING.

He tried to sit, feeling like his hands were tied. Something was blaring at him, laughing, and something else was cutting into the skin of his arm. Panic forced him up, and he noticed just in time that the thing restraining his arm wasn't rope at all, but a baby.

"Huh?" he said, blinking away the sleep to see that he was sitting on the sofa. *Cbeebies* played on the TV, Mr Tumble chuckling. Kett glanced to his right to see Alice there, playing *Minecraft* on the iPad, her face about three inches from the screen.

"Huh?" he said to her.

"Huh?" she replied, not looking up.

Somebody hammered again, and Kett understood it was the door. Moira was grumbling, stretching herself out, and he wriggled his arm out from under her. He was struggling to remember what had happened the night before, but the bandages on his arm helped. Moira had shown absolutely no interest in going to bed so after an hour or so he'd brought her in here and forced her to lie with him, the TV blaring. He had no idea who'd dropped off first, her or him.

The door again, then the flap of the letterbox.

"Mr Kett?" called Clarissa's excitable voice. "Are you in? Dad sent me over."

He hobbled to the hallway, everything aching. His arm was the worst, but the fight with the dog, and with Jeffrey Morton, not to mention the chase through the woods, seemed to have torn every single muscle he owned. It took him a couple of attempts to even turn the handle, and Clarissa's beaming smile was a little too much to take in.

"Morning!" she said. "Did I wake you?"

"No," said Kett, standing to one side so she could walk in. She had a huge box of Duplo in her arms. "I think you resuscitated me. What time is it?"

"Just after six," she said as Kett closed the door. "Sorry, dad's orders."

There was a clattering noise from the living room and Alice came tearing through the door. She thumped into Clarissa's side, almost sending the box flying.

"Yay, you came back!" she yelled in a pitch that should, according to the laws of physics, have shattered every single window in the house.

"Who's that?" came a little voice from upstairs. Evie appeared, scrubbing her eyes with both hands.

"Careful," said Kett as she slouched down them.

Moira was crying now, and he walked back into the living room to see her sitting on the floor. She looked as confused as he had when he'd woken. He picked her up and carried her into the kitchen.

"Sorry, girls, I've got to head into work again. But Clarissa is here, okay?"

"Why are you wearing a sock on your arm, Dad?" Evie said as she stumbled into the room.

"It's a new fashion thing," he said, holding up his bandaged arm. "You like it? You could wear one too."

"You look like an idiot," said Alice, and he threw her a reprimanding look.

"Is this from the dog case?" Clarissa asked. "Dad won't tell me much about it, but I saw it on the news."

"A dog?" said Evie, climbing onto a chair. "Can we get one? Are we getting one?"

"Nope, and nope," said Kett. He picked up the kettle, but Clarissa cleared her throat.

"Dad asked me to pass on a message," she said.

"Yeah?" Kett replied.

"Yeah, hang on, I wrote it down." She reached into her homemade bag and pulled out a notepad. "Kett, you miserable, uh... let's just say *person*. Kett, you miserable person, get your, uh, *flipping bottom* into work right now and give me a good reason why I shouldn't fire you, or I swear to, um, *Betsy*, that I'll tear you a new... Well, I'm just going to say *bumhole*. Does that make sense?"

"Bumhole!" shrieked Evie, delighted.

"It makes perfect sense," Kett sighed, putting the kettle back. "I'm on my way. Just let me get my *flipping bottom* into the shower first."

"THIS IS A TOSSING DISASTER!"

Superintendent Colin Clare stood at the front of the Incident Room, too apoplectic to even pace from side to side. He was visibly shaking with rage, spots of spit collecting on his lips and every vein on his face visible. If he wasn't careful, Kett thought, he was actually going to have a medical episode of one kind or another right there in mission control.

"You," he said, pointing to Kett. "What were you playing at?"

All eyes in the room swivelled to look at Kett. He cleared his throat.

"I'm almost certain you asked us to investigate the Morton property," he said after a moment. "You made that very clear."

"I didn't ask you to knock the brains out of one brother and kill the other, did I?" Clare shot back. "Let me think." He made an exaggerated show of being in deep thought. "Nope, I definitely didn't say, 'Hey, Kett, can you take out both of our main suspects with extreme prejudice and a baseball bat.'"

"It was a scaffolding pole, sir," said Kett.

"Great!" Clare said in a voice about two octaves higher than usual. "I'll pass that on to Suffolk police, who are furious at us for ending what turns out to have been a two-year operation into dogfighting, drug distribution, and a couple of murders. They'll be delighted!"

Clare was doing a pretty good impression of a crazy Nicholas Cage, and three of the detectives in the front row carefully wheeled their chairs back a little.

"At least we know they're not our main suspects anymore," said Porter. "Every cloud, and all that."

"Yes, Pete, thank you very much for reminding me." Clare clapped his hands together like he was chasing off a herd of pigeons. "Not only did you cause Thomas Morton's clogs to be well and truly popped, you also left us with absolutely nothing to go on. You could have at least caught the bastard."

"That was my fault, sir," said Savage, who was standing at the back of the room once again decked in full uniform. She hadn't slept a wink, she'd told Kett, but somehow she still managed to look as fresh as a daisy. Apart from her eyes, that was. She was starting to show the same steely coldness there that every copper did after a few years on the force. "Kett was in pursuit but I called him back, because I couldn't save Thomas's life on my own."

At this, Clare seemed to soften. He took a few great, huffing breaths, staring at the floor for a moment before looking back up.

"A lot of tossing good he did," he muttered. "Get up here, we need to know what you saw. Both of you."

Kett pushed himself out of his chair, letting Savage go before him. Clare stood to one side, offering them the floor.

"You're going to think I'm crazy," Kett said, meeting the eyes of every copper in the room.

"Too late for that," muttered DS Spalding.

"I thought it was a dog," Kett said. "It moved like one. We'd just left the Morton compound. I'd been bitten, I was running on adrenaline. It was dark. Savage was in pursuit of Thomas Morton. She's a hell of a lot faster than me. I first saw the suspect ahead, maybe thirty yards. He was on all fours, just like a dog."

"Black Shuck's real!" Dunst called out, but nobody laughed.

"He moved that way for a little while, then he just stood up and started running," Kett went on. "He was big, fast."

"You saw his face?" Clare asked. Kett shook his head.

"It was too dark. But his eyes, they glowed. They didn't

seem human. You know how cat's eyes are, and dogs, foxes too. They've got a layer of, what do you call it?"

"Tapetum," said Clare.

"That's it. It reflects, helps them see in the dark. It was like that. That's all I could make out."

"Height, build?" asked Clare.

"Like I said, he was big, taller than me. Thomas was a weedy little shit, but he was still a seventeen-year-old boy, he would have put up a fight. The suspect literally cut him open in seconds."

"That took some strength," came a voice from the back of the room. Emily Franklin, the pathologist, was pushing through the door, a bunch of files in her hand. "I've just finished, took me all night, thank you very much. Dad came in to boss me around. Retired my arse."

"Verdict?" Clare barked.

"Nice to see you, Emily," she replied with a wicked smile. "Thanks for coming in, thanks for missing all that sleep."

"It's called your job," Clare said. "Spit it out."

Franklin pulled a face as she walked to the front, barging Kett out of the way. She was wearing the same trousers as the day before, and an *Adventure Time* hoodie on top. She dumped her papers on Dunst's desk, then dug a squashed, half-eaten croissant out of her trouser pocket.

"Almost exactly the same MO as Sally O'Neil," she spat as she ate. "Morton's throat was opened up in one motion with what I can only assume is a series of parallel blades, or razors, right to left with a slight top-down diagonal accent." She imitated the strike, croissant crumbs flying everywhere. "This probably happened when they were both standing. My guess, the attacker called out or made a noise, the victim turned, and whack."

"Whack," grumbled Clare. "That a technical term?"

"Splat, then," said Franklin. "Victim hits the floor, he's going to die no matter what now. His trachea's split, his arteries are pumping blood everywhere, he's breathing it in. Digging at his own throat only makes it worse. There's a nasty scratch on his wrist, I think the attacker held him down."

She grabbed Dunst's arm, pinning it to the desk.

"Like this. Hard. Then he started to eat him."

She ripped off a mouthful of croissant, speaking with her mouth full.

"Not much, maybe three or four bites to the throat area. I can see a lot of teeth marks, all human. One ripped off a ribbon of skin all the way down to his sternum."

Across the room, Porter made a choking noise.

"No impressions from dog teeth?" Kett asked.

"None," she said. "They're still searching the woods, but Suffolk have their own Forensic team. From what I can glean, there's no evidence of a dog being there at all, apart from the hair on Morton's clothes, which came from the animals he kept at home."

"Is there enough to run a search of dental records?" Kett asked. Franklin nodded, swallowing.

"More than enough, I think. Whoever did this, he was missing a couple of teeth. Front top left incisor, and the upper right canine. Should be able to narrow it down."

She shrugged.

"That's it. I'll let you know if there's a DNA match as soon as the system chucks it out."

"We're looking into any connections that Sally O'Neil might have had with the Mortons," Porter volunteered. "It wasn't exactly a huge community. Rural. They would have crossed paths. There's no sign that Sally did drugs, but Roger smoked a fair bit of weed in his uni days."

"Who didn't?" said Spalding. Clare shot her a look that made it very clear *he* didn't.

"You think this might have been a targeted attack, rather than a random one?" the boss asked. "Morton and O'Neil being the two targets?"

Porter shrugged, so Clare turned to Kett instead.

"I don't think so," Kett said. "It doesn't feel that way. I'm guessing wrong place, wrong time, in both cases. Morton wouldn't have died if we hadn't chased him out of his home."

"Like the fox and the hounds," Clare said. "Fucking hell."

He sighed, stomping his foot.

"This arsehole is really starting to get to me," he said. "Does anyone here have anything else?"

You could hear a pin drop.

"What the fuck am I even paying you for?" he roared.

Kett popped his lips. There was a fleeting thought right at the back of his head, one that he couldn't quite put a finger on. It floated frustratingly close and he almost had it, then Clare bellowed his name and it was gone.

"Something you want to share with the rest of the class?" he said.

"I'm not sure," Kett answered. "It might be nothing. I thought I heard the suspect speak. I thought I heard him say 'bad dog.'"

"That's what he carved onto the back of Sally O'Neil's neck," said Spalding, leaning across her desk with her pen in her mouth. "Why would he say that?"

"I don't know," Kett said. "But he was looking right at me. Whoever this is, I think it's somebody who has been through something bad. Something *really* bad. Something's broken him. I don't know, maybe some*one* has broken him."

"He thinks he's punishing people?" Clare asked. "He thinks people are dogs?"

"No, I think it's more that he sees *himself* as a dog," Kett said, shaking his head. "It feels almost like he's punishing himself for his own actions."

There was that fleeting thought again, like a bird in the night.

"Sorry," Kett said after a moment. "I don't have anything else."

Clare grunted, scratching his face.

"Right. That's fucking brilliant. Spalding, Dunst, I want you to keep interviewing. Somebody out there must know something. Porter, liaise with Franklin and see if we can get something back from those dental records. Everyone else, if I don't hear some good news by lunchtime then I'll toss you all off. Understood?"

It was impossible to miss the quiet ripple of laughter that crossed the room.

"Toss you all off the top of the fucking building!" Clare finished, apoplectic.

"What about me?" Kett asked.

"You've done enough damage, Kett. For now, you and your little buddy there can head back out to the Howarth House and supervise the exhumation. Make sure the remains get back here okay. It should be impossible for you to fuck that up. The rest of you, I want him caught. I *need* him caught. We cannot let this monster take another life. And one last thing."

He stared at his feet, shaking his head before lifting it. He was no longer angry. In fact, he looked almost scared.

"Be careful out there."

CHAPTER TWENTY-THREE

IT HAD ALL THE HALLMARKS OF A FUNERAL, BUT IT WAS infinitely worse.

The Howarth property swarmed with police, far more than the situation warranted. They were all congregated around the crumbling shack beneath which Eden Howarth's body lay, their hats in their hands and their heads bowed low beneath the cold, grey sky. Two constables in surgical face masks were currently pulling the old building to pieces. It hadn't taken much effort, the sloping wooden roof coming away like it was a matchstick model, and the walls so weak that they practically dropped by themselves. A mini-digger lay in wait behind them, the driver smoking a cigarette in his cab. Kett doubted they'd need it. The ground inside the shack had been moist and loose, like a well-tended garden, and Pollyanna Craft had told him that she hadn't buried her husband deep.

Kett glanced back at her. The widow stood alone in the shade of the barn, looking almost as if she might fold into herself, as if she might just crumple into those swathes of clothes and disappear. Her eyes were puffy with tears, her bottom lip trembling. She wrung her hands together over and over and over, and her restlessness was contagious—Kett could feel the anxiety in the air, like they were all holding their breath.

"You think she's okay?" Savage asked quietly, leaning in.

"No, I don't," he replied. He'd offered to stand with Polly, of course, but she'd refused. As physically weak as she was, she was relentlessly stubborn. Kett almost admired it. "She's about to see her husband pulled out of the ground after five years. I can't even imagine how that feels."

Although he could, of course. He'd pictured it a million times—standing in the woods, or on the edge of some distant fields, or a building site, watching them pull Billie out of the ground. He'd imagined every possible version of that story.

He chased the image away, watching as the men wrestled the last wall to its knees in an explosion of dust. Past it was the grave, still drowning in flowers. There had to have been thousands of them, the ones on the top fresh but the ones beneath as rotten as the corpse they covered. He could smell them from here, they clawed into his sinuses.

The masked constables turned to him, and he nodded to them. Each of them took a trowel and began to carefully dig. Kett heard a gasp from Polly, turned to see her take a few halting steps, her hands held out. She caught his eye, her expression warped by worry and grief. But when he started towards her she sharply shook her head, rooting herself to the spot.

"Here we go," said Savage. "You done one of these before?"

"A couple," he replied. "Back in London. One was an insurance thing, the body wasn't even in the grave. The guy was alive and in hiding."

"No way," she said. "Think we'll have the same thing here?"

The answer to her question was almost immediate. One of the constables dropped his trowel and leant down, brushing away some dirt with his gloved hand. He looked at Kett and nodded.

Kett swore beneath his breath as he walked to the grave. The stench of the flowers was so strong that he had to hold his tie over his nose, and even then his eyes watered. Not so much that he couldn't see the black bag there, though, and the shard of bone that protruded from inside.

"Eden Howarth," he said. "Okay, get him up—carefully —and take him over to the morgue."

He was aware of the sobs that came from behind him, a lowing cry of grief. He leant in to the officers, almost whispering.

"And don't fucking drop him."

He watched for a moment as the officers set about exhuming the body, using brushes to clear away the dirt. Another copper in uniform was snapping pictures on a DSLR. Polly had wrapped Eden well, it seemed, but five years beneath the ground had reduced the man to a bag of bones and mulch.

"I'm sorry," said Kett as he approached Polly. He was well aware that he didn't need to apologise—she'd broken the law, after all, by not declaring his death—but she looked so fragile, so vulnerable. She wrung her hands together over and over, pausing only to scrub at her eyes.

"I should never have put him there," she said, almost a wail. "I should never have done it. I'm sorry, I'm so sorry."

Kett understood the woman well enough now to know that she would spurn any attempt at comfort, so he stood by her side and watched as the coppers uncovered her husband's body. Two more police appeared with a medical stretcher, and between them they managed to lift the bag onto it. Only once did Kett's heart almost lurch to a stop—when one of the PC's boots slipped on the rotten flowers and the whole bunch of them almost went arse over tit, Eden included. But after a pretty spectacular attempt to stay upright, all was well. There was an ambulance waiting back by the house, and it would deliver the remains to Emily Franklin so she could make the death official.

One by one, everybody began to drift away. It felt more like a funeral than ever, except for the fact that the square of exposed dirt which sat there was now empty. Savage appeared, holding her bowler hat by her side. She rested her free hand on Polly's shoulder and the woman made no attempt to shrug her away.

"I'm sorry for your loss," Savage said. "Would you like us to help you with anything?"

Polly breathed a laugh through her nose, her eyes locked to the ground.

"Not unless you want to take a horse with you?" she said. "I can't see how I'll manage them now."

"We can help with that, can't we sir?" Savage said. "We can talk to some people, see if we can get you some support."

Polly looked up, her face creasing as she attempted a smile. She cupped Savage's hand in both of hers.

"You're a good one," she said.

"I try," Savage replied. "Come on, we'll walk you back to the house."

———

KETT WATCHED the procession drive away—a squad car, followed by the ambulance, then another squad car. Savage was driving this last one. She'd offered to stay with him, but he'd told her to go. Orders were orders, after all. Clare had asked them to make sure the remains got back okay, but he hadn't specified *which* of them was to do it.

There was another reason he couldn't face going back right now. The black dog of his depression was back, and it was bigger than ever. Watching the exhumation had brought home just how stupid he was. Just how *selfish*. How many times had he done it? Put his life on the line? And for what? His efforts last night hadn't solved the case, they hadn't saved any lives. They'd *killed* a man.

And they'd almost killed him.

They'd *almost killed him.*

He could still smell the dirt on his hands, and the grave-stench of flowers sat in his nose. He could see it now, as if he was watching it on television—his body being lowered into a grave, mauled beyond recognition by the Mortons' Pit Bull. He could see his kids standing there screaming the cemetery to dust, having to be held back as they sobbed for their dad, for their mum.

He *hated* himself. It was such a violent, unexpected sense of self-loathing that it took his breath away, it made his scalp contract. Then the black dog crept onto his back, a dark, oppressive weight that felt heavy enough to push him down into the ground, into a grave of his own making.

He remembered to breathe, the sudden rush of air making him dizzier than ever as he turned to leave. Pollyanna Craft watched him go, and she offered a hand in parting.

"You sure you'll be okay?" he called to her.

"I will," she said, her words almost snatched away by the wind. "This had to come to an end sooner or later."

"You've got my number," he said. "Anything you need, just call. Someone will be back out to speak with you in due course, when we've had a chance to examine your husband. If you'd like to bury him again here, there's a way to do that."

"I don't want him back," she said. "I've caged him here long enough. It's time for him to go."

Kett nodded to her, turning away, but she called to him, fixing her dark eyes on his.

"You have an old soul, Robbie. You have a sad soul."

That was it. She shuffled back to her horses. Kett made his way to the Volvo, which was parked at a worrying angle on the main track to the house, its left-hand wheels in a ditch so that the ambulance could get past.

An old soul, he thought as he climbed inside and started the engine. *A sad soul.*

She wasn't wrong.

He couldn't see it changing, either. How could he chase the dog away when it was so attached to him, when it was so fucking loyal to his sadness that it wouldn't give him room to breathe? There was so much good in his life, in Alice, Evie, Moira, but he was finding it harder and harder to see it, even when he was around them. It was as if he was on a boat, being pulled into the night, watching his kids get further and further away from him. Sooner or later, he just wouldn't see them anymore.

He'd be gone.

He needed Billie back. Oh god, he needed her back. He couldn't do this by himself, he wasn't capable of it. It was too much, it was too heavy, it made his thoughts ache because there was no place to escape from them, no way to switch them off. If she was here now, she'd pull him close and hold him and some of that unbearable pressure would vanish. He'd be able to breathe, he'd be able to think. She would just hold him, and in the tightness of her arms, he would find himself again.

But Billie was gone. And even though the slimmest thread of hope still hung like a spiderweb in the storm of his mind, he knew that she was never coming back. It had been too long.

Another rush of panic, and Kett grappled with the wheel, revving the engine to get the heavy Volvo out of the ditch. He executed a three-point turn on the narrow track then roared back towards the main road, pulling his phone from his pocket as he did so. He was so busy looking for Bingo's number that he almost missed the junction, slamming on the brakes just in time to avoid a tractor that was barrelling down the road far too fast. Its horn bellowed at him.

"Fuck," he said, feeling as if his heart had exploded from his chest like an airbag. His pulse drummed inside his shoulder, inside the fresh wounds in his arm.

Just forget it, he ordered himself. But the Bluetooth had connected, the call blasted through the car's speakers. *No news*, is all he'd hear. *No news, no news, no news.*

What he got was almost worse than no news.

No answer.

He killed the call, pulling the car onto the road, spraying a peacock tail of grit behind him. He couldn't remember if there had ever been a time that Bingo hadn't answered his call. Whatever the time of day, whatever he was doing—even on the toilet—he always picked up. It had to happen eventually, of course. His old boss couldn't do it forever. Kett just hadn't expected it to be so soon.

It's over five months now, he told himself. *Not exactly soon.*

The black dog growled, suffocating him.

He indicated right as he approached a crossroads, waiting for the line of traffic to break before pulling out. He didn't have a destination in mind, he just needed to keep moving, and he cranked both front windows open in the hope that the cold air might shake him out of his misery. The bleak countryside unspooled around him, stubbled fields and skeletal trees, everything cold and weary and quiet. Every time he caught a flash of movement in the furrowed earth, or a flock of crows detonated from the tree-tops, he thought of the man he'd chased in the woods, that hulking shape which had sliced open Thomas Morton like he was butter.

How could you catch a killer who didn't seem human?

It felt impossible, and the black dog curled a little tighter around his thoughts.

He only realised where he was when he saw the houses up ahead. Four of them in a row, standing alone against nature. Slowing the Volvo, he crawled past them, trying to make sense of the dark windows. They looked exactly the same as they had yesterday when he had been here with Savage. *Exactly* the same.

Even the little dog in its cage in the garden of the final house.

Kett's fury was like a bomb going off inside him, fuelled by everything he'd tried to keep inside. All those weeks of grief for Billie, of madness, erupted in a chain reaction that almost overpowered him.

He slammed on the brakes, leaving the car in the middle of the road as he strode to the gate and kicked it open. The Staffy saw him coming, pushing its face against the mesh of its crate and growling. Kett ignored it, walking to the house.

"Al?" he roared, hammering on the front door. "Don't say I didn't warn you."

No answer, which didn't exactly surprise him. He walked around the side of the house to the back door, trying the handle and finding it unlocked.

"Al!" he called again, inviting himself into a kitchen that looked like it hadn't been cleaned since the house was built. "Where are you?"

The fat man appeared from the corridor, his mouth agape and his chins wobbling. He hadn't even bothered to put a vest on, and stood there in a pair of grey Y-fronts, his hairy belly hanging over them.

"What the fuck?" he spat. "Get out of my fucking house."

Kett walked towards him, walked *fast*.

"I told you, didn't I? I told you if I saw that dog in its crate again I'd fucking have you."

Al tripped on his own feet as he retreated, falling like a tree and sliding down the hallway wall. His eyes bulged, and he held out his hands like a man being charged by a bear.

"It's just a fucking d-dog," he stuttered. "What do you care?"

Kett loomed over him, his fist bunched so tight that he could feel the blood squeezing itself out of the wounds beneath his bandage. He wanted nothing more than to hit the fat fuck in his face, to keep hitting him until the pain went away. And for a terrible second, he thought he was going to do it. Al must have seen it in his eyes, because he started mewling like a kitten, actually *sobbing*.

Then, just like that, the red beast of rage passed.

Kett stood up, sucking in foul, BO-scented air and straightening his jacket. He turned, listening to Al spitting words through his wet lips.

"I won't do it, I won't do it again, I won't."

"Too fucking right you won't," Kett said.

He walked out of the house, closing the door behind him and forcing himself to breathe slowly, in through the nose then out through the mouth like Billie had once taught him. The dog was going wild, the whole crate shunting from side to side as it panicked. Its barks were like gunshots, loud enough to make Kett's ears ring.

"Hey, girl," he said, squatting beside the crate. The dog snarled at him, barking, but he held his hand out and it stopped. Maybe it recognised him. Maybe, like Savage said, he just had a kind face. "Hey, you back in doggy prison?"

The dog answered with a bark, but it wasn't an aggressive one. Its backside was thumping off the walls in the coffin of its cage, its scarred muzzle pressed to the mesh. That little tongue was poking out again, trying to lick Kett's fingers.

"If I let you out of there, are you going to bite me?" he asked.

The dog answered with another bark.

"Because I'll bite back," he said. "That's a promise."

He put his hand a little closer and the dog licked his finger, its tongue soft and warm. The laugh bubbled up inside him before he even knew it was coming.

"Good girl," he said. "Hang on, now."

He wrestled with the rusted bolt, and the dog broke free of its crate like a horse at the races. It planted its front feet on Kett's chest and began furiously licking his face.

"Oh Christ," Kett said, laughing again. "That's disgusting, dog, that's enough!"

He stood up and the dog started running in crazed circles around him, its paws drumming the ground. Kett hesitated, wondering if he was making the right decision. Then he looked into the cage and saw the layers of shit there, shit that the poor creature had been sleeping in—he smelled the cloying, bestial stench of it—and he knew that he was.

He opened his mouth, ready to call the dog, but something stopped him. There it was again, a thought that hung back in the darkness like a deer in the forest, refusing to come close. Something about a cage, about the smell. Whatever it was, it took fright and bolted. Kett shook his head with frustration, walking to the car.

"Come on," he said. "Let's get the hell out of here."

The dog followed him, its tail beating the air, its face as close to a grin as a dog could get. When Kett opened the passenger door it practically vaulted inside, shuffling its backside on the seat to get comfortable. Kett laughed, then turned back to the house. Fat Al stared at him through a crack in the living room curtains, and he looked furious. It was no wonder. Kett wasn't taking the man's pet, he was sure of that. He was taking his livelihood.

Kett made a gun with his fingers, looking Al in the eye as he pulled the trigger. Then he climbed into the car and started the engine. The dog barked again, its tongue hanging out, great globs of spit hitting the chair. It was hairy, prone to fits of rage, but it had a good heart. Even though it was a girl, there was only one name he could give it.

"I'm going to call you Colin," Kett said. "That okay?"

The dog yapped, twice, which Kett took to mean yes. He reached over and pulled the seatbelt over Colin's bulk, snapping it in. Something had shifted inside him, a little of that awful weight had lifted. Colin had done a good job of chasing the black dog of depression away, but there was only one thing that would kill the bastard completely.

In order to slay his own monster, he needed to catch another.

He needed to find out who killed Sally O'Neil.

CHAPTER TWENTY-FOUR

HE DROVE IN CIRCLES, THE WAY HE OFTEN DID WHEN HE was thinking, but after an hour or so he ended up right back where it had all begun.

It felt like a million years ago that Superintendent Colin Clare had driven him to the woods where Sally O'Neil had been murdered, his first day back on the job after six weeks away. It seemed impossible that it had been only two days.

But two days was the truth, and the evidence was right there in the fact that this was still a crime scene, the woods guarded by a fortress of police tape. Kett parked the Volvo in a muddy lay-by next to an empty squad car—Suffolk Constabulary emblazoned on its side—then turned around to look at the dog. Colin had wriggled out of her seatbelt after sniffing something the kids had left behind in the rear footwell—probably an ancient piece of cheese string just out of reach beneath the front seat—and she'd spent the better part of ten minutes trying to burrow her way to it. The dog looked at him, pleading, and he shrugged.

"It will keep you occupied," he said. "I won't be long. I would take you, but I'd get in trouble."

The dog cocked her head, the scars on her nose catching the light.

"*More* trouble, that is."

Kett scratched her behind her crooked ears, down the ruff of her neck.

"Do not shit in my car, is that clear?"

Colin went back to the cheese string, and Kett left her to it. He cranked the windows down an inch and left the car unlocked, pulling his jacket close to his chest as he made his way to the footpath that led to the fields beyond. The sun was out again, but it was keeping its heat to itself. The air felt positively refrigerated.

It was a long walk, and he needed somebody to bounce his thoughts off. Pulling his phone out of his pocket, he called Savage's number, counting the rings until she picked up.

"Everything okay, sir?" she asked.

"Yeah," he said, clambering over a stile and dropping down onto the shorn field. "You get back okay?"

"Just at the lab," she said. "Franklin's just finishing up on something then she's going to take a look at Eden Howarth. Where are you?"

"In the woods," he said. "This case has thrown me. I needed to ground myself again."

"It's a weird one, for sure," she said. "Any ideas?"

"There's something," he said. "I can feel it, I just can't get to it. It's so close."

"You're doing the right thing, going back to the start," Savage said. He heard her mutter something, the sound of a door opening. "Sometimes it can get too complicated, right? Sometimes the answer's in front of us, we just talk ourselves out of seeing it. What did Franklin say, back at the morgue?

Ockham's Razor, wasn't it? The simplest solution is often the right one."

Kett nodded, even though Savage couldn't see it. He pushed into his thoughts, trying to find the one that was evading him, but he was too tired, and the pain from his injuries was making it hard to think straight.

"Thanks," he said to her. "I'll let you know if I come up with anything."

"I'm here if you need me," Savage said. "But only in spirit. Clare wants me to stay with the remains. He's still pissed at me for last night."

"It's okay," Kett said. "I'll be back soon. I've got to do something with the bloody dog."

"Wait, what?" Savage asked. "What dog?"

And she must have read his mind because she laughed.

"You didn't."

"I did," said Kett, ending the call before she could give him a lecture. He'd reached the woods now, those same ancient trees watching him as he walked. They gossiped to each other in voices made of creaking branches and rustling leaves, pointing at him with their twig fingers. They seemed to close ranks, sealing the darkness between them, keeping whatever secrets that lay there hidden. To the other side, across the field, the land swept down towards the river, bathed in cold light, but Kett forced himself to keep his eyes on the woods. He would not let them see how much they intimidated him.

He'd almost reached the hedgerow that separated this field from the next when something jumped out of the bushes, landing hard right in front of him. Kett just about took off, and so did the woman who stood there. She clamped a hand to her heart, her expression morphing from one of surprise to the snarl of anger he knew so well.

"DS Stuart," Kett said. "A little warning next time?"

"Speak for yourself," she shot back. "What are you doing, lurking back here?"

"The same thing as you, I guess," he said. "Any revelations?"

DS Stuart chewed on her reply, frowning at him. She'd obviously been expecting a different response, because after a moment her frown fell away. She stared past Kett, down the hill to where the river sparkled.

"No," she said. "Look, sir, I'm sorry if I've been a dick."

If? Kett wanted to say. But he managed to keep his mouth shut while Stuart continued.

"The truth is, I knew Sally O'Neil. Not well, but enough. Her family used to come to my church. I'm older than her, but we hung out sometimes. We talked."

"I didn't know," said Kett. "I'm sorry."

"I really thought it was them," said Stuart, finally looking at him. "Those Morton pricks. I really did. That's why I wanted it to be by the book, and that's why I wanted *us* to go in. I wanted to arrest them so I could see the look on their fucking faces."

"I'm sorry about that, too," said Kett, resting his hand on his bandaged forearm. "It was a stupid thing to do."

"It was," she said. "It could have blown the whole thing wide open, could have been the cock-up that got them off the charge. I expected better from you, after seeing you on the news. The whole paper girls thing."

"In all honesty, that wasn't entirely by the book either," said Kett.

A pigeon took off from a nearby tree, its wings clapping as it wobbled clumsily upwards.

"Things are never as clean-cut as you want them to be," he went on. "This fucking job."

Stuart breathed a laugh through her nose.

"I hear you."

She nodded, then walked past him, patting him twice on his good shoulder as she headed back towards the road.

"One of your men was here," she called back. "I sent him away so I could get some alone time, try to figure this shit out. You okay to cover until he's back?"

"Sure," said Kett. "No problem."

He watched her for a moment more, then climbed over the slippery stile. Beyond was another field, its surface as rough as a churning ocean. More police tape marked the place where Roger and Sally had entered the woods, and Kett walked over to it. The last thing in the world he wanted to do right now was step out of the sun into that ageless dark, but he took a shuddering breath before doing exactly that. A gust of wind shook the trees, raining leaves on him. The swaying branches pulled tricks, like the moving walls of a labyrinth. He could have sworn, as he walked, that the giants had swapped places overnight, that they'd uprooted themselves, pulled their tangled limbs from each other, and danced.

The crime scene lay ahead. The forensic tent had been removed, and all that remained was a ring of tape and a circle of leaves and mulch that had been butcher-shop red when he'd last been here, but which was now brown. Death did that. It turned all that colour, all that vibrancy, into dirt. Kett ducked under the tape, then turned to look at the woods.

The woods looked right back.

"Who are you?" he asked, his voice swallowed whole. He could scream his head off here, but nobody would hear him. He could scream just like Sally did.

He tried to picture it, the same man he'd seen last night

bounding out from behind the trees. He'd been fast, power-ful. He'd have knocked Sally off her feet with the first blow —the attack to the face. Then he'd have opened her up. No hesitation, no shred of empathy or emotion.

Like a dog, he thought. It hadn't been an emotional kill, it had been a necessary one.

Because he'd *eaten* her.

Bad Dog, he'd carved on her skin, the words not there to describe his victim, but to describe himself—Kett was sure of it. Why bad? Because he'd killed? Because he'd eaten?

Because he'd *escaped*?

Kett put both of his hands to his mouth, breathing in the smell of the woods. So maybe there *was* empathy there. Maybe there was some kind of remorse, some trace of humanity. Maybe he killed because he needed to, because he was starving. But maybe he hated himself for it, enough to carve those letters into the back of Sally O'Neil's neck.

Why do that, though? And why hide them there, behind her hair? Why not carve them onto her face, her chest?

Again, a thought dashed across the back of Kett's mind, teasing him.

"Fuck!" he yelled when he was too slow to grab it. He slapped himself on the forehead with the heel of his palm. "What are you trying to tell me?"

A terrible sound shattered the silence of the woods, one that almost made Kett scream. He dug a hand into his pocket, pulling out his phone and killing the deafening blast of the Mexican Hat Dance before he could even look to see who was calling.

It was home.

"Yeah?" he said. "Clarissa?"

"It's me, Mr Kett," came the voice of Colin Clare's

daughter, as bright as ever. "We're in a bit of a pickle, I'm afraid. We can't find the charger for the iPad."

"It's not there!" screamed Alice from very close by. "I told you!"

She was gripped by a genuine panic, the way she often was when something went wrong. It was a bad one, Kett could tell. Not quite a Category Five, as Billie had called it, but certainly a Category Three or Four.

"Put her on," said Kett. He heard the phone changing hands. "Alice? It's daddy. Calm breaths, remember. A deep one in." He did it too. "Hold it. Then breathe out."

It worked, his oldest daughter was still upset, but no longer melting down.

"It's in the kitchen," he said. "Behind the toaster. I charged my phone yesterday when we were eating. I should have said, sorry."

"Thanks dad!" Alice said, her mood switching instantly. The phone thunked on something and Kett squinted, trying to work out if he'd been cut off.

"Hello?" said Clarissa after a moment.

"Sorry," said Kett. "She gets like that. She's not good with uncertainty."

"It's fine," Clarissa said. "She's amazing, just a little sensitive and prone to rashness. But who isn't?"

Kett couldn't exactly argue with that. He had a stolen Staffordshire Terrier called Colin in his car to prove it.

"She's fine," Clarissa went on. "They're all gorgeous. You want to say hi to your dad, Evie?"

"No," said Evie from somewhere in the house.

"No!" added Moira.

"Well, they miss you," said Clarissa.

"I'm sure that's not true," said Kett. "Thank you. You're so great with them, and not everyone is. We had a sitter once who said she was going to lock Alice in a cage until she'd beaten her into submission."

A cage.

Just like that, the elusive thought finally prowled out of the dark forest of his skull and found him.

Oh shit.

Kett's entire body broke out in goosebumps, his scalp shrinking.

Oh shit!

"I've got to go," Kett said, cutting Clarissa off. "I'm sorry."

He ended the call, grabbing his hair with his free hand.

The old hound's as worthless as they come, he needs a good beating to do anything.

Where had he heard that?

I need to chain the bastard up.

Pollyanna Craft. She'd said those exact words the first time they'd spoken to her, about her husband. And just now, earlier today:

I've caged him here long enough.

"Oh fuck!" he said, starting to run. He tripped on a stump, almost dropping his phone as he unlocked the screen. Before he could find what he was looking for, though, it started to ring.

"Savage?" he said, ducking beneath a branch, heading for the light. The trees grabbed at him, as if they were trying to keep him from the awful truth.

"This is messed up," Savage said. "Franklin took one look at the bones and said right away that they're not old enough to be Eden Howarth. The body's been dissolved in lye, but it's fresh. Killed with a blow to the head, probably a hammer. We have no idea who it is."

"I know who it is," said Kett. "It's Roger Carver. Polly buried Sally's boyfriend to protect the man who killed her."

"What man?" Savage asked. "Who killed her?"

Kett burst from the trees, the sunlight blinding him as he bolted for the car.

"It was Eden Howarth. He's still alive. And he's the one we're hunting."

CHAPTER TWENTY-FIVE

THE TERROR WAS TOO BIG, TOO MUCH. AT FIRST, IT *couldn't understand what it was seeing, because it seemed as if the sky was on fire. It cowered, tried to back through the door, to retreat into the dark and quiet of its cage. But the master tugged its leash, the skin on its neck blistered and raw. It squealed, but it obeyed. How could it not?*

"Good dog," the master said, scratching its head. It felt nice, but it couldn't enjoy it because of the fear. It didn't understand where it was going. The master was laughing at it. "Afraid of the sun? It can't hurt you, you stupid animal. Come, heel, we have to say our goodbyes."

It knew what it was saying goodbye to. The room where it had been kept for as long as it could remember was now empty. One by one, all the other dogs had grown old and died. One by one, the master had collected them from their cages and taken them outside for the last time.

All the dogs except for it, that was.

The last one had died that morning. It had hated the other dog, because they had fought for food every mealtime. A great big black thing, the other dog had owned big teeth and it had liked to bite. It had some of the other dog's teeth tucked into the folds of its fur, the ones it had found in the dirt. Because it wanted big teeth too.

Yes, it had hated the other dog. But it had felt sad when it had watched the dog fall still, because the creature had been its only companion. They had barked together at the fingers of moonlight that crept through the boarded windows, sometimes even slept together in the big room, when the cages had been left unlocked. Now, though, there was just it and the master.

"I said come," the master shouted, yanking the chain again. The movement cut off the air and it grunted, uttering a shrill whine. It crawled forwards on all fours, out through the doors into the open. It couldn't believe it was here, that it was being allowed out into the roaring noise of the day. How long had it been? It didn't understand time the way it used to, but it knew it had been years. The air here was cool, the touch of the wind gentle. And the sun, so big, so bright, but so warm. It could almost remember a time when it had enjoyed the sun, but then it shook its head to warn the memory away. Memories were bad. Memories got you the stick.

"It's not far," said the master. She walked briskly, her skirts gathered up in her free hand so they wouldn't drag in the mud. It followed, trotting now, its back aching and its palms—no, paws, always paws—already bleeding from the rough ground.

It was still too bright to see anything clearly, but its night-blind eyes could make out a path that wove through crumbling buildings. And there, on the grass, a small rectangle of dirt that held its last friend. The master stopped beside it, one hand on the spade that stood there, the other holding its chains.

"That will be you soon," the master said. "Look."

It *did* look, it stared at the black-furred body which lay there. No life. No energy. Nothing at all but hair and teeth, all mud-stiff and silent. It whined again and tried to turn away, but the master snapped its chains again.

"Look, dog. I brought you out here so you could see what you'll become. That's all that's left, when the last part of you grows dark, when the fire goes out. A hole in the earth. Nobody will remember you, not even me."

The master smiled, and it was cruel. It remembered a time when that smile wasn't cruel, when that smile was a welcome sight, when it had loved that smile. Again it chased the thought away, but it was too late. Pieces were turning inside its head, as if the daylight had awoken something, awoken some*one*.

What had happened? What had happened to it? Was there a life before the cage? Before the stick? Before the master? It growled, trying to think past the darkness, past the knots of matted, stinking hair that seemed to grow on the inside of its skull. All it could feel was the same hunger it always felt, that aching, awful absence right in the middle of it. It turned away from the grave, from the animal that lay there. It turned and saw the room it had just left, the cages inside, and the house that grew around it. What had happened to it?

What had happened to him?

It was right there, a memory. Him and the master walking hand in hand past the stables. In the memory he laughs, and so does she.

"Dog?" the master said. She tugged the chains again. "Time to go back to your cage, I think."

He growled, slinking back on all fours, still looking at the house.

At *his* house.

"Heel, dog," said the master. She began to walk back, pulling him with her. But he resisted.

"No," he said, the word like a pebble in his mouth. "No."

"Bad dog!" the master screamed, and her face crumpled into a mask of outrage. "How dare you! Bad dog!"

She didn't have the stick, but she balled her hand into a fist and struck him in the nose. He growled again, retreating, fighting the leash.

"Bad dog!" the master shouted again. "Enough!"

She hit him again, hard enough to make him feel like he was back inside his cage, inside the dark. The thought of it was too much and he lunged at the master, sinking his teeth into the flesh of her leg. Her skirts were in the way, but she must have felt it because she opened her mouth and screamed. He bit her again, and again, and the last time he pulled something free with his teeth, something warm and wet and impossibly delicious.

The leash grew loose and he scrambled away, dragging it after him. The master howled behind him, a sound of pure fury, but he didn't stop. He couldn't have stopped even if he'd wanted to, because the sheer exhilaration of running was like nothing he had ever felt. It was joy.

"Dog!" the master shrieked. "Dog, come back!"

He ran, clumsy on all fours. It had been too long for him to remember how to stand on his back legs, but maybe he would, in time.

"Dog!" came the cry from behind him. Then, finally, a word that almost floored him. "Eden!"

Eden. Had he been called that once?

"Eden, stop!"

But he knew he was not Eden any more. Not now. Not after all this time. Not Eden, not human. Not dog, either.

Just free. Just hungry.

CHAPTER TWENTY-SIX

It took Kett less than ten minutes to chase the winding roads back to Pollyanna and Eden's house—even without a siren. Twice the Volvo thumped off the high verges as he took a corner too fast, once lurching so hard he thought it was going to tip. The dog howled from the back seat, scratching the leather to pieces.

"You still alive?" Savage said to him for the second time, her voice rattling from the speakers. He could hear a siren behind her, knew that the cavalry was on its way.

"Just," he replied. "Hang on."

He swung right, the car juddering around the bend. Then he turned left, sweeping onto the track that led to the riding school. He put his foot down, the engine roaring as he rounded the cluster of trees and skidded to a halt in front of the house.

"Please wait," Savage said. "We're twenty minutes out. Suffolk are closer."

"I won't go into the house," Kett said. "But something tells me Polly's not going to hang around."

Something in the words she'd spoken as they parted.

This had to come to an end sooner or later.

"I'll call you back, give me a sec."

He ended the call, grabbing his phone as he climbed out of the car.

"Stay, Colin," he told the dog as she pressed her face to the window. "I'll be right back."

The house looked as deserted as it always had, its windows blind. One half of the grand double-door still hung off its hinges, perfectly still. Kett paused for a moment, listening past his pulse for any sign of movement. But there was nothing, not even the clop of hooves or the snort of a panicked horse. The old red Land Rover was still in the garage, though. She was still here.

"Polly?" he yelled as he made his way along the front of the house.

He could be wrong about her, he knew. But something had clicked inside his head, the machinery of his thoughts turning like tumblers in a lock. The more he thought about it, the surer he was that Eden was alive, and that it was Polly who had turned him into a monster.

There isn't much he doesn't stick his muzzle into.

How she'd done it, how she'd reduced a grown man to the snarling, bloodthirsty *bad dog* Kett had seen last night, was anyone's guess. But one thing was certain, she'd had all the time in the world to do it. Nobody had seen Eden for five years, nobody had suspected a thing. And given five years, surely you could turn a man into anything.

"Pollyanna Craft," he bellowed again as he reached the end of the house and turned into the courtyard that led to the stables. "It's DCI Kett. I need to speak with you."

Something answered him, a gentle whinny from the stables. He jogged across the weed-strewn cobbles, pushing through a door into a fug of horse-smell. Ahead were seven stalls, three of which had horses in them. They watched him with their dark eyes, their hooves skittering. Kett peered over each gate in turn, finding nothing, then moved back the way he'd come.

Eden always liked the barn.

He broke back into the sun and ran to the barn, his arm and shoulder both aching from the effort. The door was a bastard to move, but he used his boot to give it some encouragement and it finally opened. Nothing ran at him, nothing burst from the shadows. He searched it quickly, finding old farm equipment, a workbench littered with scraps of metal, but little else.

"Where are you, Polly?" he called as he walked out into the sun. "I know what happened. I know what you did to Eden. You said you wanted it to come to an end, so let it be over."

He scanned the shallow grave where Roger Carver had been buried, then the surrounding buildings—none of which looked like they would survive the elements for much longer. Finally, he turned back to the house.

The house.

I'm too ashamed to let you see it, Polly had said.

Too ashamed of what they might find.

He ran, ignoring the pain as he crossed the courtyard once again and clattered down the stairs to the servant's door. A quick glance through the glass told him nobody was there, and he took a big step back before driving his boot into the old lock. The window cracked, the wood splintering. The next kick split the door wide open, sending it crashing into the wall behind.

"Polly?" he shouted.

He stepped into the darkness of the cellar, instantly assaulted by the smell of raw sewage. Gagging, he covered his nose with his tie and pushed into the shadows, using the torch on his phone to see where he was going. The small space was packed with boxes and crates, all of which were so caked with dust that they couldn't have been opened in years. Past them was a pile of what looked like laundry baskets. The closer he got, the more he understood that this is where the smell was coming from. Each basket was filled with cloth, and those rags reeked of faeces.

Human faeces.

Eyes watering, heart hammering, Kett crossed quietly to the only door he could see. It opened willingly, revealing a staircase that rose into a dusky, unfriendly light. He took the steps two at a time, paying no attention to the squeals of alarm from the old wood. It wasn't like he was trying to be stealthy.

"Polly," he yelled when he reached the top. "You're making this harder than it needs to be."

He was standing in a narrow servant's corridor, and the stench up here wasn't any better. It had a different quality to it, though—wilder, more *bestial*. He'd smelled it before, in the woods where Sally had been murdered, and again when Thomas Morton had been attacked. It made the hairs on the back of his neck rise, made something primal, something instinctive, rush through his veins. Kett crept down the corridor, opening a large door at the end of the hallway. Ahead was a huge room baking in the sunlight that flowed through the dirt-streaked windows at the back of the house. It was utterly empty, and he crossed the bare, creaking boards in a heartbeat.

"There are others on their way, Polly," he called out as he stepped into a dark corridor, this one leading past a sweeping staircase to the front doors. "It will be better if you show yourself to me now, if you come willingly."

Something answered him, a soft squeak from further down the hall. Kett walked slowly, cocking his head to try to make sense of the sound.

Sounds.

There were more of them. Scratches, a muffled cry, and that same relentless *squeak, squeak, squeak.*

An arched door stood closed at the end of the corridor, lit by the finger of sunlight that came through the broken entrance. Kett put his ear to it. The noises were there, but they were muted—as if they were trying to be as quiet as possible. He grabbed the handle and turned, pushing the door into an ocean of darkness and rot.

"Christ," he said, gagging at the rolling waves of stench that seemed to swallow him whole. He fumbled for his phone, the blade of torchlight sweeping across a space that looked more like a torture chamber than a formal dining room. Metal crates stood against every wall, some with bars, others solid steel coffins with hatches on their tops. The floor was crusted with filth, the walls too. On the far side of the room was another door that led outside, the glass boarded up.

"Polly?" he called through his fingers. "Where are you?"

He stepped into the room, into that awful, festering hell.

There, right ahead of him, movement.

He swung the torch up, finding the ceiling, the ornate chandelier, the rope that hung from it, the bulky figure that swung to and fro, to and fro, a noose tight around its neck.

Squeak. Squeak. Squeak.

"Shit," Kett said. He ran, his boots slipping in the muck, tripping on the detritus that littered the floor. "Polly!"

He reached her, grabbing hold of her body to try and lift her, noticing too late that she had no legs, no arms, and that she made no noise at all other than those relentless squeaks.

What the—

He stepped back, shining the torch, finding a weighted bag of sand and rags that hung from the ceiling. It was covered in slashes and what might have been bite marks, repaired countless times with fresh scraps of cloth and leather. It made no—

Slapslapslap.

A noise behind him—the slap of feet on bare wood and a grunting roar of fury. Kett spun around, but he was too slow. Somebody thumped into him like a freight train, knocking him back into the bag. His feet caught one another and he fell, landing on his bad shoulder and screaming a cry of agony into the dark. His phone fell from his hand, sliding away, a beam of light cutting up towards the ceiling.

Kett kicked out at the figure but it was fast, and it was strong. It grabbed his ankle with a grip of iron and twisted it hard.

"Fuck!" he roared.

A flash of agony in his thigh, something that might have been teeth. He kicked out again, this time making contact. The pain slid out of his leg and he sat up, throwing a punch and hitting flesh. His attacker grunted, letting go of his ankle as it staggered back. Kett rolled away, snatching his phone from the floor, aiming the flashlight as he struggled to his feet.

Pollyanna Craft stood there, heaving in breaths like a horse. She no longer looked hunched over and weak. Her back was straight, her hands flexing, her eyes bright and full of malice. She grinned at Kett, and it took him a moment to work out why she looked so happy.

She was holding a hypodermic needle.

He slapped a hand to his leg, but it was too late. It was like something had cut his thoughts loose from the rest of him, his mind suddenly liquid. His legs crumpled, and for a second he didn't even notice that he'd hit the floor, because there was no pain. He tried to push himself up but his arms were suddenly boneless.

Polly, he tried to say, but his lips wouldn't shape the word. It dribbled from his lips.

"O-ee."

"It's a shock at first," Polly said. She squatted beside him, her skirts spilling out around her. She put a cold hand to his forehead, stroking her thumb across his temple. "But it will make you feel better. Ketamine. I use it on the horses. I used it on Eden, too."

Kett swore, trying to make his arms work. His mind was a rush of emotion, a blast of sunshine in the dark, like somebody had turned on a golden tap. But behind that was a nausea he seemed to feel inside his very soul—and a dark tide of swelling terror.

"He was an arrogant beast, just like you. He thought I was weak, pathetic. I swear it's the only reason he married me, because he thought I'd do everything he said. And I did. For fifteen years I was at his beck and call. He used to call me his little bitch, you know. 'Pollyanna, my beautiful, obedient little bitch.' Until one day I decided I didn't want to be his dog anymore."

She smiled, and in the muted light she looked utterly insane.

"I wanted him to be mine."

Kett managed to get his legs beneath him, pushing himself away from her.

"Where do you think you're going?" she said, grabbing his ankle again and hauling him across the floor with surprising strength. She was dragging him towards a cage, he saw, maybe three-foot high and made of solid steel, a wide hatch in its ceiling. "You'll forget about all this soon enough. The drugs will erase all those memories. It took a year with Eden, more or less, before he forgot his own name. But he did. A cocktail of ketamine and other drugs every day, a strict training regime, a cane across the nose every time he spoke, or cried, or used those little fingers. He was eating out of my hand after eighteen months, he was shitting with all the other dogs soon after. After all those years he couldn't even remember being human."

Kett struggled against her, and she turned around and kicked him hard—right between the legs. Even with the drugs in his system, he felt it, a hollow ache that made him double up.

"They're on their way," he tried to say, but the words fell out of him in awful clumps.

Polly wasn't listening. She grabbed him under the arms, hauling him up like he weighed nothing then rolling him into the cage. He landed, turned, managed to lift his arm. She slapped it out of the way.

"At least, that's what I thought," she said, leaning through the hatch. She had his phone, he realised, using it to blind him. "But maybe some nugget of shit held out in that brain of his, some morsel of the insolent arsehole he'd once been. Because he fucking got away from me. After all these years I let my guard down, I let him outside, and he ran."

She slammed the hatch shut, catching Kett's arm. Past the roar of painless agony he heard her speak.

"He killed the girl. He ate her. I can't say I'm surprised, it's what I made him, I suppose. But I was disappointed." She laughed, and it wasn't kind. "The boy, the one who was with the girl in the woods. He came here. Can you believe that? He ran right to my front door and asked for help. Couldn't let him live. Couldn't let him find out the truth."

She shoved the dead weight of Kett's arm into the cage and he dropped like a bag of bricks. He blinked up at her from the dark, feeling like he was sinking into the floor, into a grave.

"I told you I was stronger than I looked, didn't I?" she said. "I warned you. I never had a riding accident. Strong as an ox. Only limping because that arsehole dog Eden bit me in the leg."

"Not... alone..." Kett said, shaping the words as best he could. He wasn't sure if she'd understood him or not, until she nodded.

"I'm not naïve enough to believe more of you aren't coming," she said. "Such a pity. You would have made a good dog. Like Eden. Like the others, too. Sad souls always make good pets, because they know things are better when you don't have to worry about them. When all you have to do is eat and shit."

She leaned in, her eyes so dark they looked like empty pits.

"It doesn't matter," she said. "I'll find someone else to make my dog, I'll do it someplace else. And it's not like you'll see out the day."

She looked back, cocking her head.

"No doubt they'll catch my stupid bitch when they get here," she said. "I know Eden's close, I can smell it. But it's hungry. I haven't fed it in a long time. As soon as I'm gone it will slink out of the shadows and come looking for a meal. It's been busy since it escaped, my dog, my Eden. It's been making things. *Sharp* things."

Kett growled, and she grinned down at him.

"Good boy," she said. "Good dog."

Kett reached for her, his arm too heavy.

"Don't you dare," he shouted, the words too big for his mouth. "Don't you fucking dare."

"Goodbye, Robbie," Polly said, adjusting her skirts. "Goodbye, my sad, old soul."

She smiled her lunatic smile, then the hatch of the cage closed like a coffin lid.

CHAPTER TWENTY-SEVEN

Alone in that boundless dark, Kett understood how easy it had been for Eden Howarth to lose his mind.

His own sanity was already retreating, his thoughts unwinding then blowing out of his skull like the seeds from a dandelion clock. He snatched at them, feeling only the sides of the cage, the filth that encrusted the floor. His body still buzzed, beautifully numb. Pain was nothing but a memory, and with it went everything that the pain had stood for, everything it reminded him of. All those fights, all the hurt, it was as if somebody had simply washed it all away.

He sat back, giddy with exhaustion. Lights exploded in his vision, fireworks that blazed red and green and blue. They weren't real, he knew. But then how could he know what was real? He could hear a car engine, too. The crunch of gravel from outside as somebody drove away. Was that real? Or was he hallucinating it too? He floated on a dark ocean; his mind was an empty vessel. Maybe *he* wasn't real. Maybe he never had to be real again. No more pain, no more fear, no more arguments, no more stress.

Just a dog. He was just a dog.

Even Billie was fading. He tried to find her in the still-ness, in the quiet, but she'd gone. A rush of gratitude passed through him, because if he couldn't remember Billie then he couldn't remember the horror of what had happened to her, he wouldn't have to spend every waking second feeling like he had let her down, that he'd let her be taken.

And he almost let her go again now, he could feel her hanging on to the edge of his mind with the tips of her fingers—one peeling loose, then another, then another, ready to fall.

Then... *anger.*

An inferno of it that burned inside him, that illuminated the gaping abyss of his thoughts. He saw Billie there and he howled to her, furious with himself for even thinking that he would be better off without her, without her memory. He reached out a hand and in his mind's eye he saw her take it.

I won't let you go, he said, the words like cathedral bells. *I won't let you go again.*

And that anger roared, crackled, snapped—not just anger at himself but at the woman who had locked him in here.

The adrenaline ripped through him, chasing away some of the numbness. He punched upwards, a whisper of pain in his knuckles as his fist met the roof of the cage.

"Come on," he said, the words barely words at all. "Come on!"

He threw a punch again, somehow finding the centre of the hatch. Another one, another. But the cage was solid. It was designed to keep the strongest of dogs.

I'm not a dog, he told himself. *I'm not a fucking dog.*

He flexed his hand, aware of the blood that ran from his knuckles. Reaching up, he found the lip of the hatch, running his fingers along it. It had some give to it, although his fingertips were so numb he wasn't sure how much.

Come on.

There had to be a latch somewhere, or a bolt. He pushed his fingers further out, aware of the pain even through the haze of the anaesthetic. There was no way of knowing the damage he was doing to himself, but it didn't matter. Nothing mattered, other than getting the hell out of this cage.

Come on, motherf—

There, something hard right on the lip of the hatch. Kett pushed it with his finger, wincing at the stickiness he felt there—his own blood, he was sure of it. The fucking thing wasn't moving, it was wedged tight.

"Fuck!" he said, pulling his hand back inside. At least the word had some shape now, there was some feeling back in his lips.

Where the hell was his backup? Surely they should be here? He prayed that they'd intercepted Polly as she fled, that they had her in the back of a police car. But what if she'd slipped away? How long before she did this to somebody else?

The fear and frustration boiled inside him. He lay on his back, driving both of his legs up into the hatch. Again. Again. Flakes of metal rained down into his eyes so he screwed them shut. Kicking, kicking, kicking—so much noise that he didn't hear the sound of snuffling until it was right next to him.

He stopped, listening past the thrash of his pulse, past the pain that was starting to creep back inside him.

Footsteps, padded and quiet.

"Savage?" he called out, slurring the word and knowing he wasn't going to be that lucky.

Panting breaths, a whine that might have been human or animal. Something scratched at the cage, fingernails on metal.

"Eden?" Kett said, the fog clearing even more from his mind and from his speech.

A low growl that morphed into a word, spoken over and over and over.

"*Nononono.*"

A snort, the noise that a drowning man might make as his head went under for the final time.

Something brushed against the cage again. It sounded sharp.

"Eden, I need you to listen to me." It wasn't a fully legible sentence, but it was close. He was pretty sure he'd managed to kick the needle out of his leg before the full shot of ketamine had gone into him. "You're not what she made you. Your name is Eden Howarth, you're a man, not a dog."

"*Nonono.*"

"She's gone," Kett said. "Your wife, Pollyanna, she's not here anymore. She's going to prison, Eden, for a long time. You can get your life back. We can fix you."

The bolt squeaked, then snapped back. Kett rose as quickly as he could, ramming his good shoulder into the hatch. It hit something as it opened, and past the flare of pain Kett saw a dark shape staggering back. Eden dropped onto all fours, growling, two eyes as bright as silver pennies glaring at him. He looked angry. He looked *dangerous*.

It's hungry, Polly had said. *I haven't fed it in a long time. As soon as I'm gone it will slink out of the shadows and come looking for a meal.*

Eden made a soft, wet noise, like he was licking his lips. Kett grabbed the outside of the cage and hauled himself over the lip of the hatch. He hit the ground hard, but the drugs in his system cushioned the agony.

Eden growled at him, snarling, snorting. Kett grabbed the cage and pulled himself to his feet, his legs hollow tubes that threatened to buckle at any moment.

"Eden," he said, hoping that if he repeated the man's name enough times he'd find himself. "Eden Howarth. You need to snap out of it."

Kett took a step. It wasn't exactly pretty, but it did the job. He took another, using the cage for support. Eden crouched between him and the door, his growls growing more and more aggressive.

"You're a man," Kett said. "You're human. Polly's gone, she won't be able to hurt you anymore. I promise."

He kept walking, adrenaline pumping the drug from his system. It felt as if the entire room was moving, swaying back and forth, and he had to swallow down an acidic ball of vomit that burned up his throat.

"Don't be scared," he said. "We'll get you out of here. We'll get you to a hospital. We'll get you some food."

Eden skittered away as Kett drew near, the man's eyes never blinking. He scratched at the floor with something sharp, something metallic. Kett tried walking backwards, so he wouldn't have to turn away from him, but he didn't have the coordination for it. He spilled over, only the cages holding him up.

"You're going to be okay," he said, facing the door again. It was half a dozen yards away now, he was almost there. "You're going to be okay."

He grabbed the handle and opened the door, light rushing past him and filling the room. Eden cried out—the most human noise he'd made so far. Kett thought it was a sound of pain, but then it came again and he understood it was a cry of fury.

A cry of *attack*.

Eden was bounding towards him, moving clumsily on all fours but still so fast. Kett grabbed the handle, trying to close the door, but Eden suddenly rose onto his feet and sprinted, his filthy face twisted with something that wasn't rage, wasn't anger.

It was *hunger*, pure and simple.

He was on Kett in a heartbeat, thumping into him and sending them both crunching to the hallway floor. He pinned Kett with one filthy hand, his head drawing back, his mouth wide open. Two of his teeth were missing, the rest more brown than yellow. His face was streaked with dirt and blood, and he wore a filthy beanie hat which bore two green, marbled stones that caught the light like eyes.

His real eyes were wild and bloodshot, devoid of emotion and yet somehow full of need. They were the eyes of a creature that had no urge other than to sate its hunger, to end its crippling starvation.

On his right hand was a glove tipped with bloody razors.

"No!" Kett shouted, but Eden wasn't listening. The man's head snapped forward, more like a cobra than a dog as it whipcracked towards Kett's throat.

He threw up a hand, Eden's teeth locking around the sleeve of his suit and the bandages that were wrapped beneath. For once, Kett was glad of the ketamine, because the pain was just a shadow of what it might have been. Even so, it still took his breath away. The man bit hard, his head thrashing from side to side. His right hand was rising, those razors flashing in the light from the front door.

He brought it down but Kett bucked hard, roaring with defiance. Eden's razors hit the ground, scraping over Kett's ear. Kett bucked again and bunched the fist of his free hand, throwing a punch into the man's ribs. Eden grunted and Kett hit him again, this time a straight shot to the man's chin. He rocked his body, managing to roll his attacker off him.

Eden landed hard, but he was back on his hands and feet in a heartbeat. He threw himself at Kett, spit spraying from his lips. His clothes were a patchwork of skin, the patterns unmistakably those of dogs. Long teeth had been sewn into the fur, and they rattled like castanets as he charged.

There was no time to stand up. Kett managed to get to his knees just as Eden reached him. They tumbled together, rolling, a thunder of pain roaring in Kett's chest as the razors slashed through his skin. Eden's head darted down again, those yellow teeth snapping.

Kett called Eden's name. But the man was an animal. Wherever Polly had taken him inside his head, he was still there.

"Bad dog," Kett roared, firing out each word with force and praying it would work. "Bad dog!"

Eden whined, backing away and covering his face with a hand. Kett struggled to his knees again.

"Bad dog!" he shouted.

Eden growled, his hunger overriding his shame. He coiled, ready to lunge again, but Kett moved first. He threw himself onto Eden and pinned him to the ground. The man writhed and snapped, his teeth *clacking* together as he lunged for Kett's throat. It was too much, the horror of it boiling up inside Kett's veins, exploding from his mouth.

"Enough!"

He brought his head down, a demolition ball that smacked into the bridge of Eden's nose. The sound it made was like a concrete block being cracked in half, and the man's movements immediately slowed. Eden groaned, twitched, then fell still, his breaths bubbling up through his bloody lips.

Kett wasn't sure if he could stand. The drugs might have been wearing off, stripped from his veins by adrenaline, but the headbutt had left him reeling. Eden was down, if not entirely out. Grunting, Kett managed to pull off his jacket. He rolled Eden onto his front, then tied the sleeves of the jacket tight around the man's hands. He couldn't help but notice those razors again, still caked in blood that had once swum through the veins of Sally O'Neil and Thomas Morton.

Kett grabbed the wall and slid up it, listing wildly. Shaking his head, he tried to assemble the shattered fragments of his thoughts into some kind of order.

Polly.

That was all he needed.

He left Eden where he lay and staggered to the broken front doors, pushing his way through them. His car was where he left it, Colin's face steaming up the window as the Staffy eagerly awaited his return.

"Come on, girl," Kett said as he climbed inside. "Let's finish this."

CHAPTER TWENTY-EIGHT

HE ALMOST COULDN'T REMEMBER HOW TO DRIVE.

He started the Volvo's engine, darkness creeping into the edge of his vision, his limbs no longer numb but still terrifyingly disobedient—as if they were somebody else's arms and legs stitched onto his body. He managed to close the door, then immediately opened it and vomited onto the drive.

"Fuck," he groaned as he slammed the door shut again, wiping his sleeve over his lips. Colin paced uneasily on the passenger seat, smelling blood and shit and fear. She whined at him, and he did his best to smile at her. It must have looked more like a grimace, because she retreated, her head low, her backside hitting the door.

He reached into his pocket for his phone, then remembered that Polly had taken it. He floored the accelerator instead, sweeping the Volvo round in a wide arc and almost taking off the wheel arch on the verge. The garage door was open, the old Land Rover no longer there.

He hit forty on the track, barely slowing as he skidded onto the main road. For a second it felt like his mind hadn't made the turn with him, vertigo turning the world upside down. He grabbed the wheel with his right hand—his knuckles swollen and split—and used his left hand to squeeze the dog bites in his arm, the pain blasting through the confusion, sharpening him.

"Where are you?" he said, scanning the open fields ahead.

He rounded a bend, too fast, and almost collided with the back of a BMW—swinging out and around it without hesitating. The driver leaned on his horn but Kett ignored him, hitting sixty on a bumpy straight and praying that nothing was coming the other way. Something had to be listening, because the Volvo roared around the next corner unopposed, the Norwich road right ahead.

He had to slow because there was traffic here. But he didn't stop, poking the nose of the car through the junction and blasting the horn until people let him out. He smacked his hands on the hazards, clipping a Golf as he turned and ripping the smaller car's bumper off. He didn't care. All that mattered was finding Polly before she disappeared. The car rattled as he floored it, the road here wide enough for him to drive right along the centre line. Cars whumped past on either side, blurred faces full of anger and shock. Then he wheeled around another hairpin and saw a tractor ahead, too wide to pass.

"Come on!" he yelled, punching the horn again. "Move!"

It didn't, the driver smirking at him in the rear-view mirror. Kett swore, flooring the pedal again and crossing onto the other side of the road. He had to pull back in almost instantly as a bus rumbled past, but then the road was clear and the old car chugged past the tractor, cutting back in again seconds before a lorry flattened it.

It was only then that Kett noticed the smoke up ahead. It towered to his left, over another harvested field, too thick and too dark to be a bonfire. He followed the road as it curved towards it, the slope rising. The traffic had built up here, a line of cars waiting patiently, and when Kett crested the hill he saw why.

Ahead, at a junction, sat a red Land Rover, its bonnet smoking.

And crumpled around it was a police car.

Kett pulled the Volvo out, overtaking the waiting cars. A few pedestrians were already at the scene, covering their mouths with their hands as they peered inside the police car. He cut the engine and jumped out, staggering down the road.

"What happened?" he called out.

An older man in a peaked cap looked up, frowning at Kett. It wasn't hard to work out why—Kett looked like he'd been in an accident too, his shirt torn in half a dozen places and soaked with blood.

"Police," said Kett, reaching for his warrant card before realising he'd lost his wallet. He reached the mangled cars, seeing the uniformed officers inside. They were both moving, thank god, but they were hurt, and badly. For a moment he thought that the woman in the driver's seat might be Savage, then he noticed the Suffolk Constabulary logo on its crumpled side.

The Land Rover was empty, the driver's door open.

"Where is she?" Kett said.

"She ran," the man replied, pointing to the field that sat alongside the road. "She went that way."

"I need you to get them out of there," Kett said, nodding to the coppers. "Get them away from the car, then move everyone back." He turned to the crowd. "I need you all to help. Does anyone have a phone?"

To their credit, three people held out their phones. He took the nearest one, which was already unlocked, and dialled 999. Then he climbed the bank, stepping onto the hard earth of the field. He heard a bark, looked down to see Colin scampering up beside him, her tongue hanging out and her eyes bright.

"Where are you going?" the old man asked from the road.

Kett didn't answer, putting his free hand to his brow to cut out the glare of the sun. The field was huge, and it ended in another stretch of woodland. He scanned it, squinting, until he saw movement.

A figure drowning in dresses, limping for the trees.

"Got you," he said.

He started after her, the effort blasting the last scraps of nausea from his system. Polly might have been strong, but she wasn't fast, especially not with the injury to her leg. She was going to reach the trees before him, though, and if she did that then there was a good chance he would lose her.

"What's your emergency?" asked a voice on the line.

"My name is DCI Robert Kett," he said between breaths. "We have an RTC on the Norwich to Bungay road, just past the White Lion pub. Two officers in need of urgent medical assistance. I am in pursuit of a suspect, in a field to the... east of the accident. Would appreciate air support."

He didn't wait for the message to be confirmed. He pocketed the phone and put his head down, halfway across the field now. Polly had vanished, sucked into the trees.

"Fuck," he said.

He looked down at the dog that ran by his feet.

"Get her," he said.

Colin looked up at him, oblivious.

"Go on, get her! *Fetch!*"

Somehow, she understood. She accelerated, her feet kicking up great arcs of dirt as she blasted towards the woods. Kett raced after her, everything aching, his heart clattering against his ribs so urgently that he half-expected it to stop dead.

Colin made it to the woods in seconds, and almost instantly there was a piercing scream. Kett puffed and wheezed his way to the tree line, leaning on a trunk and peering into the muted light. He couldn't see much past the flashing beat of his pulse, but he could hear growling from right ahead, and Polly screamed again.

"Get off me!" she yelled. "You stupid fucking dog!"

Kett found the last of his strength, tripping his way over the branch-strewn ground until he saw Polly. She lay on her back in a ditch, breathless, Colin standing victoriously on her chest. The dog's lips were drawn back, her teeth bared.

"Colin," said Kett, and the dog looked around. All he wanted to do was order her to bite, but he kept the words locked behind his lips. He ducked down beside them and patted Colin on the head. "Good girl," he said. "You got her."

Polly looked catatonic, as if she had injected *herself* with ketamine. She lay in the ditch, in a bed of filthy water, her eyes blinking at the branches that swayed and cheered above her. She wasn't going anywhere, Kett knew, and it was just as well because he didn't think he could stay upright for much longer. He manoeuvred himself onto his backside beside Polly, close enough to be able to beat her down if she tried to get up, and sucked in great lungfuls of air.

"Pollyanna Craft, you are under arrest for the false

imprisonment and torture of Eden Howarth, and for the murder of Roger Carver."

There was no doubt whatsoever that she was responsible for the deaths of Sally O'Neil and Thomas Morton too, although proving that to a jury of her peers would be difficult.

"You do not have to say anything, but it may harm your defence if you do not mention when questioned something which you later rely on in court. Anything you do say may be given in evidence."

He paused to scratch the dog's head. Colin wiggled her behind, still perched on Polly's chest. Polly was muttering something, and Kett had to lean in to hear it.

"Just animals," she said, still staring at the scraps of sky overhead. "What does it matter? Animals. At the end of the day, isn't that all we are?"

"No," said Kett. "It's not."

He heard shouts, looking over his shoulder to see shadowy shapes darting through the trees.

"Kett?" came a voice that could only belong to DI Porter.

"Robbie?" added Savage.

"What the tossing hell is going on?" said a third voice. "Where are you?"

Colin answered for him, unleashing one of her ear-shattering barks. Kett patted the dog's head again, then Savage skidded down beside him.

"What happened to you?" she asked. "You look like shit. Like *actual* shit. Like you've been rolling in it. What *is* it with you and faeces?"

Kett laughed, the noise of it surprising him. It might have been the ketamine, but he couldn't seem to stop himself. Colin jumped off Polly and ran to Savage, licking her fingers.

"Is that dog dangerous?" Clare asked as he ran over. "We need a leash. Somebody get me a—"

"She's fine," said Kett. "She's the one who took down Pollyanna."

"Get that woman out of there," Clare said, putting his hands on his hips and staring at the sky. "Give me strength."

Two uniformed constables appeared, working together to haul Polly's bulk out of the ditch. There was no fight left in her. There was barely *anything* left in her. She looked like the living dead as she was escorted out of the woods, her eyes as lifeless as the marbles that Eden Howarth had worn on his hat.

Porter offered Kett his hand.

"You okay to get up?" he asked, genuinely concerned. "I can get a stretcher back here. Paramedics are on their way."

"I'm fine," said Kett. He offered his own hand, and Porter pulled a face.

"Christ, Robbie, what have you been *touching*?"

Porter grimaced as he pulled Kett to his feet, and Kett kept hold of his hand until the dizziness had passed. Savage took his other arm. The pain was really starting to burn through the numbness, and he grit his teeth against it.

"What happened?" Savage asked.

"I'm not sure you'd believe me if I told you," he said. Clare snorted.

"You bloody well will tell us, Kett," he said, pointing a finger at him. He glared for a moment more, then seemed to soften. He breathed out a sigh. "But for now, just tell me this. Is it over?"

"Eden Howarth is back at the house," Kett said. "He's

out cold, and tied up, but you need to get to him as fast as possible. He's still extremely dangerous."

"And he killed our victims?" Clare asked. "Both of them?"

Kett nodded.

"Eden killed Sally and Thomas," he said, looking to where Polly could be seen walking across the field, a circle of police around her. "But she's to blame. She turned him into a... a monster. And she killed Roger Carver."

They stood there in silence for a moment, the woods quiet except for the beat of a distant helicopter. Kett closed his eyes, taking a moment. He'd done it again, he knew. He'd thrown himself into a situation that could have left him dead—or worse. Richard Johnson, the psychologist, had been an arsehole, but he'd been right about one thing.

There is a self-destructive streak inside him that could go off at any time and take everyone else out with it.

He thought of his kids, of Alice and Evie and Moira, and felt a craving for them that was physical, that was almost overwhelming.

"I need to get home," he said, his body starting to shake, his teeth chattering.

"I'll drive you," Porter said. "We'll get you back. Via the hospital, I think."

Kett nodded his thanks, too tired to argue. He felt, for a moment, that he might just fall asleep right there in the woods, standing up. He peeled open his eyes again, grateful that both Porter and Savage were still holding him.

The dog whined, squatting next to Clare's feet. Its eyes bulged.

"Please tell me it's not doing what I think it's doing," said the boss. A sudden smell answered him, and they all clamped their hands to their faces.

"Jesus," said Porter. "What the hell has it been eating?"

"Cheese strings," said Kett. "And whatever else she found in the back of the car. Isn't that right, Colin?"

The dog barked, grinning.

"Enough of this," roared Clare, sweeping his arms in an effort to move them all out of the trees. "You lot are going to be the end of me. The paperwork for this is going to be..."

He paused, looking at Kett.

"Wait, did you call the dog *Colin?*"

And Kett was laughing again—Porter and Savage too—as they made their way back into the sun.

CHAPTER TWENTY-NINE

Wednesday

KETT STOOD IN THE LITTLE GARDEN OF THEIR HOUSE, his eyes closed, the sun warm against his face, and for the first time in what felt like forever he took a breath.

Then something thumped between his legs, almost knocking him over. He opened his eyes to see Moira running right for him as she chased the dog, Evie behind her, both of them screaming with delight. They dived between his legs, and it took some fast footwork to stop himself from falling over and landing on the pair of them. Even three days after the fight with Eden Howarth his entire body sang with pain, but for once it felt like a good pain. Pain meant you were still alive, after all.

Colin the dog was doing another lap of the garden, her feet like drums, her tongue almost touching the floor. She lapped the girls in seconds, catching up to Evie and loosing a friendly bark. Evie giggled hysterically as she rubbed the dog's nose, Moira grabbing Colin's mangled ear.

"Easy, girls," Kett said. "She's still getting used to you."

She was, but there was no doubt in Kett's mind that the dog already loved them. He'd introduced Colin to his daughters bit by bit over the last few days, and the Staffy hadn't shown anything but kindness and friendship.

"I'm her favourite," said Evie. "Colin's my best friend."

"Est end," Moira echoed, trying to push Evie away so she could get closer to the dog. "Mine!"

"Remember," he said. "It's only for a little while, just until we find her a home."

"This is her home," said Evie. "She can live in our room."

Kett opened his mouth to reply, but he was gripped by another bout of vertigo. He walked to their little wooden picnic table and perched on it, closing his eyes until the universe stopped dancing. The powerful anaesthetic that Pollyanna Craft had injected him with had pretty much been flushed from his system, but he could still feel the drug inside him, infecting his thoughts and his movements. He wondered if he'd ever stop feeling dizzy.

"Look, dad!" Evie squealed. "She licked me! She licked me!"

The dog had done nothing *but* lick the girls. The paramedic who'd seen to him after he caught Polly in the woods had also checked out the dog—completely against protocol. It had been her educated guess that Colin hadn't been a fighting dog—although it was clear from her injuries that she *had* fought, a lot—but rather a breeding dog for champion pit fighters. Kett wasn't entirely sure what was worse. Colin had been through hell, over and over and over.

She deserved a good home, a family.

But Kett had enough on his plate.

"Dad, can I come out now?"

He looked over his shoulder to see Alice hovering in the kitchen, peering through the back door. She'd been scared of dogs for as long as Kett could remember, especially fast dogs, *especially* loud dogs. Colin was all of those things, and it just wasn't fair on her to bring the panting, barking, farting whirlwind into the house.

Not yet, anyway.

"Five more minutes," he said. "Then I'll put her on the lead, okay?"

Alice didn't reply, she just retreated into the dark with her iPad.

Kett closed his eyes for a moment more, taking long, deep breaths. For the first day or so after he'd got home, all he could smell was shit—even after shower after shower after shower. He could taste it, too, as if the filth of Eden's lair had got inside him. Even though he'd been there himself, caged like a dog, he found it almost impossible to imagine what the man had gone through, the horror of being locked up for days, then weeks, then months, and finally years. *Five* years—all while Pollyanna drugged his food and beat him and screamed at him over and over that he was no longer human.

That he was a *bad dog*.

Eden had been collected by an ambulance crew and taken to hospital, of course. His body had been riddled with injuries, including the broken nose that Kett had given him. Those would heal, in time, but Kett wasn't sure if his mind would. How could anybody come back from that?

"Knock knock," came a voice. Kett opened his eyes to see DI Porter poking his head through the gate. "Is it safe?"

Colin answered with a volley of barks as she bolted

across the garden. Porter yelped, closing the gate before the dog could reach him.

"Can, uh, can somebody get her away?" he called out from behind it.

"You're such a baby, Porter!"

The gate opened again and Savage appeared, bending down and accepting a barrage of kisses from Colin. She laughed, scratching Colin's back until the dog started turning in tight circles.

"Come on!" Savage said, pretending to throw a ball. Colin broke into another sprint, chasing shadows all the way to the far fence.

"Have you ever met anything with so much energy?" she asked as she walked to Kett. He lifted an eyebrow and nodded to where Evie and Moira were chasing each other, both of them trying to bark.

"You're kidding, right?" he said. "My girls make Colin look like a bloody sloth."

"Did somebody say my name?" came another voice. Superintendent Clare loomed through the gate, scratching his hairy nose. Porter craned past him like an anxious child, looking for the dog.

"It's not your name anymore, sir," said Savage as she sat down on the opposite side of the picnic table. "It's the dog's."

Clare grumbled as he crossed the lawn. He nodded to Kett.

"Good news," he said. "We won't need you in the interview room. Pollyanna Craft gave us a full confession."

"That's great," said Kett. He hadn't exactly been looking forward to sitting opposite her, after what she'd done to him. There was a good chance he'd have ripped her head clean off her shoulders. He flexed his hand, his knuckles still swollen.

"She's been charged with three murders," Clare said.

"Sally and Thomas's too?" Kett replied, frowning. Clare shook his head.

"Forensics found two more bodies on her property, in shallow graves."

"*What*?" Kett said. "Who?"

"We don't know, yet," Clare said. "Both young men, boys really. Both buried naked apart from a collar around their neck—buried alongside a number of actual dogs. It's hard to tell, because of the lye, but Franklin thinks they were choked to death."

"Jesus," Kett said. He remembered Polly's basement, the piles upon piles of old sheets covered in human excrement. It hadn't all belonged to Eden after all.

"She's insane," Clare said, shaking his head. "But we're not going to let them push for an insanity plea. Not on my watch. She'll pay for what she did, and most importantly she won't do it again."

Kett nodded. But there was little satisfaction to be had from closing the case. Sally O'Neil was still dead, so was Roger Carver and Thomas Morton. Two more young men had died, and Eden would never recover. The world wasn't a better place at all.

Kett could feel the black dog creeping closer, and he turned to his children.

"Evie, come here," he said. She did as she was asked, squealing again as she ran towards him. He scooped her onto his lap and she put her head to his chest, heaving in a sigh. She'd been playing with Colin all day, and she was knackered. So was Moira. They'd both sleep like logs tonight.

Maybe he *should* keep the dog.

"Help, she's coming," said Porter, skittering away from Colin like an elephant from a mouse. He skirted around the table, almost running.

"Oh for Christ's sake, Porter," roared Clare. "It's just a tossing dog. Say hello to it."

"No!" objected Porter.

"That's an order," Clare said, jabbing his finger at the giant DI to show how serious he was. Porter squealed, then leant over. Colin planted her feet on his legs and stood up, her pink tongue flashing between his fingers.

"Ew!" he said. "I don't like it."

"You think that's gross," said Kett. "Just wait till you have a baby."

Porter's frown was instantly replaced with a grin.

"I forgot to say! Allie said yes, she said we could try! We *have* tried!"

"*Way* too much information, Porter," said Savage, pulling a face.

"So you don't want the dog, then?" Kett asked.

"Me?" said Porter, shaking his head. "No way."

"Sir?" said Kett, turning to Clare.

"I would," the boss replied, looking fondly at Colin. "We used to have Staffies, when the kids were little. They're beautiful dogs. But no. One Colin is more than enough in my house, thank you very much. You're not keeping her here?"

"Alice is scared of dogs," Kett said, sighing. "She's been through enough, I don't want to make her life any harder. I'm hoping that maybe, if she spends a little time with her, she might come to accept her eventually."

Colin seemed to know she was being talked about,

looking up at Kett and cocking her head. He held out a hand and she trotted over, sniffing him then licking Evie's feet. Evie burst into rippling giggles, and her happiness was contagious. Kett found himself laughing.

"I'll take her," said Savage. "If you like? She can live with me, keep me company while I take my exams. When Alice is used to her, she can move back in here."

"Really?" said Kett. Savage nodded, holding her hands out. Colin walked to her, yawning. The dog turned in circles then curled up into a ball by Savage's feet, as knackered by the kids as they were by her. "She likes you."

"Maybe I've got a kind face too," she said.

"No, I told you, my face is angry," Kett protested. "Fierce. Hard as nails. Grr."

Evie yawned too, sliding her little hand into his. He hugged her close, putting his face to her hair and breathing her in. She smelled like Evie, but she also smelled like Billie, too. All the kids did. Because she was inside them, always. She would live there forever.

There was a sadness to the thought, of course there was, but at least there was *something*. He'd come to understand that the black dog of his depression was absence, a terrible void inside him. When it had been at its worst, he'd felt himself leaking out into that abyss, everything that made him who he was—the joy, the warmth, sure, but also the sadness and the grief. It hurt to hold onto the bad things, but they were important, and having those feelings was infinitely better than losing them. He didn't understand it, not really, but he knew that sometimes grief was the only way of keeping someone with you.

He was starting to accept that maybe grief was the only way of keeping Billie alive.

"Mine!" yelled Moira, waddling up to him and making grabby-grabby hands. "Uggle."

"In a minute," Kett said. "I'm cuddling your sister."

"No!" Moira replied, the tears already forming. "Mine! Daddy!"

"Okay, okay," he said. He patted Evie's behind, lowering her to the grass. "Sorry, I just can't handle the noise."

Evie walked straight to Porter, holding out her hands and letting him lift her. He booped her gently on the nose.

"Nearly time for bed, champ," he said.

"I need a poo first," she said. Porter's eyes widened in horror.

"If you're holding her, you take her," said Kett. "Them's the rules."

"No!" he said.

"Call it practice," added Savage, shooing him on his way. She stood up, stretching. The dog rose with her, wagging its tail. "I'll go help. He'll only cock it up."

Clare looked like he was about to add something, then his phone started to ring. He excused himself, walking back to the gate.

"Just me and you, then," Kett said, smoothing back Moira's springy hair.

"Mine," she said, pushing his hand away.

"I know it's yours," he told her. "I wasn't planning on stealing it."

He smiled at her, and she grinned back. He stood up, fighting another sweeping blast of vertigo. His shoulder throbbed, his arm burned, and everything else pulsed somewhere on the spectrum of pain. But he was alive. He had to keep telling himself that.

He was alive.

"Come on, let's go grab some supper."

"Bis-kit," she said, pointing a chubby finger at the house.

"Well I was thinking more fish fingers and chips, but biscuits sound good too."

He set off, noticing Clare pacing back and forth by the gate. The Superintendent's face was creased with worry, and he kept glancing over. Kett's Spidey-sense suddenly tripped, his heart revving. Something had happened, something bad. Another murder? Or maybe something to do with the Pollyanna Craft case? He slowed his pace, watching as Clare ended the call. The boss clenched his giant hand around the phone like he was trying to crush it.

"Trouble, sir?" Kett asked.

And Clare replied with a look, one that made Kett feel as if he'd been thrown into a lake of icy water. He knew what that look meant. He understood it perfectly.

"Billie," Kett said.

Clare nodded, taking a long, hard breath.

"That was Bingo, your old Superintendent," he said. "He wanted to speak to me first, to make sure you didn't do anything stupid."

"What?" Kett said, taking a step towards Clare. The boss held up his hands the way he would against a charging bull. "What did he say? Is Billie okay?"

"I don't know," Clare said. "He doesn't know. Look, let's take Moira inside and—"

"Tell me *now*, Clare," Kett said, his voice like thunder. "Tell me what he said or I swear I'll wring it out of you."

Clare swallowed hard, looking at Moira then back at Kett.

"They haven't found her," he said, speaking slowly and clearly. "I'm sorry, they haven't found Billie. But they have found *him*. The Pig Man. They know who he is, and more importantly, they know *where* he is."

He shook his head, and Kett knew what words he was going to speak next long before they spilled out of his mouth.

"Robbie, they know what happened to your wife."

HE WILL FIND THE TRUTH
EVEN IF IT KILLS HIM

THREE LITTLE PIGS

A DCI ROBERT KETT NOVEL

ALEX SMITH

THE INTERNATIONALLY BESTSELLING SERIES

THREE LITTLE PIGS
THE THIRD DCI KETT CRIME THRILLER

He will find the truth. Even if it kills him.

Five months ago, DCI Robert Kett's wife Billie was snatched from a London street.

Five months of no leads, no evidence, and no suspects.

Until now.

When a routine police search uncovers a chamber of horrors beneath one of the city's most expensive houses, detectives find a clue that points to Billie's fate, and to the identity of her kidnapper—an enigmatic serial killer known as the Pig Man.

Desperate for closure, and still reeling from his last investigation, Kett returns to London for his most personal and most dangerous case yet—a case that pits him against a terrifying evil.

He doesn't know if Billie is alive or dead. He doesn't know if he's too late to save her. All he knows is that he swore he'd go to hell and back to find out what happened.

And now, he's about to.

You won't be able to put down this fast-paced British crime thriller from million-selling author Alex Smith.

PROLOGUE

Somebody had once told DS Adam Ridgway that London was hell.

Today, more than ever, he was sure they were right.

He pulled the Ford Focus over to the side of the road and stopped, leaving the engine running. The wipers beat back and forth, back and forth, like an agitated heartbeat, but even at full speed they couldn't keep the rain off the windscreen. People had been saying to him all day that the heavens had opened. If they had, it was to finally wash the stink out of the city. Maybe if it rained hard enough, London would finally be clean.

Fat chance, he thought.

He squinted through the downpour, making out a street that belonged in a fairy tale. Behind towering lime trees and fortified walls sat a parade of mansions, too aloof to reveal anything other than the peaks of their roofs. Dozens of chimneys rose like gun turrets on a destroyer, fighting back the rain. None of the houses had numbers, which Ridgway found both strange and intensely annoying.

He reached into the pocket of his jacket and pulled out

a slip of paper. It was greasy to the touch, and it had been folded so many times that it resembled a piece of parchment pulled out of a medieval tomb. There was only a small cluster of marks on it, written in a hand that looked as if it had been shaking wildly as it wrote.

Bishop 73.

"Are you gonna lead me somewhere or not?" he asked the paper.

The chances were the answer would be *no*, like every other scrap of evidence he'd uncovered. Not one clue had led anywhere except around in circles. Not a single witness testimony—not that anyone had dared to give more than their name—had shifted the darkness from around this fucking case. Ridgway had been tasked with finding Billie Kett, and the men who had taken her. But he might as well have been asked to reel in the Moon. Finding Billie was impossible, because whatever the truth was, this city was hiding it well.

Hell didn't give up its secrets easily, after all.

But *Bishop* 73 was what he had, and if he didn't use it then how could he look his old friend Robbie Kett in the face ever again? He'd given Robbie his word that he'd help him find his wife, and even though five long months had passed since he'd made that promise, he wasn't about to give up on it anytime soon.

"Seventy-three," he said, folding the paper back into a lozenge and returning it to his suit pocket. "Where are you?"

He put the Focus in gear and crawled along the street. Rain drummed off the car like it was under attack, like people were lobbing stones at him from behind the tall walls. He wasn't welcome here, he knew that much. This was an unfriendly street. An *unkind* street. He'd only been a Met detective for a handful of years, but he knew the city well enough now to understand which parts were dangerous. It wasn't the estates where the gangs waged war, it wasn't the corners where the drugs were sold. It was places like this, because these houses were castles, they were *kingdoms*, and the people here could get away with anything.

He passed a wrought iron gate with the number 67 stretched across it. It was all he needed. He drove the car past two more colossal homes before stopping outside the next and cutting the engine. The cold began to creep inside immediately, and he rubbed his arms through his suit. Over a high gate and through sheets of rain he made out the top of a palatial white house, a row of eight wide, dark windows staring back at him. They looked like spider eyes, he thought, and despite the fact he was thirty-two years old he still shuddered uncontrollably at the thought.

Pull yourself together, Adam, he thought. He didn't speak aloud, though. Even though the rain roared, the street felt too quiet, too empty.

Too dead.

"Ah fuck this," he forced himself to say, clicking his fingers like he was warding off demons. "It's just a house."

He popped the door and scampered out, wet through after a handful of seconds. His coat was in the boot and he ran to collect it, slinging it on as he splashed across the wide pavement. There was a little shade here from a giant conifer that grew beside the eight-foot wall, and he hunkered into it. He half thought about calling the boss, Superintendent Barry Benson, but Bingo—as the entire force called him—wouldn't want to be disturbed unless there was something concrete. He pulled out his phone and texted him instead:

Checking out 73 Bishops Wells, update to follow.

The rain did its best to wash the phone out of his hand,

to carry it away with the water that streamed into the gutters. The screen was so wet he couldn't even get the text to send. Then it *whooshed*, and he slid the phone back into his pocket.

"Right," he said, blowing raindrops off his lips. "This had better be worth it."

There was an intercom mounted on the wall, complete with a camera, but Ridgway knew it wasn't working because none of the lights were on. He dutifully pressed the button anyway.

"Hello? This is DS Ridgway of the Metropolitan Police. Could you open the gate, please?"

Nothing. No reply, no static. Ridgway sighed, pulling his collar around his neck and taking a few steps back. The wall that surrounded the property was tipped with ornate curls of black metal which looked pretty but which, he knew, were designed to slice open anyone who tried to climb over. The gate was lower, and smooth—two security cameras mounted on either side provided all the protection it needed. Ridgway waved at them, fairly sure that nobody was there to wave back.

He looked mournfully back at the car, wondering if he should just leave it. Then he asked the question he knew he'd have to ask at some point, but which he really didn't want to.

What would Robert Kett do?

It was a question, in fact, that Bingo had specifically ordered him never to ask, because the answer was always something ridiculous, impulsive, and probably illegal.

But the answer was also something that, more often than not, would solve the case.

"What would you do, Robbie?" he asked. "What would you do to find your wife?"

Anything, came the reply. *Everything*.

Bishop 73 wasn't much. The informant who'd got it for him hadn't even told him where it was from, hadn't told him whose shaking hand had written down the word and the number. *Bishop 73* could be a name. It could be an age. It could mean anything, or nothing at all.

Or it could be an address. *This* address.

What would Robert Kett do?

"Fuck it," he said.

He took a breath, then ran at the gate, jumping high enough to get his hands on the top and one foot on the brace. The wood was so wet his shoe almost slipped off, and he squeaked as he grappled for purchase. Then he planted his other foot, shoving hard and managing to get a leg over the top. It wasn't a graceful dismount, not at all, but some quick footwork stopped his arse from going for a swim in the Serpentine-sized puddle that had grown on the other side. He hop-skip-jumped to safety, brushing his hands down his lapels to try to find some composure.

If anyone *was* watching him from inside the house, they'd be pissing themselves with laughter.

It didn't matter. It wasn't like he had much of his shift left to ride out. After this he was done, which was just as well as he was already late. A quick look around then he could head home, peel off his sodden suit and sit down to dinner with his wife—who'd lecture him about the fact it was almost seven, then plaster him with kisses anyway. His permanently irritating nine-year-old son Cal would be there too, but hey, you couldn't win them all.

Ridgway smiled, chastising himself for giving Cal a hard time. He loved the boy more than anything, of course. And seeing him waiting right there at the living room window every evening when he pulled the car into the driveway was the highlight of his life.

I'm running late, he told them, spinning the message across the city in the hope he'd somehow become telepathic. *But I'll be there*.

He splashed over the vast brick-weave driveway to a front door that would have felt at home at Buckingham Palace. The lights on the buzzer were out, so he rapped as hard as he could, feeling the ache of it even in his cold-numbed hand.

"Police," he called out. "Open up."

The house kept its mouth shut, those dark eyes still glaring at him. He knocked again, waited a moment, then stepped back. It didn't exactly look like the kind of house that would belong to somebody called the Pig Man. *If* the person who had taken Billie was even called that. According to Robbie, the source of that particular nugget of intelligence had been the dying words of a pathological liar and murderer called Raymond Figg—not exactly your first choice when it came to workable info.

But he had nothing else. Nobody did. If the Pig Man even existed, only one person seemed to know anything about him, and all that person had revealed was a name, and a number.

Bishop 73.

Ridgway smoothed back his prematurely greying hair, only for the rain to immediately knock it over his eyes again. He moved to the nearest window, peering in to see a room that was entirely bare. The next window over revealed a similar sight, except this one seemed to have ivy growing up the inside of the glass. The house was deserted, which wasn't surprising—half the seven-figure properties down the street had been bought up as investments and left to rot.

It was only as he rounded the rear of the house, entering a surprisingly small garden that cowered beneath a perimeter of enormous trees, that he found his access point. And he wasn't the first person to have used it. A pair of Georgian double doors had been forced open, fragments of glass littering the wide sandstone patio. A pair of curtains billowed in a wind that Ridgway hadn't even noticed on the street.

"Hello?" he called out. "Is anyone there? This is the police."

Still nothing, but it was a weird kind of nothing. It felt *too* nothing. He could almost picture Kett standing next to him, the way he always did when they'd partnered up. He could almost imagine him saying it:

This house isn't empty.

"Police," Ridgway called again, his voice quieter than ever.

He took a step towards the open doors, glass crunching beneath his shoes. It was only then that he realised something: the glass was outside the house. Somebody had broken *out*. The curtain whipped and snapped at him, like a guard dog, and he pushed it to one side as he entered.

The first thing he noticed was the dark. It was far darker than it should have been with the windows uncovered, even with the rain and the overcast skies. He didn't understand where the light had gone, as if it had been somehow sucked out of the space in front of him. He pulled out his phone again, switching on the flashlight. It did absolutely nothing to chase away the shadows.

"Hello?" he called out. "This is the police. If somebody is here, make yourself known."

It was like the house replied, a shuddering groan passing through it. Ridgway came so close to screaming that he had to slap a hand over his mouth to stop it from spilling out of him. He groaned into his palm, hearing the noise again.

Just the wind, you pillock. The fucking wind. What are you, nine years old?

Although that wasn't really fair because Cal was nine, and his son wouldn't have been afraid. He'd have been racing through these corridors like it was soft play.

Ridgway almost called out again, then thought better of it. If there was anyone here who wanted to speak to him, they'd have replied by now. That *probably* meant the place was empty. It was clearly abandoned, after all—it was almost raining as hard in here as it was outside, great puddles of water warping the expensive oak boards. The ivy in the other room hadn't grown alone, the walls were slick with mould and what looked like ferns hung down from the exposed rafters. It was surreal, like the world had ended and he'd only just realised.

He was halfway across the room when he noticed the second thing: the smell. It was the stench of rot, sure, of a house left to decay. But there was something past that, something sweeter. By the time he poked his head through the door into the wide corridor beyond he recognised what it was. Joss sticks. His wife used them in the bath, even though he pleaded with her not to because the smell got into his clothes and drove the drugs dogs crazy whenever he went near them. He cleared his throat.

"Hello? Police."

There were four doors along the corridor, all closed except for the one he'd just come through. The dark grew deeper and thicker with every step, as if it was swallowing him, working him down its throat with snake-like peristalsis. The torch on his phone did its best, but it seemed to be as intimidated as he was, the light shrinking into itself.

I'll just check a couple of rooms, he said, nodding to himself. *Just to make sure.*

The first room wasn't a room at all, it was a cupboard—bare of anything except rat shit. The next led to a small utility room, and here Ridgway frowned, because there was a washing machine against one wall, a new one, an expensively quiet one.

And it was halfway through a cycle.

What?

It was probably squatters. The street had to be full of them, because who would pass up the chance to live in a house like this, even if it was falling apart? Squatters were usually harmless, but not always. He lifted his phone, inadvertently blinding himself as he dialled Bingo's number. The boss picked up after two rings, the way he always did.

"Detective Sergeant," he said in his distinctive baritone. "Got your text. Is this my update?"

"House is abandoned, but not entirely," Ridgway replied, blinking the pattern of his retinas out of his eyes as he walked to the next door. "Electricity is on, and somebody is here. Washing machine's running. Squatters, I think."

"I'll send a team," Bingo replied. "Just to be sure."

Ridgway opened his mouth to object, then shut it again. There was something about the house that was creeping him out, big time, and he wasn't about to say no to some company.

"My advice, clear out until they're with you. Any sign of anything illegal?"

"Other than the squatting?" Ridgway asked.

"You know, *properly* illegal," said Bingo. "Any sign of Billie Kett? Or the Pig Man? Did your lead pan out?"

Ridgway turned the handle and pushed open the final door. Darkness seemed to scurry past him like swarming rats, and another wave of that awful, rotting smell wrapped itself around his face. The windows here had to be curtained, or boarded up, because barely a crack of light slipped through. It was utterly silent, even the rain outside seemed to be a long, long way away. Ridgway felt somehow cocooned, mummified, and the thought of it made him want to turn tail and flee.

He didn't, of course. He was police. He was better than that.

"Adam?" said Bingo from the phone, and once again Ridgway almost screamed.

"Hang on, sir," he replied, hearing his heartbeat in his voice. "I'm on my way out now. I just wanted to check..."

He squinted into the dark, taking a step. The floor creaked beneath his shoe, and he felt the sudden and unexpected slope of it. Pulling the phone from his ear, he angled the flashlight beam into what had once been a huge kitchen, but which was now more like a warzone. Almost the entire floor was missing, a crater of absolute darkness filling the room from wall to wall.

He grabbed the door for support, leaning over the hole as far as he dared. Behind him, the washing machine whined into its spin cycle.

"Hello?" he said.

He angled the light down into the crater.

"Oh god," he said, the words falling out of him in low, groaning clumps. "Oh fucking hell."

He heard Bingo calling his name, but he couldn't make himself lift the phone. He didn't want to see what he was seeing, and yet he couldn't stop looking.

He *could not* stop.

Picked out in the trembling beam of his torch was a basement—boarded floor, expensive rug, ornate green wallpaper. Joss sticks sat on a walnut table, curls of smoke rising past surreal, fleshy sculptures mounted on the walls. There was something not quite real about it, especially nested here in this ruin of a building. It was too perfect, like something from a doll's house.

The dolls were there too.

Three women lay on the rug in the middle of the room, almost close enough for their elbows to touch. They each wore an elegant red dress, and their faces were covered with what looked like cheap children's animal masks: a giraffe, a lion, and a monkey. Their legs were straight, their hands folded over their hearts—the same way as a corpse in a coffin.

But they weren't dead. Not *all* of them, anyway.

Because the woman in the middle stared up at Ridgway through the holes in her lion mask, and even though the slits were small he could read her expression perfectly.

She was completely and utterly terrified.

"Hang on!" Ridgway called down. "Fuck, just hang on!"

He lifted the phone to his ear, darkness flooding the basement again like a tide of ink.

"Get everyone here now, we've got three women in the basement, I think they're tied up. Animal masks. 73 Bishop's Wells. I'm—"

Ridgway became aware of the whine of the washing machine behind him, and past that something else—maybe a sound, maybe just some kind of primal warning that made his hackles rise. He turned, the beam of light turning with him, picking out the man who stood halfway down the corridor. He wore what looked like pyjama trousers, his obese top half naked apart from curls of hair and a sheen of sweat. His face was covered by a mask.

A *pig* mask.

"Shit shit shit!" said Ridgway, the warmth draining from him. "It's him!"

"Get out of there," ordered Bingo. "Run, Adam!"

Run where? Behind him the chasm yawned open in the kitchen floor, and in front of him the Pig Man lifted his arms and loosed a monstrous squeal. Something flashed in his hand, something sharp, but there was no time to see what because he was running, his bare feet pounding on the boards, his entire body swaying as he grunted forwards.

"Wait—" was as far as Ridgway got, then the man thumped into him, and death slid between his ribs in a blast of cold heat.

There was no pain. There was nothing much at all, to be honest. He felt himself fall back, fall hard, fall and fall and fall—too far for the basement, surely, he had to be falling deeper than that, into hell. Then the ground caught him, and it was not gentle. He tried to breathe, but his body had forgotten how. It had forgotten how to do anything, it seemed. Above him, picked out in the light of the torch that had fallen beside him, a pig's face watched him, grunting quietly.

Ridgway's head lolled to the side and he saw the three women from the floor on their feet now, walking out of the room in a neat little line. The first one opened the door, vanishing into the dark. The second stopped to let the third through, and when she looked back he saw tears in her eyes through the holes in her mask.

I know those eyes, he thought. *I'm sure I do.*

She gazed at him a moment more, then from somewhere overhead came a snort, and she too vanished into the gloom.

"Adam?" came a shrinking voice from the phone. "Adam?"

Ridgway closed his eyes and saw his wife setting the

table, saw his little boy sitting at the living room window, waiting for him.

I'm going to be late, he told them. *I'm sorry.*

Silence, and the last of him fell away.

I'm going to be late.

ABOUT THE AUTHOR

Alex Smith wrote his first book when he was six. It wasn't particularly good, but it did have some supernatural monsters in it. His latest books, the DCI Robert Kett thrillers, have monsters in them too, although these monsters are very human, and all the more terrifying for it. In between these books he has published thirteen novels for children and teenagers under his full name, Alexander Gordon Smith—including the number one bestselling series Escape From Furnace, which is loved by millions of readers worldwide and which is soon to become a motion picture. He lives in Norwich with his wife and three young daughters.

Find out more at alexsmithbooks.com